# ROOM
# SERVICE

# ROOM SERVICE

## AMY GARVEY

𝓑
**BRAVA**

KENSINGTON PUBLISHING CORP.
http://www.kensingtonbooks.com

BRAVA BOOKS are published by

Kensington Publishing Corp.
850 Third Avenue
New York, NY 10022

All Kensington titles, imprints and distributed lines are available at special quantity discounts for bulk purchases for sales promotion, premiums, fund-raising, educational or institutional use.

Special book excerpts or customized printings can also be created to fit specific needs. For details, write or phone the office of the Kensington Special Sales Manager, Kensington Publishing Corp., 850 Third Avenue, New York, NY 10022. Attn. Special Sales Department. Phone: 1-800-221-2647.

Brava and the B logo Reg. U.S. Pat. & TM Off.

ISBN-13: 978-0-7582-1591-8
ISBN-10: 0-7582-1591-6

First Kensington Trade Paperback Printing: June 2007
10  9  8  7  6  5  4  3  2  1

Printed in the United States of America

*For Stephen, who makes sure we're
never out of fudge marble ice cream.*

*And for Barb, Deb, Mica, Kris, Chris,
Molly, and Carol, who absolutely get it.*

# Chapter 1

Olivia Callender was fed up with Monday even before she stepped outside her family's hundred-year-old hotel and found the brass nameplate above the door listing to one side like a drunken sailor. From now on, she thought to herself as she frowned at the tarnished sign, Monday was on notice.

What she needed was a time machine. Really, it was sort of amazing that no one had invented one yet when you could watch TV on your cell phone and your refrigerator could talk to you. At any rate, a time machine would certainly solve a lot of her problems.

If she had one, she mused as she backed away from the hotel's revolving door, she could skip today altogether and avoid lunch with her uncle. She could spend the crisp September day walking around Manhattan instead. She bit back a smile as two businessmen strode by like a pair of matched horses in their gray suits and black briefcases. If she had a time machine, she could spend the day walking around the Manhattan—or the hotel—of her childhood.

Poor old thing, she thought as she tilted her head to glance up at the building's eleven sturdy red brick floors, and the gabled windows on the top story. She was no

Eloise, and Callender House certainly wasn't the Plaza, but this hotel was home, and had been since Olivia was born.

It wasn't the hotel's fault it had begun to resemble a faded old dowager whose stockings were bagging around her ankles and who had lipstick on her teeth.

She patted the rough brick beside the revolving door fondly. And it wasn't the hotel's fault the nameplate had come loose on one side. The thing had to be nearly as old as the hotel. Still, she wished it hadn't come loose today. Maintenance would fix it, but whether or not it would get done before Uncle Stuart arrived for lunch wasn't what she would call a sure thing.

What was certain was that he would notice it, and re-mark on it, and roll his eyes, and exude condescension the way some men left a cloud of aftershave in their wake. And she would have to soldier through it, the way she always did, until he'd reached his quota of criticisms and taken off again.

A time machine was looking better and better.

She didn't understand why he insisted on seeing her in the first place. For the first twenty years of her life he'd barely acknowledged her existence. But now that her father was dead, he called like clockwork, every six months, to schedule lunch with her right there in the hotel restaurant.

Family loyalty was out, and so was affection. Olivia couldn't remember the last time he'd even hugged her, and if he tried it she'd have to make a superhuman effort to keep from shrinking away from him. Stuart Callender was about as snuggly as a rattlesnake. With a porcupine hide.

As for loyalty . . . Well, Olivia's father was the one who inherited Callender House, not Stuart. Apparently even her grandfather hadn't much liked his younger son. Then again, Stuart had always made it clear that the hotel business was not for him.

Which made these twice-yearly lunches as difficult to understand as they were to sit through. Especially when Stuart's primary aim seemed to be pointing out every one of what he believed were Callender House's flaws.

The lobby, for instance. Every time he stepped through the door he had something to say about the faded marble floor, the circular red velvet banquette, and the dark leather settees. "Scratched," he'd say, pointing to a tear in the leather. "Stained," he'd say, raising his eyebrows at the banquette. "And the ferns? It's the twenty-first century, Olivia. This isn't Casablanca."

Well, she liked the ferns. There were a lot of them, true, and they were a little bit old-fashioned, yes, but they were part of the lobby's charm. There had always been ferns in the hotel's lobby, and she had hidden behind the extravagant green fronds more than once when she was a kid.

The ferns weren't going anywhere, she thought to herself as she ambled away from the building. Her father had entrusted Callender House to her, and she intended to preserve it just the way he had when he inherited it from his father. Callender House was a New York institution. Just like hot dogs, and Central Park, and traffic.

She frowned at that thought. Okay, traffic wasn't exactly a *good* institution, but New Yorkers were used to it. Without traffic they would have one less excuse for being late to work.

"Morning, Ms. Callender."

As if on cue, Declan Sweeney arrived, nearly—Olivia glanced at her watch—two hours late for work as the daytime doorman. At least he was always charming about it.

She'd hired him mostly because of the pure Ireland in his voice. His face didn't hurt, either. He had the dark hair and blue eyes of the black Irish, and he'd come to the States only this spring to be an actor. Or was it to paint? No, to study photography. That was it. She was almost sure, anyway. Not that it mattered. He was only twenty-four—or was it twenty-two? He'd probably change his mind about his career a dozen times in the coming year.

"You're late again," she informed him, but she couldn't hold back a smile.

"I'm in love, I am," he announced happily, pausing to stare with fondness into middle distance. "Althea's her name. I'm doomed."

How this explained him being late to work, Olivia wasn't sure she wanted to examine. And since Herb, the night doorman, had left hours ago, she urged Declan inside for his uniform with a wave of her hand.

"Sign's crooked, you know," he said with a cheery smile, and pushed through the revolving door.

She frowned at his back.

So the sign was crooked. It wasn't a tragedy. It wasn't a crisis. It required a ladder and possibly a screwdriver. Or a drill. She wasn't sure about that part, but she was sure that the lopsided nameplate hadn't required an urgent call from Angel, the head of maintenance, before she'd even had her first cup of coffee.

The same went for all of the discussions about replacing the carpet upstairs. Olivia liked that carpet, even if it was getting a bit worn. Okay, threadbare. Still, you couldn't find carpet like that anymore.

"And I don't know why you'd want to," Josie Gallo, her guest services manager, had responded to that with raised eyebrows. "There are no avocado-colored flowers like that in nature. It's mutant foliage carpet. It's *awful*."

It was sort of awful, but it had been there forever. And the avocado-colored flowers matched the avocado-colored stripe in the wallpaper. She'd run down those halls, on that carpet, when she was a kid.

No one appreciated tradition, she thought with a spark of mutiny as she stepped backward toward the curb. Her gaze was trained on the hotel, counting floors and picking out the windows of the suite where she had grown up. Everyone wanted everything to change, all the time. Newer, improved, bigger, better. It was absurd. Some things deserved to stay just the way they were. And Callender House was one of them. Her father had entrusted her with it, and she wasn't going to let him down.

It was a little disconcerting that she couldn't pick out the old suite's windows automatically, however. Once upon a time, she'd been able to do it in her sleep—she'd spent the first eighteen years of her life there, after all. She took another step backward, craning her neck as she counted up each floor, then over five windows—or was it six? The perspective was a little different now that she was taller.

She stepped backward again, squinting now, trying to remember—until a pair of very strong hands thrust her forward and a cab blared its horn.

She was still stumbling for balance when she heard something else hit the pavement with a wet splat, and then an irritable, "Oh, bloody hell."

Uh-oh.

She grabbed hold of a parking meter to right herself and turned around to find a cabbie giving her a one-fingered salute as he drove off—and a rock star covered with what looked like a mocha latte, an exploded suitcase and a dropped backpack at his feet. The sidewalk was littered with jeans and T-shirts.

He looked like a rock star, at least. First there were the faded jeans and what looked to Olivia like motorcycle boots, black leather that had seen better days and plenty of wear. Then the layered shirts, a long-sleeved gray one under a short-sleeved dark blue one with Mick Jagger's luscious pout on the front. Finally there was his hair, dark and shaggy around his face—and splattered with creamy white foam, just like his face. And the white snakes of his iPod, which he pulled from his ears and shook over the sidewalk, spraying foam and coffee.

She swallowed hard. "I'm so sorry. *So* sorry. You don't even know . . ."

"I can imagine well enough," he said with a dry smile, shaking latte out of his hair like a wet dog. His eyes were gray, she noticed. Deep, stormy gray, and fixed on her face. "You and that cab would have ended in blood and tears, now wouldn't you?"

"Um . . ." She knew, vaguely, that her mouth was hanging open, but she couldn't seem to close it, much less find an intelligent response. She hadn't expected the British accent. Something inside her melted into a warm puddle.

She'd dreamed about men like him. Well, fantasized was probably more accurate. In her sleeping dreams, men tended to be a strange combination of Cary Grant and that guy from the Verizon commercials.

But men like this one, those were the kind in her daydreams. Except this one was possibly better.

And she'd . . . splattered him.

"You're all right, yeah?" he asked, wiping his face. "I didn't mean to shove you quite so hard."

"You . . . Well, you saved me from being hit by a cab." She shrugged as a heated blush spread over her cheeks. "I'm fine. You're . . ."

"A bit of a wreck at the moment, I know." He grinned at her then, a sudden flash of mischief and sunshine. Licking his upper lip, he added with a wink, "Brilliant latte."

Completely cool. Completely confident.

Completely unlike any man she had ever met.

In her head, there was no problem. She would say something witty, or smart, or maybe even flirty. He would lean in and flirt back, invite her to dinner. She would give him a mysterious little wave when she left, maybe flip her hair a bit. In her imagination, hair-flipping got them every time.

But this wasn't her imagination. This was real, right here, right now. This was overwhelming.

Especially when he pulled up the hems of his T-shirts and wiped his face off, revealing a lean, muscled abdomen.

So much for offering him a towel from the hotel. So much for any hope of getting her racing pulse under control.

And he wasn't even going to give her a chance to try. "Bit of a trick, walking backward, yeah?" he said, letting his shirts fall and wiping his hands on the back of his jeans.

"Oh. Right." Her cheeks were on fire. She wouldn't have been surprised to see an actual flame lick at the tip of her nose. "That was . . . dumb."

"Not in an empty meadow, maybe." His grin was as lopsided as the hotel's nameplate now, and a lot more appealing. "On a Manhattan street now . . ."

"I know. I am sorry." She gestured helplessly at his ruined shirts, at the empty cup on the pavement.

"No worries, love. Pleasure to meet you . . . ?"

"Olivia." She put her hand in his when he offered it, and an actual thrill of excitement raced through her. Which was silly, because he was simply being nice. It was probably a British thing. Nothing to do with her at all.

"Rhys," he said, and she realized he was still holding her hand. His was nice, firm and warm and stronger than she would have imagined for a man with such long, lean fingers.

But she couldn't stand here all day holding hands, mooning after him like some teenager, even if she wanted to. It was time to step away. Get back to work. Take her tattered dignity back to her office and mend it with a big fat muffin.

Right. She was stepping away now. Yes, *now.*

Except for the fact that it wouldn't be polite to leave him to the scattered contents of his suitcase all by himself, would it?

She untangled her fingers from his and knelt down to pick up a pair of jeans—and found a jumbled pile of boxer briefs beneath them. She dropped the jeans with a little gasp of embarrassment, and looked up to see Rhys grinning at her.

"I'll take the unmentionables, love."

If she kept blushing like this, she was going to have to stick her face in the freezer to cool off.

When Rhys had crammed the last of his shirts and a scuffed dop kit into his suitcase and zipped it up, Olivia straightened up and took a step toward the curb. "It was very nice to meet you, Rhys." Her cheeks were still flushed with heat, but she managed another smile before she said, "I have to . . . well, I have things . . ."

There was no denying it. She couldn't flirt if her life depended on it. She sounded as if English wasn't even her first language. Finally, tearing herself away from the amused grin that still lit up his face, she ended with, "Well, good-bye."

Then she turned around and started for the hotel, pretending she couldn't feel him watching her go, and trying not to wonder what her butt looked like in her old gray trousers. Not sexy, she was sure. Definitely not cool.

Not that it mattered. She could dream about guys like Rhys, but that was where the sentence ended. Guys like Rhys were all rock and roll and straight-up whiskey and motorcycles. She was Top 40 and hot tea and the occasional bicycle. Some things definitely weren't meant to change.

Guys like Rhys were what daydreams were for.

And as she pushed through the revolving door of the hotel, she figured daydreaming about Rhys could happily take her right through lunch with Uncle Stuart.

If nothing else, she did daydreams like a pro.

Not what he'd expected from New York, Rhys Spencer thought as he righted his battered suitcase and slung his backpack over his shoulder again. All right, yeah, getting knocked over and splattered with latte was a bit what he'd expected, but Olivia whatever-her-name-was? Not in a million.

If you believed the movies and the telly, which he usually didn't, New York women wore black like a bloody uniform and were about as likely to be caught woolgathering on a sidewalk as they were to be wandering alone through Central Park after dark.

But Olivia, whoever she was, had been doing just that, hadn't she? Daydreaming, staring up at that old hotel as if it were a castle, completely oblivious to the traffic gunning down the street behind her. If he hadn't looked up from his latte when he did, she would have backed right into that sodding cab.

He glanced at the building. Callender House. A hotel, it looked like. He'd never even heard of it. A bit down at heel now, if you asked him. All faded old brick and stained brownstone. Even the sign over the entrance was crooked. Olivia needed a better travel agent.

She wasn't wearing black either, was she? Wouldn't suit her, he decided as he stared at the revolving door of the hotel, where a young doorman was whistling under his breath. She was too ... dreamy. As old-fashioned as her name was. All that curling brown hair, and those enormous brown eyes, like something out of a Kate Greenaway illustration. She'd blinked so prettily at him, her cheeks blooming with mortification, and that lush mouth ripe for a kiss. He smiled, despite the sticky remains of his drink on his shirts and hands. The woman had him spouting poetry.

He should have asked for her number. Or at least her last name. But he'd found himself staring into those sleepy eyes instead, and then she was gone. Funny, that she was so shy. She looked about near nervous collapse when he'd simply asked for her name.

Which made following her into the hotel a truly bad idea. Not at all the thing. She wouldn't like it, he'd lay money on that.

But in his head, he heard her tentative voice. *Olivia.*

And he realized his feet were already carrying him through the hotel's revolving door, which groaned as if he'd wakened it, and into the dim hush of the lobby.

Of course she wasn't there, conveniently waiting for him. So he strolled off to the right, in search of the bar, running an idle finger along the red velvet banquette in the center of the lobby's marble floor as he passed it.

The bar was empty. It was a bit early, of course. And Olivia didn't seem the type to swill down a cocktail before noon. When he walked back into the lobby, no one was waiting at the pair of lifts, either, both of which looked as if they'd come straight from a theatrical props department, filed under "obsolete."

Bloody foolish notion anyway, following her in here like a stalker. He'd been in Manhattan for all of an hour and he needed a hotel room himself, since he never bothered to make a reservation in advance. Limited your options when you tied yourself down to a strict plan, didn't it? It wasn't as if he had anything particular to do anyway. *Fork in the Road* was through filming until the first week in November, which was when he'd need to get himself back to L.A. for the finale. And cook up a sodding storm, if he wanted to win the competition and the two hundred grand that came with it, but he wasn't especially worried about it. In the meantime, he had enough dosh in his bank account to last for a while, and no better ideas than following a pretty woman into a hotel.

He glanced around the bedraggled lobby. He felt as if he'd stepped back in time, but that wasn't a point for the plus column in this case. Crikey, there was a vintage wall of mail slots behind the desk, fitted with tarnished brass doors and miniature keys. It had probably been built when the hotel first opened. Olivia should count herself lucky if her room had a loo instead of a chamber pot.

And just then, as if he'd conjured her, she walked into view. Without thinking about why, he stepped behind a giant fern and watched her. She'd come not from the ladies' room or the bar or the lift, but from a door behind the front desk. Strangest of all, she'd stopped there and reached for a piece of paper under the counter before pushing that cloud of glossy hair behind her ears.

He strained forward to listen when the young girl at the desk, outfitted in a rather severe black jacket and a brass nametag, smiled at her. "Two new guests scheduled for this afternoon, Olivia," she said.

Olivia's smile was sudden and surprisingly sunny. Her whole face lit up when she smiled, and something inside him warmed to the sight. "See?" Olivia said, with a happy little shrug of her shoulders. "I knew it. I've got a staff of worrywarts. Josie was just complaining about the registration numbers this morning."

A staff? The pretty little bird with the shy smile and the

big eyes had a *staff?* He leaned in an inch too far, rustling the leaves on the plant, and had to grab them to silence the noise when Olivia glanced across the lobby in his direction. Sod it all. There was a reason he was a chef and not an MI6 operative.

"It's your hotel," the desk clerk said with a firm nod of her head. "You'll show 'em."

It was Olivia's hotel? This time, Rhys was lucky he didn't knock the fern over completely, because he stumbled forward in shock as a bell went off in his head.

He frowned. Chances were it was an alarm. A "bad idea, mate" alarm.

Didn't matter, he thought, a grin spreading. So the place was down at heel, and he wasn't at all looking forward to getting acquainted with that suspicious-looking lift. He'd stayed in worse places. But none of them had been owned by a soft, curvy woman with brown eyes and a mouth he wanted to taste about as much as he wanted to draw his next breath.

Yeah, he'd just found his digs for the next little while. Right here in Olivia's strange old hotel.

# Chapter 2

Two hours later, Olivia realized it was going to take a lot more than daydreaming about a flirty British guy to get through lunch. The way things stood at the moment, lunch for anyone was only a distant possibility.

"Josef, it's all right," she said gently, patting her chef's arm. Beside him on the long stainless steel counter were the ruins of a German chocolate cake. "Bake another one."

"Bake another one, she says." The older man rolled his eyes to the ceiling, his bushy black brows meeting in a frightening line. "So simple, yes? No! Is not so simple!"

Olivia cast a pleading look at Rick, Josef's sous chef, but he was no help. Arms folded over his chest, he lifted his chin and snorted.

"All right," she said, vaguely aware that in the back of her mind something was knocking, only a faint, distant sound so far. Panic. She ignored it. If she ignored it, it would go away. There was no time for panic today. Anyway, Josef was simply in one of his moods. Happened all the time. "Why doesn't someone tell me exactly what happened?"

The cavernous kitchen exploded with voices. Josef, Rick, Jesus, one of the line cooks, Willie, one of the servers—all of them chimed in with their version of the Great Cake Disaster.

"The man is insane. Like, certifiable. I'm just saying."

"Sous chef? This is what you call a sous chef today? Bah."

"You know, this kind of atmosphere is exactly the kind of thing that they write about when it comes to toxic workplaces."

"I didn't know the butter was bad! Who left it out?"

Olivia took a deep breath and stepped back as she checked her watch. Ten minutes to one. Uncle Stuart would be here any minute, and she had mutiny in the restaurant kitchen.

Which wasn't surprising, or even uncommon, but it was one more reason to put Monday—this one, at least—on the list.

She couldn't get angry. Not really. Josef Vollner had been the head chef at the Coach and Four since she was ten, and she had more experience sneaking into the kitchen for pieces of Linzer torte and leftover pasta than in treating him like an employee. He was pushing seventy, he was notoriously sensitive, and for a man who claimed he would never feel at home anywhere but Berlin, he loved Olivia and the restaurant with remarkable loyalty.

"I didn't do it," Rick was saying, shaking his head. "I don't do pastry. That's Jesus's job."

"Hey! I don't make the frosting, I just put it on the cake!"

"Amateurs!" Josef railed, stomping his foot so hard Olivia jumped. "Forty years in this business, and I work with amateurs!"

"Forty?" Rick snorted as he leaned against the counter. "Try fifty. Plus."

Panic was being a little more insistent, pounding instead of knocking now, but Olivia straightened her spine and ignored it. "Gentlemen! I'm ashamed of you all. Now can't we—"

A crash from the dining room cut off her plea for cooperation, and a moment later Helen, one of the waitresses, flew through the swinging doors. Her face was as white as her starched shirt.

For a moment, she simply gaped at them, her mouth moving without emitting any sound.

"Helen?" Olivia urged.

"The chandelier . . ." She shook her head slowly, eyes still wide. "I . . . it . . . fell."

Panic had given up knocking and barged right in, Olivia realized as a shiver of alarm buzzed up the back of her neck. "Fell? *Down?*"

Helen nodded, and Olivia pushed past her, heart pounding, and into the dining room.

Where the central chandelier that had hung in the restaurant's main dining room just this side of forever lay on the carpet, its brass and crystal bones scattered over the floor and the nearest tables.

"I have crystal in my soup," an older woman in a bright purple suit said in amazement before she fished out the broken piece with her spoon.

"Don't eat that," Olivia said. Her voice sounded far away even in her own ears. It was a ridiculous thing to say, but chandelier carnage moments before her uncle was due to arrive for lunch was even more absurd. Of all the luck, she thought to herself, watching as Willie, who had followed her out of the kitchen, knelt to brush some of the glass into a pile with a dust broom. She had always liked that chandelier, too.

A man across the room stood up, smoothing down his tie. "I'd like a refund. This is unacceptable. Dangerous. Really, when you think of what—"

Olivia held up a hand to stop him. "Not a problem, sir. The maitre d' will help you with that." The man was seated miles away from where the fixture had fallen, but she didn't care. It *wasn't* acceptable to have pieces of the restaurant committing hari-kari while you were finishing your Chicken Veronique and house salad. She didn't want to talk about it, though. If she could just stand here, frozen and more than a little numb, maybe the whole mortifying situation would end up being a dream.

Wait, make that a nightmare. Heart sinking, she managed a weak smile as Uncle Stuart strolled into the dining room.

"Here we are, sir," the porter said cheerfully as he opened the door to Rhys's room. Setting the suitcase on the luggage rack, he crossed the room and hauled open the drapes. "The sunshine's free."

Rhys lifted an eyebrow at him, but he smiled anyway. Bloke was trying, at least, although he hadn't stopped chattering all the way upstairs in the creaking lift.

"Phone's here," the porter said, pointing unnecessarily at the telephone on the ancient maple desk. "And this is the bathroom." Opening a door beside the closet, he poked his head inside to find the light. "You can always call for more towels if you need them. And the menu is in the drawer in the desk."

"Menu?" Rhys said absently. He was testing the mattress, which most likely had a good five years on him. The bedspread alone looked to be vintage 1950.

"Yes, sir." The kid beamed. "Our restaurant is an institution here in the city. The Coach and Four. We don't offer room service, but the restaurant is open for breakfast, lunch, and dinner. There's a menu in the drawer."

No room service, eh? Rhys found the menu and scanned it. Crikey, even the food was from another era. Chicken Veronique? He thought that had gone out with girdles, black-and-white TV, and party lines. And French onion soup? Holy hell. He'd have a word with Olivia about that posthaste.

"Anything else I can do for you, sir?" the porter asked. He was shifting from foot to foot, hands behind his back. If he was trying not to look too eager for a tip, he was failing miserably, Rhys thought. Not that he blamed him. He hadn't seen anyone else in the lobby or in the halls on the way upstairs. Tips must be few and far between at Callender House. And the kid had already recognized him as one of the contestants on *Fork in the Road*, with a blurted, "Hey, you're that British chef on the TV show!"

He pulled a five out of his jeans pocket and handed it to the kid. "Thanks for the help."

"Thank *you*, sir." Just short of bowing and scraping, the porter backed out of the room, closing the door behind him.

Rhys turned in a circle once he was alone. Then he sniffed the air. Musty, just a bit. As if the room had been shut up for too long. Someone should tell Olivia to have housekeeping air the place more often. Better for business all around.

Dull green and blue, stripes on the walls and flowers on the bed, a Renoir print over the bureau and a telly that would have looked more at home with rabbit ears. The room was really a bit shabby, wasn't it? Vintage or not, the coverlet was threadbare, and the rug underfoot wasn't much better. Once upon a time, the furniture and fittings must have been the height of style, but that time was far in the past. As in, decades. The cornices and cross-and-bible doors—old solid wood ones, he bet—were a brilliant touch, though. Probably wouldn't find them in the new hotels, unless they were made of MDF.

It was a bit sad, really, he thought as he pulled out the desk chair and sat down. The room seemed to know it had been neglected. The armoire was practically cringing in embarrassment, and the curtains were stiff as a dowager at the vicar's Sunday tea.

Bloody hell. He ran his hands through his hair restlessly. *No more metaphors, man!* He'd gone absolutely barking mad. What was he doing? Callender House, shabby or not, was none of his affair.

But it was a bargain, he told himself as he dumped the contents of his suitcase onto the bed and rummaged through his things for a clean shirt. He was amazed tourists weren't banging down the doors to take advantage. It was a wonder that Olivia didn't look into advertising, a few mentions on a travel Web site or two . . .

There he went again. He grunted as he pulled off his sticky shirts and replaced them with a new one. He wasn't the sort to let a cabbie run down some innocent woman, but following her into a hotel? Checking into that hotel? Ticking off all the ways she could save said hotel from ruin, if not bankruptcy? He was no knight in shining armor. He snorted at the idea as he tossed clothes into the bureau drawers. And as far as he knew, Olivia wasn't a damsel in distress.

Even if she looked a bit like one. Soft around the edges, like a full-blown rose, round and sweet. Even if it was beginning to feel a bit like fate had drawn him to that very spot on the sidewalk this morning, to her. He could still hear the bell going off in his head, a happy silver peal, as if his wandering had come to an end.

"Oh, *bloody* hell," he barked into the silent room, slamming his suitcase shut. He really had gone mad. He didn't even know her, for Christ's sweet sake.

But there was always the chance that he would see her if he strolled down to the restaurant for a quick meal. And that was the point of it, wasn't it? He wanted to see her again. Wanted a chance to actually talk to her, when he wasn't covered in mocha and facing the strewn contents of his suitcase on the sidewalk.

That was all. A bit of flirtation. A welcome-to-New-York meal with a pretty girl. Nothing more.

Shaking his head at himself, he pocketed his room key and walked into the hall—and nearly collided with a tiny little woman in a hot pink turban and enough lipstick to coat the walls of his room.

"Oh dear," she murmured, pressing a hand to her breast and batting a pair of frightening false eyelashes at him. "You almost knock me over, young man." *Almost* was pronounced with a very Russian Z.

"My apologies, ma'am," he said, backing up against the wall when she drifted closer, a trio of scarves fluttering at her throat.

"Yelena Belyakova," she said, grasping his hand before he could snatch it away. When he didn't respond quickly enough, she added, "Madam Belyakova, formerly of the Ballet Russe and the Joffrey."

He shook her hand, which was little more than a bundle of bird bones weighted down with several heavy silver rings. Good God, was he supposed to kiss it? He pumped it instead, and flashed his most charming smile. "Rhys Spencer. Formerly of . . . London."

"Beautiful city," she said, and slipped her arm through his. "I have lover there once. And what brings you to New York?"

A lover. Right. Aware that his mouth was hanging open, he snapped it shut. "I'm a chef, ma'am—madam."

"You cook?" She smiled up at him from beneath a layer of heavy blue eye shadow. "I love a man who knows his way around kitchen. I will teach you to make blini."

It was a declaration, not a suggestion, so Rhys wisely didn't argue.

Madam Belyakova had led him down the hall, he realized with a start, tottering on a pair of heels he wasn't at all sure it was sensible for a woman of her age to wear. Not that he intended to argue that point, either.

"What brings you to the city, then?" he asked when she gazed up at him expectantly. Anything to keep cooking lessons out of the conversation.

"I live here, silly boy." Her laugh was a rough bark, full of gravel.

She lived here? Then why was she wandering about this hotel, way up here on the ninth floor? He searched for something else to say, but she beat him to it.

"My apartment is on tenth floor," she said with a sage nod. "Almost thirty . . . well, many years now. I like to walk in the halls sometimes. Is easier than the streets. So many brash young men out there, with their falling-off pants and their big radios. Is not music, what they play. Music is Stravinsky and Mozart."

Rhys was trying to keep up, with her words if not her pace—they were practically crawling along the hallway. "You live here . . . in the hotel?"

"Why yes, silly boy." She laughed again, another grating rasp. An old-school smoker, he bet. "Top two floors are for residents. Have been always."

He lifted a brow as he considered this. Maybe meeting Madam Belyakova was a blessing in disguise. "You must know Olivia then."

She gave an artful shrug, and fluttered one of her scarves with her free hand. "Olivia Callender? Of course, darling. I know her since she was child!"

"Really now." That was a convenience he would be a fool to pass up, wouldn't he? He gave the old woman's arm a companionable squeeze. "I'm sure you don't like to gossip . . ."

"Gossip? Bah. I am too old for such things." But her hot pink smile was sly.

"Of course, it wouldn't really be gossip to tell me, say, if Olivia was married, now would it?"

"Married?" Amusement echoed in her laugh. "Oh no, not our Olivia. I tell her she must find young man—or older man, for they are sometimes better, you see—but she say she is too busy here. Too busy with hotel, too busy dreaming her life away. Is a shame, really. She is lovely young woman. She does not have dancer's body, but lovely nonetheless."

Rhys bit his lip to hold back a snort of surprise. Olivia's body was lovely, all right, dancer or not.

And she was single. Too busy for men, Madam Belyakova had said. Brilliant.

Well, not brilliant, really, because it meant she might decide she was too busy for him, he realized with a stab of alarm. Then he remembered the flash of heat in her eyes when they shook hands, and smiled to himself. He could persuade her to make time for him. Show him around her city, perhaps.

In the meantime, though, maybe Yelena could be persuaded to not gossip some more.

"Madam Belyakova?" He stopped at the ancient brass doors to the lift and pressed the DOWN button. "Would you do me the honor of accompanying me to lunch?"

Clearly, she was still asleep, Olivia told herself as she stood at one end of the Coach and Four's dining room, Uncle Stuart beside her. It would certainly explain the crooked nameplate, the cake debate, and the fallen chandelier. Not to mention the sexy Brit who'd rescued her from certain maiming, if not death, via taxi cab.

It was, quite simply, a nightmare. A nightmare with one very pleasant interlude, but who could explain dreams, really? The subconscious was a strange place.

And hers had apparently had a nervous breakdown.

"If this is a typical afternoon around here, you're in more trouble than I thought." Stuart arched a brow and waved at the chaos. Most of the diners were huddled at the maitre d's station, clamoring for refunds. Willie and Helen were arguing over the best way to clean up the remains of the chandelier, and in the kitchen, Rick and Josef were apparently still arguing, oblivious to the newest disaster.

For a dream, it was uncomfortably realistic.

"This isn't a typical afternoon," Olivia said, and realized she was actually wringing her hands. That was bad. *No more hand wringing*, she admonished herself. It was a dead giveaway. "Not at all."

Stuart's response to that was a snort, and Olivia took a deep breath. She wasn't going to panic. Or cry. Even if she really, really wanted to.

Most afternoons at the Coach and Four were lovely. Dinnertime, too. It was never too crowded, for one thing, and it was . . . friendly. Comfortable. A bit like family, really. Which wasn't what Stuart seemed to think a hotel restaurant should be, but Olivia liked it that way. Some nights the hotel's permanent residents ate together, taking one of the big tables in the corner, and on really quiet evenings Frankie Garson sometimes played the old baby grand piano and everyone gathered around to sing show tunes and old standards.

When she was a child, her father used to play that piano the same way.

All right, she was wringing her hands again. She had to somehow move from this spot, and more importantly move Uncle Stuart from this spot. To Siberia, preferably.

"I'm so sorry about this," she said after another deep breath. Wow. The man had eyebrows like a villain out of a silent movie, she noticed. Black and bushy and somehow malicious. "Can I take you to lunch somewhere? My treat."

"I highly doubt you have the funds to take me anywhere but the corner deli." He rolled his eyes and folded his arms over the neat gray pinstripes of his suit jacket. "I'm not particularly interested in lunch, in any case."

"Well, we can talk in my office," she said. Pretending the idea didn't make her want to run screaming from the room. "It's quiet in there."

"Yes, I've been there," he said with something uncomfortably close to venom in his voice. "It was your father's office, too, as well as your grandfather's."

There wasn't really an answer to that, since it was true. It didn't explain why he seemed so angry about it, of course, so instead of answering she simply swallowed hard. Any minute she would be back to wringing her hands. Or very possibly hiding under the piano.

"Well?" Stuart demanded, spreading his hands in impatience. "Let's go on with it, shall we?"

Oh, there were no words for how much Olivia didn't want to do that. Nothing Stuart could say now would be good. How could it be? No one looked that frightening when they were about to tell you they'd bought you a pony, after all.

So she sucked in another deep breath, aware that she was probably overdosing on oxygen, and said, "Yes, let's go into my office. I'll have the kitchen send in some tea."

But when she turned to head for the door, she saw something so strange it took her a moment to process it. It was

Rhys, gorgeous, funny, rock star Rhys from this morning, with Yelena on his arm. Her pulse gave a startled little kick and she heard, as if from far away, her own gasp of surprise.

That couldn't be right. It couldn't be him, could it? With Yelena? Maybe this really was a dream. A bad one, yes, but a dream nevertheless. Only in a dream would Yelena flutter her fingers at Olivia while Rhys winked, slouched in the door with the tiny little ex-ballerina hanging onto his arm.

She didn't have time to consider it any further, though. Just then Josef came storming out of the kitchen, bellowing, "I quit! Yes, quit! Is lunacy, this place! *Wahnsinn!*"

For an instant, there was complete silence as every head turned to look at him, standing in the chaos of the dining room, broken crystal at his feet. His chef's hat was bunched in his hands, his coat was smeared with chocolate frosting—and then he was making a beeline for Olivia.

Beside her Stuart took a step backward as Josef huffed to a halt in front of them, but it was too late. Because Rick was pushing through the swinging door behind Josef, doing his own ranting. His hat was gone, too, and his face was the color of an overripe tomato. And in his hands was the disputed cake.

"I'm crazy? You're crazy," he shouted. A woman at the closest table dropped her fork in surprise, and it clattered against her plate. "It's just a cake! A bad one!"

Josef whirled around to face him, which Olivia guessed Rick had been counting on. Because in the next moment the remains of the cake were sailing through the air—and smacking Uncle Stuart in the face with a wet, heavy splat as Josef ducked.

Olivia desperately wanted the next noise she heard to be her alarm clock's horrible shriek, but instead it was an outraged grunt from her uncle.

"You see, yes?" Josef barked to the room at large, spreading his arms wide. Despite the fact that an innocent bystander was covered with German chocolate cake, and his sous chef had fled into the kitchen—probably for some rotten eggs, Olivia thought with another vague stab of alarm—the chef was positively triumphant. "A lunatic!"

Well, yes. Apparently it was going around.

Even further than she'd thought, too. Because as Uncle Stuart managed a muffled "Mmmppff!" she felt an arm slide around her waist, and looked up to see Rhys beside her.

Her mouth fell open, but nothing more coherent than Stuart's outburst emerged.

"Here you are, sir," Rhys said to her uncle, pressing a clean linen napkin into his hand. "So sorry about that, really. We were supposed to have the run-through for the dinner theatre later. Mixed signals, yeah? What can you do?"

Those dark gray eyes of his were wide and busy, she noticed as she stared up at Rhys in amazement. They were darting around the room, in fact. Probably because it was difficult to make up an enormous lie like the one he'd just told off the top of his head.

"Dinner theater, yeah," Rhys continued, as if he weren't facing a furious man with chocolate frosting all over his face and his suit. "Hasn't Olivia told you about it? Interactive, we're thinking." He grinned, a bright flash of amusement that lit up his whole face. "Maybe not so interactive as this, you see, but with the customers participating. It's all the rage in . . . in the West End. Of . . . Manchester."

Olivia bit her bottom lip as Stuart raised his sticky eyebrows. As liars went, Rhys was pretty awful. But the fact that he was doing it at all was . . . well, confusing, for one thing, but sweet. So very sweet.

The feel of his strong arm around her was something different, though. Not sweet. Hot was the word for that. Tempting.

And dangerous. Very, very dangerous.

"You expect me to believe that this . . . this pandemonium," Stuart sputtered, "is going to be a regular feature here?" He wiped another glob of icing from his chin and a glistening cherry from the top of his head.

"Well, regular is a relative term, yeah?" Rhys squeezed Olivia closer when she opened her mouth. "More of a special event, I'm thinking."

If Stuart raised his brows any higher, they were going to end up on the back of his head. "And you are?"

Oh, this should be good, Olivia thought with a distant flutter of panic.

Her unlikely rescuer didn't miss a beat. "Rhys Spencer." He stuck out his free hand, and withdrew it gracefully when Stuart simply stared. "Friend of Olivia's."

"I see." Stuart tossed the smeared napkin on the closest table and brushed off the front of his suit with distaste.

Olivia had a feeling "I see" didn't mean what it usually meant. And in the sudden ringing silence, she had an even more frightening feeling that the next words out of Stuart's mouth weren't going to be anything she wanted to hear.

But Rhys was still beside her, his arm draped around her as casually as if they'd known each other for years. As if they were, in fact, friends. As if stepping in to save her from horrifying situations was the thing he'd been waiting all his life to do.

That was silly, of course. If she was honest with herself, she had to wonder about a complete stranger barging into her life and taking over. He was probably unbalanced. An escapee from a local mental hospital, even if he was a gorgeous, unbelievably charming one.

She should really move away from him, gently untangle

his arm from around her waist, and take Uncle Stuart into her office. Call the police. Or the men with the butterfly nets.

But the truth was, standing next to Rhys felt . . . right. Perfect, in fact. Even if that delicious aura of danger hadn't completely faded.

Maybe she'd gone crazy, too. Today, it didn't seem impossible.

"This is exactly what I warned your father about," Stuart said. He looked ridiculous—still faintly smudged with chocolate, cake crumbs on the front of his wrinkled suit coat—but there was nothing ridiculous about the tone of his voice. "This hotel is a dinosaur and you have no idea what to do with it."

He laughed then, shaking his head as he surveyed the room. The people who hadn't stormed the maitre d's station for refunds stared at him, forks in midair, drinking glasses halfway to their lips. Maybe because his laugh was more of a bark, and gleefully nasty. "Do you know what this place is worth?" he said, turning back to Olivia. She stiffened, and felt Rhys's arm tighten around her. "Millions, Olivia. *Millions*. Every year, I've waited for you to give up, to understand that you can't make a go of this place. Your father could hardly do it, after all, and he actually had business sense."

"All right then, you—" Rhys began, but Olivia tugged him back, even though her heart was pounding so violently, it was hard to hear anything past the roar in her ears. A fistfight wasn't going to improve this situation. Even a real prince on a white steed wouldn't improve this situation.

"If I needed any more proof that you don't know what you're doing here, I got it today," Stuart continued, unruffled, ignoring a grumble of fury from Rhys. "If you don't know it by now, you should. And you're going to learn it before the year is up, I guarantee you that."

Olivia opened her mouth to respond, even though she had no idea what she was going to say, but this time Stuart was the one to stop her. He raised a hand with weary disgust.

"Don't bother." He brushed off his suit coat one last time as he started out of the room and threw his last words over his shoulder. "This hotel *will* be mine."

# Chapter 3

It was hard to think straight during an adrenaline rush, Olivia decided as Rhys steered her into a chair. And that's what she was probably feeling—adrenaline zooming through her bloodstream, pure and simple. Fight or flight, panic response, there were probably a dozen terms for it.

But she really didn't care what it was called, she thought as she stared at a star-shaped piece of chandelier on the carpet not three feet away. She felt as if someone had slapped her, hard, and it was all too clear that no matter how weird this day had been, it was definitely not a dream.

"You all right?" Rhys said, leaning in to offer her a glass of water.

She stared at it, wondering where he'd found the glass, and said without thinking, "Ella Fitzgerald once sang to Mayor LaGuardia under that chandelier. I don't remember what song, but I know it's written down somewhere."

He seemed to consider this for a minute. "Uh, yeah, that's brilliant. What happened here anyway?"

She sighed and took the water from him, checking for broken glass before she took a sip. "Nothing good." Then she smiled up at him. "Except for you. That's the second time you rescued me today. Or tried to."

"I can still take a swing at him, you know." He winked at her, and lounged back in his seat. "Old guy like that can't run very fast, I warrant."

There it was again, that thrilling flicker of arousal.

Which was just as surreal as everything else about this moment. The glittering bones of the chandelier on the carpet, the sound of renewed shouting coming from the kitchen, the diners who were no longer even pretending to eat and were staring at her instead.

It would be so much better if this really were a dream.

Rhys was still watching her, she realized, raking his fingers through his hair restlessly. He'd changed his shirt—Mick Jagger was gone and the word "Arsenal" had replaced it, whatever that meant.

"Who was that bloke?" Rhys said suddenly, narrowing his eyes.

Who was *he?* That was the question Olivia wanted to ask. But before she could answer him, Josie's voice broke the silence and Olivia saw Josie and Roseanne heading toward the table, Josie's auburn ponytail bouncing over her shoulder and Roseanne's graying brow knitted in concern. Her heart lifted, just a little bit, which was good since it had sunk so low it was practically down at her ankles.

Josie raised an eyebrow at her, and gestured toward the fallen chandelier. "I thought I told you no more wild parties."

Roseanne squeezed past Rhys and took the chair beside Olivia, winding an arm around her shoulders. "Oh, leave her alone. What happened, honey?"

Roseanne was in charge of bookkeeping, and she had worked at Callender House since Olivia was a baby. Any minute now she'd be petting Olivia's head the way she had when Olivia was still in kindergarten, and Olivia wasn't about to argue.

"Should I start with the cake or the chandelier?"

"Start with Stuart," Josie insisted. "I saw him marching through the lobby. Weren't you supposed to have lunch?"

"That was right out after the cake in the face," Rhys put in with a naughty smirk. "Lost his appetite, he did."

Josie was horrified. "You threw a cake at him?" she asked Olivia.

"Of course not!" Olivia sighed. "Unfortunately, Rick did. Actually, he didn't really throw it at Uncle Stuart, but Josef ducked."

"What does Josef have to do with it?" Roseanne asked, glancing back at the doors to the kitchen as if either one of the chefs would come charging out any second, armed with more baked goods.

"He was mad about the cake," Olivia said, brushing more crumbs from the tablecloth.

"So he . . . pulled down the chandelier?" Josie asked.

"No!" Olivia sagged against Roseanne's arm, but she couldn't help smiling when Rhys bit back a laugh. The whole thing sounded ridiculous. It *was* ridiculous. Except for the part where she was pretty sure Stuart meant to take the hotel away from her.

"Someone start from the beginning, yeah? Because I still don't know who that sodding bloke was," Rhys said.

Josie turned confused eyes on him. "Who are *you?*"

"Rhys Spencer," he said, offering her a hand. "Friend of Olivia's."

Both Roseanne and Josie raised their eyebrows at this in a silent plea for explanation.

"I met Rhys this morning," Olivia said, glancing up at him as her cheeks heated. Again. God, why wasn't there a cure for blushing? "Outside."

Then she stopped, mouth still open. She didn't even

know the rest of the story, and certainly not why or how he'd appeared in the restaurant out of nowhere.

"I'm a new friend," Rhys said smoothly, and winked at her.

More raised eyebrows. It was an epidemic.

And also a little insulting, Olivia realized as she sat up and shrugged off Roseanne's arm. As if she couldn't have a friend who was gorgeous and sexy and had the most delicious British accent she'd ever heard.

Just because she'd never even met a man like Rhys before didn't mean anything. Much.

"Very new," she added pointlessly, and was rewarded with another wink. So new she didn't know anything about him, but Roseanne and Josie didn't need that little detail.

"Wait a minute," Josie said, holding up both hands. "You're on that TV show, the cooking one. You're the British chef all the fan sites are rooting for."

Rhys gave Olivia a sheepish smile as her mouth fell open in surprise. He was on TV? Now?

"Yeah, I'm that British chef," he admitted. "Show's on a break until we film the finale a month from now."

"I thought you looked familiar," Roseanne said, clearly sizing him up with even more appreciation now, but Josie was unimpressed.

"Reality TV aside," she said, "what happened in here? It looks like the place got raided."

"Josef and Rick were arguing about a chocolate cake that got ruined, and then there was a crash, and then Helen rushed into the kitchen to say the chandelier had fallen down, and then Stuart showed up, right on time as usual, and then Stuart got a cake in the face," Olivia said with a weary sigh. "I think that about covers it."

"Not quite, love," Rhys put in. "There was that nasty bit about the hotel at the end."

Roseanne bristled, and sat up straight. "What does that mean?"

"I'm not sure, to tell you the truth," Olivia admitted. Suddenly crowded by the questions, she got up and paced a few feet away.

Which only attracted more attention from the noneating diners. Except for Yelena, who was chatting up Willie from her usual table in the corner, turban bobbing.

"Maybe we should take this discussion elsewhere," Josie suggested when she followed Olivia's gaze to the interested patrons watching from their tables. "I'm thinking the bar might be appropriate."

"Brilliant," Rhys said, and got up to slide his arm around Olivia's shoulders. Just the weight of it made her tingle with awareness. "Lead the way."

The bar was deserted, which wasn't unusual for a Monday afternoon. Still, it was a little too deserted, she thought as she pulled a stool away from the polished length of mahogany and sat down. Where was Tommy?

"No barkeep?" Rhys said, leaning over the counter to scope out the selection of bottles. "And no Grey Goose? I think the occasion calls for some quality spirits, love."

"I don't usually drink before dinner," Olivia protested, wondering if she should tell Rhys to come out from behind the counter before Tommy appeared and waved his offended dignity around. Rhys had flipped open the bar's hatch door and walked right in as if he belonged there, and was even now taking glasses down from the racks.

"Who *is* this guy?" Josie whispered fiercely in her ear as she pulled up another stool. "I mean, aside from some random reality TV person?"

"I don't care," Roseanne said before Olivia could answer. "I sure like to listen to him. Imagine if I brought *him* to the next Renaissance Faire with me. God, can you picture him in leggings?"

"Shhh!" Olivia warned her when Rhys looked up, a bottle of Stoli in one hand and a bottle of Jim Beam in the other.

"Pick your poison, ladies," he said with a grin.

"I actually need a drink," Josie said in amazement. "Has the whole world gone whacko today?"

Olivia shrugged. "Pretty much."

"Tell them what the sodding fool said to you," Rhys suggested as he poured a shot of bourbon and passed it to Roseanne.

"Yes, please do," Josie said, reaching across the bar for the bowl of pretzels. "The suspense is giving me a headache."

Olivia stared into the tumbler of vodka Rhys had poured for her. She'd never had liquor straight up, and she wasn't sure she wanted to start now. But when she thought about Stuart's voice as he hissed, "The hotel will be mine," she decided to give it a shot.

"Oh my God, it burns," she choked out a minute later. "I think my eyes are actually watering."

"Make her something foofy, will you," Josie said. "She's not exactly a shot drinker on a good day."

"One Flirtini, coming right up."

"Are you a renegade bartender, too?" Josie demanded. "And will someone *please* tell us what Stuart said?"

"He said the hotel will be his." An echo of her earlier panic vibrated in the back of her head, like a headache threatening to take hold. "Exactly like that. He sputtered and criticized, just like he always does, but this time he said—"

"The hotel will be his," Josie repeated. Her eyes flashed fire when she glanced up from her drink to look at Olivia. "Who does he think he is, Darth Vader?"

"Oh, honey." Roseanne bit her bottom lip and fingered the end of her long, gray braid. "I've been afraid of this."

Olivia gaped at her. "What do you mean? He's always hated this place."

"Doesn't mean he doesn't know what it's worth." Roseanne's voice was softer now, and she reached out to pat Olivia's hand. "You're going to have to be very careful, sweetie."

"Careful about what?" Josie asked. She set down her glass and crunched into a pretzel with a little more violence than was strictly necessary. "The hotel is Olivia's."

"That may be," Rhys said, sliding a martini glass toward Olivia, "but there are a million ways he could make that very difficult for her, yeah?"

"Driving me out, you mean?" Olivia said. There went her pulse again, fluttering like a caged bird.

"Exactly."

"Well, he won't." She stood up, ignoring her drink, and paced toward the middle of the room, absently pushing chairs into place at their tables as she went. "He can't."

When she was a child, the bar had always been off limits. "Nothing for little misses to see in there, sweetie," her father would say with a laugh. Her mother had agreed, but as often as not Olivia would run down the service stairs and creep through the lobby when she was supposed to be in bed. She'd find parents seated with friends or hotel guests at one of the round tables in the dark, smoky room, her mother in a cocktail dress with her good pearls on and her hair done, her father in his customary blue suit, his glasses polished but still sliding down his nose when he laughed.

And now it was hers.

She couldn't remember the last time the bar had been as crowded as it was in her memories. Now, more nights than not, half the tables sat empty. She squinted and crossed the room to run a finger over one of the picture frames. The Chrysler Building reached for the sky from beneath a film of dust. The place wasn't even getting cleaned regularly.

The fact that she was here, not in a cocktail dress, not in pearls, but in her old gray pants and an even older sweater, drinking vodka on a Monday afternoon, didn't exactly lift her spirits.

She turned around and faced the others, all of whom were sipping their drinks and watching her as if she were about to break into song.

"He's not taking this hotel away from me," she said after a deep breath. "He can't. There's nothing in the world that will make me give up this place."

"Bravo!" Roseanne said, clapping. The bourbon had already pinked her cheeks.

"It's a landmark," Olivia continued, confident now. "It's history, it's my legacy. *Mine*."

Even Josie clapped this time, and Rhys whistled, long and low.

Olivia sketched a bow, pleased with herself. Stuart couldn't scare her, the big bully. Callender House *was* hers, and that was the way it was going to stay.

Just then Angel pushed open the door and stuck his head inside. "Um, Olivia?"

She smiled at him. "Yes?"

"The nameplate outside just fell off completely."

Perfect. She sighed. "Where's my drink?"

Josie helped herself to another shot when Olivia left the room, with the yummy Brit following her. It was a workday, but around here, that didn't mean much.

"Hit me, too," Roseanne said, holding out her glass.

Josie poured bourbon for both of them. "It's not usually this crazy around here, is it?"

"Not quite," Roseanne admitted. "How long have you been here now?"

"Two months." Josie knocked back the shot, and coughed when she'd swallowed. "And I really don't want to look for another job. Again."

She wasn't even sure why she'd taken this one. Okay, well, part of the reason was being "let go" from the St. Regis, but she refused to feel ashamed of that. If the manager couldn't stand to hear the truth about what one of the guests had been found doing with a member of the housekeeping staff, it wasn't her fault. A little flirtation between consenting adults was one thing, but fur handcuffs? In the linen room? Please.

And Olivia had offered her a big promotion. Not a big salary, but at least a promotion. Guest Services Manager. It looked good on a business card, and it would have taken her a decade or more to get to the same position at one of the big hotels.

"How long have you been here?" she asked Roseanne idly.

"Twenty-seven years," Roseanne answered with a placid smile. "Olivia's grandfather hired me, and then I worked for Olivia's dad. Who was just a little less eccentric than his father."

"Twenty-seven years, huh?" At the idea of twenty-seven years in one job, another drink seemed tempting, but Josie stifled the urge. Drunken subway riding was never a good idea, and passing out on her keyboard probably wouldn't win her any brownie points around here either.

"I wouldn't change it for the world." Roseanne set her glass down and propped her head in her hands. "I get my time off every year for the faire, I have my own office and

free lunch, and I know if I ever get kicked out of my apartment, I can move in here."

"That's a ... plus," Josie said dubiously. "Unless the
hotel closes down. I have to say, registration is not exactly
at an all-time high. And the residents? Most of them are
paying circa-1978 rent." She considered that for a moment
as she lined up pretzels on the bar. "Which is a good deal,
actually. Maybe I should move in here."

Roseanne snorted, but a moment later her grin faded. "I
am worried, you know. Stuart's never actually threatened to
take the hotel away from Olivia before."

"I don't know why he is now," Josie pointed out. "I
mean, I like it here, and Olivia's great, but this place isn't
what you'd call a cash cow."

"Nobody knows that better than I do."

"Reassuring to hear from the woman in charge of my
paycheck," Josie said dryly. "I hope Olivia's thought of
some ways to get more paying guests in here."

Roseanne sighed, her faded blue eyes sorrowful. "If she
hasn't, she will now."

"Who will what?"

Josie looked up to see Gus Fitch ambling toward the
bar—and then ducking beneath it, just as Rhys had.

She threw up her hands in defeat. "Did I miss the memo
about fix-your-own-drink day or something?"

"I'm filling in for Tommy," Gus explained, squirting
water into a glass he'd filled with ice. "He pulled out his
back."

"But ... you're a guest," Josie sputtered, looking at
Roseanne for backup.

The older woman shrugged and took a pretzel from Josie's
pile. Apparently, bourbon did nothing to fuel her righteous
indignation.

Gus had been a guest since Josie had started work at the hotel, but Olivia had told her he'd actually been at Callender House for nearly a year now.

Which was, in Josie's opinion, pretty weird. Gus Fitch had written two best-selling books, one on his childhood as the son of a famous film director and another exposing the truth about the Riverside Institution, a mental hospital. He'd been on *Oprah*, for heaven's sake.

Not that he looked it. Josie wasn't sure what a best-selling author was supposed to look like, but it seemed to her it should involve a little more bling than Gus indulged in. He was wearing his usual uniform of faded jeans, loose cotton sweater, and baseball cap today, and Josie didn't think she'd ever seen him in anything else. Even on *Oprah*, come to think of it. Coupled with his sad puppy dog eyes and his low, soft voice, he reminded her of an overgrown kid who'd just witnessed his baseball team losing the pennant race.

But he was sweet. In fact, he was sort of the default hotel mascot, as far as she could tell. He knew everybody, and everybody loved him. Including Tommy, she guessed, who was famously territorial about "his" bar. There was even a plastic sign tacked up beside the mirror: *Tommy's Parking Only.*

"So what's the occasion?" Gus asked as he refilled the pretzel bowl. For a volunteer bartender, he took his responsibilities pretty seriously, Josie noted. "You guys don't usually knock back shots in the midafternoon."

"Stuart got nasty with Olivia at lunch today," Roseanne said with a weary sigh. She settled back on her stool, which creaked under her weight.

"Right after the chandelier fell down and Rick threw a cake at him," Josie added.

Gus blinked. "That's not good."

"You're a master of understatement," Josie said, but she smiled as she did, and Gus blushed a little bit.

And then he smiled at her, a real smile, a shy, just-for-her smile. Maybe it was the bourbon, but suddenly she understood why everyone liked him so much. Because she did, too.

"That's going to take some fixing," Olivia said as she stood on the sidewalk outside the hotel and examined the now dented nameplate.

"Fixing?" Rhys grunted. "Time for the rubbish heap, I think. Get a new one."

"No!" Bending to pick it up—and finding it far heavier than she'd thought—Olivia propped the tarnished brass gently against the wall. "This is the original sign. It's . . . it's . . . *historic.*"

"Not everything old is historic," Rhys argued, and slouched against the bricks as he folded his arms over his chest.

Well, the Callender House nameplate *was* historic. Whether it was or not, Olivia decided, frowning at her own logic. After the cake and the chandelier and, frankly, the vodka, she wasn't prepared to argue about it with a stranger.

Which reminded her that Rhys Spencer, for all intents and purposes, was just that. Scowling at him, she asked, "Where did you *come* from?"

"Right about there, I think," he answered, pointing at a spot on the sidewalk with a wicked grin.

She sighed. "I mean it. You just turn up out of nowhere, saving me from disaster. I can't decide what kind of penny you are."

His brow lifted in confusion, disappearing beneath that shaggy, dark fringe of hair. "What kind of what now?"

"Penny. You know." She wasn't going to blush this time, damn it. "See a penny, pick it up, all day long you'll have good luck? But then there's 'turning up like a bad penny,' too."

"I think you're undervaluing me either way," Rhys teased, but when she scowled harder, he threw up his hands in surrender. "No need to get narked, love. I'm a chef. I just arrived in town this morning, as a matter of fact, by way of London and lately L.A. In fact, I have to head back there for the finale of the show in a month."

"A chef? Really?" She tried to picture him in a white chef's coat—and, even sillier, a white chef's hat like Josef had always worn—and had to stifle a giggle.

"I don't wear the hat," he said, and scowled right back at her. Goodness, the man was practically a mind reader. "And yeah, I cook. Always have. It's the one thing I do brilliantly."

As she watched his lips form the words, she highly doubted that cooking was the only thing he did brilliantly, as he put it. Look at that mouth. He was probably an excellent kisser.

A flicker of surprise skittered up the back of her neck. What was she thinking? No one had said anything about kissing.

She realized she was still staring at him and dragged her gaze away to ask, "So what brought you to New York?"

"Don't know." He grinned and pushed away from the wall to reach out and take her hand. "Hadn't been here in a long while, and I needed a change after all that blasted Los Angeles sunshine."

It was hard to take in everything he was saying with his lean fingers clasped around hers. "Where are you staying?" she managed, trying to ignore the warmth of his hand, and the distracting way he was running his thumb over her knuckles.

"Didn't I mention that, love?" He pulled her closer, just an inch or so, but it was enough to send an electric tingle of awareness through her body. She glanced up into those smoky gray eyes, and felt her mouth fall open when he spoke again. "I'm staying here. I'm your newest guest."

# Chapter 4

Desperate times called for desperate snacks. Well, maybe not desperate as much as industrial-strength, Olivia mused as she flipped on the lights in the restaurant kitchen close to midnight. Most of the time, the idea of trekking downstairs from her small tenth-floor apartment was enough to keep her from raiding the stash in Josef's pantry, but not tonight.

Tonight she needed something big. Something strong. Preferably something chocolate. And the only thing that even came close in her tiny kitchen upstairs was an aging box of Count Chocula she'd bought on a whim one day, in a fit of nostalgia. But cereal—especially stale, not-really-chocolate cereal—was not going to get the job done tonight.

All remnants of the Great Cake Battle had been cleaned up, and the dinner service had proceeded without disaster. Mostly because Rick had thrown his apron on the counter and quit shortly after Olivia found her way back to the kitchen.

Which was after she'd heard that Rhys Spencer was ensconced in a room on the ninth floor.

Boy, did she need chocolate.

She padded across the clean swept floor to the pantry and

swung open the door. Rhys Spencer could stay anywhere in the city. But to hear him tell it, he'd met her—for all values of "meeting" that included pushing her out of a taxi's path—followed her into the hotel, discovered it was hers, and checked in without a second thought or a backward glance.

It was . . . a little alarming.

And she really hoped his bed had been made with the newest sheets.

Staring at the neatly arranged contents of the pantry, she couldn't help wondering what it meant. Rhys hadn't only checked into her hotel, he'd come downstairs in search of her and tried to salvage the bizarre situation in which she'd found herself. And then he'd made her a drink. And followed her outside, where he'd been charming and sexy enough to make her head spin, lounging against that wall, all indolence and sly grins.

It was . . . well, weird. Unexpected, at the very least. Men didn't really do things like that, did they? Not outside of fairy tales and romantic movies, at least.

But it was also sweet, and flattering. And completely nerve-wracking.

She didn't know what to do with a man like Rhys, she thought as she cut a piece of leftover cake from the dinner service and put it on a plate. She knew what she'd *like* to do with a man like Rhys, and that was surprising enough, because it entailed the kinds of things she'd only read about in books.

The kinds of things that made her a little dizzy with desire just imagining them.

Forking up an enormous bite of cake, she bit into it and sighed. Chocolate was never a bad thing, but she was afraid even Josef's sinfully rich dark chocolate cake wasn't going to cut it tonight. If she wasn't thinking about Rhys and all the ways he made her restless, she was thinking about Stuart and all the ways he made her nervous. She'd tossed and turned in bed for nearly an hour before she came downstairs. Usually she was asleep the minute her head hit the pillow.

But not tonight. Today had been one long, strange wakeup call. If she ever got to sleep again, she'd be lucky.

Taking her plate, she flicked off the lights and padded toward the door. It was eerily quiet tonight, and once the lights were out, she needed a moment for her eyes to adjust to the dark. She knew the hotel like the back of her hand, but since her father had died it seemed . . . bigger. It was all hers now, even the few nooks and crannies she had never explored, and Stuart had managed to scare her into wondering if those unknown corners held anything but trouble.

And her father was no longer around to reassure her. To call the plumber or the electrician, or handle the odd guest who tried to short them on the bill. It was up to her to make sure the elevators were running and the upstairs hallways got vacuumed.

And the chandelier was checked out occasionally, she reminded herself grimly. Too late for that now.

Too late for a lot of things. But not for a soothing cup of tea with her cake, and maybe some mindless television. She needed to sleep tonight. She could deal with everything else tomorrow. Or possibly the next day.

Stepping into the service corridor outside the kitchen, she turned left to head toward the back elevator—and smacked into something that felt very much like a tall, strong man.

She let out a nervous shriek as her plate—and her cake, damn it—hit the floor, and two strong hands grabbed her upper arms.

"Olivia? Olivia, it's me. Rhys."

She blinked in the dim hallway, wriggling away from

him. Rhys? My God, he *was* a bad penny. A big, gorgeous, sexy bad penny. "What are you doing down here? You scared me to death."

"Couldn't sleep," he admitted, kneeling to examine her ruined snack. "Not a good day for cake around here, yeah?"

"Apparently not." She groped for the light switch, and then knelt beside him. There was a dark smear of chocolate frosting where the cake had skidded across the floor, and the plate had cracked down the middle when it hit the concrete of the service corridor. She sighed. "Let me get a broom."

"No, let me. My fault, after all." He followed her down the hall to the broom closet, and she couldn't help cursing herself for coming downstairs. Or at least for coming downstairs in her oldest jeans and her ratty gray NYU sweatshirt. And her slippers! Oh yes, very attractive.

Not that she'd expected to run into anyone down here, of course. That was the whole reason she'd taken the fire stairs and had planned on using the service elevator on the way back. It wasn't a good idea to run into guests in the lobby after midnight with pilfered food, in clothes that were essentially pajamas.

But Rhys Spencer was a lot of things she hadn't expected, wasn't he?

She propped open the door to the broom closet and reached for the light switch, but nothing happened when she flicked it on. "I guess the bulb burned out," she said, and then gasped because Rhys was following her into the closet.

"Don't—" she started, but it was too late. He'd knocked the door away from the wall, and it swung closed behind them with a bang.

Uh-oh.

"Bloody hell," Rhys mumbled. "Sorry about that."

She shook her head in the darkness as he rattled the knob.

"Hey, what's this now? It won't open," he said.

"That's because it sticks." She fumbled toward the wall, kicking a bucket as she went and drawing her slippered foot backward with a wince.

"What do you mean, it sticks?"

"I mean it sticks," she explained, squinting into the dense, stuffy darkness. Where she was standing with a man she barely knew. A very sexy, currently outraged man.

She sighed as he rattled the doorknob again. "And now we're stuck."

Seven Minutes in Heaven. That was the name of the kissing game, wasn't it? She'd heard stories about it—plenty of them, with a lot of wet, slobbery details—in the cafeteria during seventh grade, even though she'd never played it herself.

A boy and a girl, alone in the dark. In a closet, in fact. With nothing to do but kiss.

Well, actually, based on some of the stories she'd heard, quite a few things aside from kissing went on, but still. She'd never wanted to play the game with anyone but Joshua Burkle, and that was mostly because he had soft brown eyes and he'd been nice to her when she dozed off during Shannon Kesslar's reading of Juliet's death scene in English and fallen out of her chair.

Rhys was certainly a much more appealing candidate. As far as she could tell, he wasn't a mouth-breather, at least.

Or he would be a more appealing candidate if he'd stop pounding on the door, she thought, wincing as he launched a fresh assault. His knuckles were probably raw by now.

"Bloody hell," he muttered for the tenth time in as many

minutes, and she heard him crossing the floor. Toward her, she thought. "Why hasn't the sodding door ever been fixed?"

"The handle's on back order." She was fairly sure she was talking directly to his chest. It was distracting, because he smelled wonderful—a combination of something woodsy and sharp, and something she suspected was simply Rhys. "It's an old door."

"No," he said with exaggerated surprise.

She poked him—or tried to. The space was so dark, she couldn't even see her hand in front of her, and instead she wound up jabbing a mop handle, which clattered over backward.

"I'm over here, love," he said, and the smile in his voice was as bright and warm as a well-lit room. Then she felt his fingers close around her hand, and she swallowed hard.

"I can tell you one thing good about a broken doorknob," he added. "Being stuck in this closet with you."

"What's good about that?" The question came out in a whisper.

"Oh, I can think of a few things," he murmured, and let go of her hand to wind his arms around her. "We can . . . uh . . . keep each other warm."

*Seven minutes in heaven, here I come,* the part of her brain not overwhelmed by his nearness whispered. But what she said was, "It's too hot in here already."

"We can keep each other company," he murmured into her ear.

God, he was . . . so close. So big. So warm and strong and firm and . . . absolutely unknown. A kiss was one thing—a kiss would be, she was sure, so very, very nice—but the rest? Here? *Now?*

Ignoring the voice of her hormones, which was nodding and shouting, *Here! Now!,* she said in the most teasing tone she could muster, "I like being alone."

His lips hovered against her earlobe, hot and soft. "I don't believe you."

"You're very sure of yourself, aren't you?"

"I was doing better before I knocked over your cake and locked us in the closet," he admitted, but as he did he left a trail of light kisses down the side of her neck, and she trembled.

"That wasn't very smooth, no," she said, and wriggled out of his reach, bumping into what felt like a broom in the process. "And you have to stop that. I can't even see you. I don't even know you!"

He sighed, a soft breath of disappointment in the close, dark space. "What do you want to know?"

Good question. The obvious one was, "Why are you flirting with me?" but that wasn't exactly a confident way to begin a discussion. A dozen more whirled through her head—*Are you going to kiss me? Do you know how sexy your accent is? Why couldn't you sleep? Oh God, you're not in the room with the squeaky box spring, are you? When are you going to kiss me?*—but when she opened her mouth, she heard herself asking, "What's your favorite color?"

Clearly, she was beyond help.

But Rhys simply snorted, a good-natured sound. "Don't have one. You?"

"Sky blue," she said automatically, and then stopped. "What do you mean, you don't have one? Everyone has one."

"Everyone picks one so they can answer that question," he argued, and she heard shuffling as he lowered himself to the ground. "Sit. We may be here for a bit."

She did, feeling her way past the broom and brushing her hand against something that felt like a stiffened string mop. Shuddering, she settled onto the concrete beside him, aware of the warm length of his thigh. "You really don't like one color over another?"

"I like green apples, and ripe pumpkins, and a nice, bloody, purple piece of filet mignon," he said after a minute.

"Okay, what's your favorite food?"

"No such thing," he said with a laugh. "I'll eat almost anything if it's prepared just so."

"You're not making this easy," she said with a frown. "Come on, what's . . . what's the meal you'd want if you were on death row? Your last meal."

"Why? What have you heard?"

She slapped his thigh gently. "Come on. Play along."

"All right then." He grabbed her hand before she could pull it away and twined his fingers with hers. "Kobe beef, a bottle of fifteen-year-old Laphroaig, and a dark chocolate torte. You?"

"*I'm* not going to death row," she said with a laugh. "What's Laphroaig?"

"Single malt scotch, love. Best on the planet."

"So you intend to go out drunk and sick to your stomach?"

"I don't intend to 'go out' at all," he protested. "And you said play along—it's your turn."

The feel of his thumb tracing circles on the back of her hand was hypnotic. She did her best to ignore it, and said, "Okay. Um, mashed potatoes, turkey, and apple pie."

His snort this time was incredulous. "Blimey, love, I need to teach you how to eat. There's more to life than plain potatoes, yeah?"

Food snob. "Well, I like them," she answered. "New question. What's your favorite . . ." She trailed off, thinking. "I know. What's your favorite swear word?"

"I don't think you'd want to hear it."

"Try me."

"You'll blush."

"I don't . . . blush," she said weakly, feeling her cheeks flaming already.

"You don't blush, and I'm the king of England," he laughed. "My turn. Why wouldn't you go out for dinner with me tonight?"

She sighed. The man was nothing if not persistent.

"The sous chef quit this afternoon," she said lightly. "And Josef was still in a temper about the whole thing. I can't cook, but I can run interference. Or try to."

"Well, why didn't you tell me?" he demanded, letting go of her hand.

Bewildered, she said, "That I can't cook?"

"No, that you were short a sous chef." She could feel him shaking his head in disgust. "I could have stepped in, you know."

"Rhys, you're a guest," she protested. "*My* guest. I know this place is a little . . . well, eccentric, but usually we don't require guests to make their own drinks and fix their own meals. I mean, we do have some standards."

"Brilliant," he said dryly. "I'll keep that in mind if something falls on my head."

"Hey!"

"Something to think about, love." She heard rustling, and then he was closer, his arm winding around her shoulders. "If your uncle is determined to run you out of this place, you've got to be on top of your game, yeah?"

"I don't think I have a game," she said wearily, but she didn't shrug his arm away. The weight of it was a comfort in the dark, as much as a temptation. It was horrifying to admit how easy it would be—and how good it would feel—to crawl into Rhys's lap and forget everything but what they could do in seven minutes. Or seventy. "Maybe you can teach me."

He squeezed her shoulders gently. "Don't worry, love. I'm not going anywhere."

"Bloody hell, I've got to get out of this sodding closet," Rhys grumbled sometime later, pounding on the door for the third time in as many minutes. "Does your custodial staff keep banker's hours? Where is everyone?"

Still curled on the floor, Olivia answered sleepily, "It's probably not even four yet."

"Are you mad? We've been in here for days," he protested, rubbing the side of his hand, sore from pounding.

"Rhys, are you . . . are you claustrophobic?"

If only. It would have been much more pleasant, if not exactly more manly, to pass out from terror than admit to Olivia why he needed out, and now.

"Certainly not," he said with authority, shifting his position against the stubbornly stuck door. Bloody hell, if he didn't take a piss soon, he was going to explode. "But this isn't my idea of a brilliant way to spend the night, you know."

"You're the one who let the door shut," she pointed out with a yawn.

Oh, sure, it was a perfect time to cast blame. "You're the one who didn't mention that I shouldn't!"

"Well, I didn't think you were going to follow me into the broom closet."

"Yeah, my fault completely," he said dryly. At least arguing was a distraction.

"A baby was born in here, you know," Olivia said suddenly. "In the forties. An unmarried maid was trying to work as long as she could, and the baby came early. She named her Callie, too."

He blinked, momentarily confused. "And this has what to do with me locking us in the broom closet?"

Silence. "Nothing," she said finally, and the embarrassment in her tone produced a stab of guilt. "Just something I thought you might find interesting. I guess you don't want to hear about the Balinese sword swallowers who were here in the early sixties."

He laughed out loud at that. "You are quite a surprise, Olivia Callender."

She was, too. A bit more every minute. It was a miracle that she'd let him kiss her neck earlier, for starters. He was moving fast, especially for someone like Olivia, and he knew it. But a tiger didn't change his stripes, and he wasn't sure he wanted to try.

He was honest, at least. It was part of the reason he liked food, in fact. Food didn't lie. An apple was an apple, however you sliced it.

The thing was he thought Olivia was, too. After the women he'd encountered in L.A., especially, she was a breath of fresh air.

He hadn't expected it, the women. Sure, there'd always been some, food groupies for Christ's sweet sake, at the restaurants in London. But L.A. was a whole new kettle of fish. One that had been left out in the California sun, too.

The competition had been bad enough. The producers had prided themselves on their mad challenges. A fusion of Italian and Asian cooking—for breakfast. A lunch menu for six-year-olds featuring mushrooms and broccoli. A wedding reception menu for a hundred—on a five-hundred-dollar budget.

Wankers, he thought darkly. As if most chefs had to face any of those particular issues. Still, he'd made it to the finale—on sheer will power alone, he sometimes thought. There weren't many people you could trust not to stab you in the back when two hundred thousand dollars was at stake. In fact, there were exactly none. Not that he'd expected to trust anyone in the first place—his mother, and later Clodagh, had taught him the folly of that long ago. But it was still a bit of a shock to find himself swarmed with women who made Barbie dolls look natural. Not a genuine thing about one of them, from their breasts to their noses to their motives.

But Olivia . . . Olivia was nothing but real. Just the memory of her blinking at him on that sidewalk was enough to make him grin. She hadn't a shred of artifice in her bones. He liked that.

And if she asked outright, he'd have to admit to her that he hadn't been wandering around the hotel only because he couldn't sleep. He'd been lying in that lonely bed upstairs, and every time he closed his eyes he'd seen her face.

Stunned and scared when her uncle made his nasty threat. Determined when she announced in the bar that the bloke would never take the hotel away from her.

And his brain had spun into gear again, clicking through everything he'd seen of the hotel, everything Olivia probably needed to change to make the place a success—all the ways he could help her save it, not that she'd asked, or he'd ever done anything remotely like it before.

And he'd known he had to get a look at the Coach and Four kitchen, when no one was about to interrupt him. He was a chef, after all. If she was going to pull this rotting old mausoleum out of the trash heap, that was one of the places to start.

Not that he'd planned to *call* it a rotting old mausoleum, of course. Not to her face. It wasn't lying if you simply omitted part of the truth.

He was no white knight. Nothing humble about that, just plain truth. But Olivia . . . what *was* it about Olivia that had him stumbling all over himself to come to her rescue?

He already knew all the reasons why he wanted to kiss her. And touch her. And listen to her sigh . . .

Stifling a groan, he moved away from the door. Christ, he had to piss. That last glass of beer after dinner had been a mistake, not that he'd expected to be stuck in a closet overnight.

He expelled a noisy sigh, and he heard Olivia shifting her position on the floor.

"I think you're going to kill me," she said matter-of-factly.

He blinked. "Kill you? Why?"

"Because I just remembered that there's a transom over this door."

He could practically feel her blushing. "A transom, yeah?"

"Yeah." She bumped into something and mumbled, "Ouch."

"Shouldn't it be a bit brighter in here with a window over the door?" he said absently, turning to reach as high as he could above the door.

"It's wooden," she explained, and he felt her, soft and warm, beside him. "It still cranks open, I think, but no one ever uses it. We'd need a ladder, though, and I think there's one against the back wall . . ."

"Hold on," he said through gritted teeth. He'd find the sodding ladder if he had to trip over every bucket and mop in the place, and break both legs to do it. If there was a transom up above that door, he was going through it.

Before he exploded.

"I'm sorry," she repeated, as he clattered past God only knew what, pawing the air for anything metal with rungs.

"What are you sorry for, love?" His knuckles scraped against something solid and cool. Bingo!

"For not remembering sooner." She sounded humiliated

and very small in the darkness. "We could have been out of here hours ago."

They wouldn't have been in here in the first place if the bloody door wasn't broken, but he wasn't going to remind her of that. Not her fault, he told himself as he maneuvered the ladder—none too gracefully—through the cramped space. Something crashed to the floor and Olivia yelped.

"Not to worry," he said as he propped the ladder against the door. "If you'd remembered earlier we wouldn't have played getting to know you."

Brilliant, the way he could feel her blushing in the dark.

"Stand back now," he said as he set his foot on the lowest rung. "I don't know how sturdy this thing is."

"Rhys, no!" Her fingers closed tentatively around his calf. "Let me do it. I'm smaller than you are, for one thing. I don't want you to hurt yourself. Or, well, get even stucker."

No chance. He reached down to untangle her fingers. "I don't think so, love. For one, whoever goes through needs to do it backward. You're not about to dive headfirst out of the transom, are you? And I'm taller. When I drop, the fall won't be so far."

He hesitated when she was silent. It made sense, didn't it? Not that he relished the idea of twisting into some pretzel of a position to get his legs through the thing first.

When she spoke, she sounded doubtful. "Okay. But I'm beginning to feel a little too much like the proverbial damsel in distress today."

"You can save me later, yeah?" He clambered up the ladder rung by rung. Bloody difficult to do in the dark, when he had no idea where the blasted thing would end. Or where, for that matter, the transom's crank was.

Then he banged his head into it.

Muttering and hoping like hell he wouldn't have a nasty goose egg later, he yanked on the thing. Painted shut, or rusted, most likely. It gave way with a groan a moment later, even though he had to smack at the transom a few times to get the thing open.

"Got it," he announced when the blasted thing had swung open as far it would go.

"Well, be careful," Olivia warned him. "Maybe you should just yell for someone instead of climbing through it."

Like hell. Any minute his bladder was going to explode, and that was hardly the way to entice a woman to give you a whirl.

"I'll be fine," he said, twisting on the ladder and hanging onto the bottom edge of the window for dear life as he angled his first leg up and through it. A contortionist he was not, and he was already fairly certain the situation was going to require a bit more flexibility than he could lay claim to.

So it wasn't going to be easy, or graceful. It wasn't as if Olivia could see him, as he was blocking most of the dim light coming through the open window.

And that was truly a saving grace he realized a few minutes later, when he'd finally stuffed both legs through the window and wriggled backward in an attempt to slide through.

Because he was stuck. Again.

"Olivia."

"Yes?"

He heard her foot hit the bottom rung of the ladder. "Love, I think it's time you rescued me."

# Chapter 5

"He didn't really say that, did he?" Josie asked the next day as she and Olivia circled the empty ballroom on the second floor.

"He really did." Olivia smiled as she said it. By the time she'd finally shoved him through the window—where he landed with an ungainly thud—he was about ready to murder someone. Or maybe pass out. He'd barely opened the closet door before tearing off down the hall in search of a bathroom.

She hadn't gotten that information out of him very easily, although he'd come back just moments later to find her standing in the hall wondering where he'd gone.

"But he wasn't hurt?" Josie said now, striding across the floor to open the dusty drapes.

"Just his ego," Olivia assured her.

At least she'd try to convince herself that was the case. He'd ridden upstairs in the elevator with her, slouched against the wall and looking as petulant as he was sexy, but he hadn't even suggested coming into her apartment. Of course, he probably figured there wasn't much point. They'd spent six and a half hours locked in a closet together, and the most action he'd seen was from a bucket and the ladder.

"So . . . what is it you want to do in here?"

Olivia glanced at Josie, who was drawing a heart in the grimy dust on the window with one fingertip.

"I'm not sure," she said with a frown. "Yet."

The huge space was kind of a mess. Actually, there was no "kind of" about it. It was closed up almost one hundred percent of the time these days, and she hated to waste the small housekeeping staff's time with it when it wasn't used. The parquet floor was dull and thick with dust, the molding on the walls needed to be repainted, and the drapes were . . . well, falling apart, she noticed as she walked over to the windows.

It had been pretty once. Of course, it had also been filled with tables and chairs, and candlelight, and the wall sconces had all been polished. Every year it had been decorated with white twinkle lights and silver streamers for the New Year's Eve ball and banks of roses for summer cotillions . . . Well, until about eleven years ago, it had.

And then the swankier hotels had begun hosting bigger, more lavish New Year's Eve parties, and the summer cotillions dwindled into memory as the East Coast debs discovered the Hamptons and the hip clubs in Alphabet City and the Village.

Olivia rested her arms on the windowsill and stared down at Madison Avenue. A cabbie leaned on his horn as a hot dog vendor pushed his dented silver cart across the street. "We can't really afford to do anything, can we?" she said to Josie, who was examining her thumbnail with interest. "Even if we charged the sun, moon, and stars for tickets to some kind of ball, we can't afford the promotion and the catering costs beforehand. And if we didn't sell enough tickets, we'd be out all that money."

Josie shrugged, but her eyes were sympathetic.

"I can't figure out why we don't have more guests in the

first place," Olivia continued, and pushed away from the window to pace. "It's impossible to get a room in this town half the time, and our rates are really low compared to a lot of other hotels, aren't they?"

Josie held up a hand to stop her. "We're filling rooms. Mostly. But we're not offering much aside from the basic room, so we're just breaking even. Guests would spend more money here if we offered something else, like room service or massages or, I don't know, a gift shop."

"But we never did that before!" Olivia protested. In the huge space, her voice echoed with frustration. "Why isn't it enough to have a lovely room?"

Josie shook her head, her ponytail swinging back and forth in sympathy. "Honey, we need to get you into the twenty-first century. Nothing's ever good enough anymore. The American Way can be summed up in one word: More. High-speed Internet, hot towels, concierge floors, mini-bars. . . . Are you getting the picture? *More.*"

Olivia expelled a noisy sigh. "But we have antiques! And atmosphere! And . . . and Mayor LaGuardia used to eat here!"

Josie blinked at her. "I'll be sure to spread that last part around."

"Spread what around?"

Olivia glanced over her shoulder at the sound of Rhys's voice and found him slouched in the double doorway, arms folded over his chest, one eyebrow arched in curiosity.

Josie answered him before Olivia could find her tongue. "The dangers of broom closets."

"Where were you yesterday?" Rhys drawled, and walked into the room. His boots echoed on the bare floor. And the sight of a pair of black leather pants on his long, lean legs and narrow hips made an entirely different noise—a voice in Olivia's head that whispered, *Oh my.*

"Yesterday I was safe and sound in my own bed," Josie retorted with a mischievous smile. "With the bathroom just steps away."

Olivia felt the blood drain from her face as Rhys turned a murderous gaze on her, but all he said to Josie was, "There's a busload of Japanese tourists down in the lobby, love. Better scarper off to see to them."

"Be still my heart," Josie answered, and they both laughed as she strode out of the room, ponytail bouncing behind her.

"Telling tales out of school, are you?" Rhys asked, pinning her against the window with his arms outstretched on either side of her. His eyes were the color of smoke this morning, but at least they were smiling.

"Maybe one or two," she admitted. Fibbing wasn't an option when he was so close, his gaze pinning her as surely as his forearms were.

"I think you need to pay for that." He leaned even closer—his forehead was practically touching hers, and she could feel the heat of his body. In fact, his mouth was right there, those gorgeous lips curved in invitation. All she had to do was close her eyes and tilt her head up just a little bit and they would be kissing . . .

"Take me on a tour of your hotel," he said.

She blinked and stumbled forward a step as he straightened up. "A tour?"

"Show me around, yeah? All the best bits, all your favorite things." He winked at her. "But no more broom closets."

It was silly to feel as if the most popular guy in school had asked her to the prom, Olivia told herself as she led Rhys into the library across from the ballroom.

Silly, but there it was anyway. Rhys flirted, she melted.

Like a sixteen-year-old who had never been kissed on the arm of the boy all the girls drooled over. He was even wearing leather pants, for heaven's sake. And she'd bet money he owned a motorcycle, or at least knew how to ride one with style.

She'd had fantasies like this. Well, not exactly like this, but close. Her, a gorgeous guy, a dimly lit, romantic room . . .

An eagle-beaked old man peeking out from behind the wing of a brown leather chair.

Rhys started, and she touched his arm. "Hello, Mr. Mortimer," she said brightly. The room was dimly lit, that was for sure. Only one lamp was burning on the library table against the far wall, and the drapes were closed. In the gloom, Mr. Mortimer's unfortunate nose and long, bent neck looked alarmingly vulturelike. So much for romance.

"Good morning," the older man said, turning back to his newspaper.

"Who's he?" Rhys whispered into her ear.

"Harold Mortimer," she whispered back. "He's lived here for years. He likes the library."

"I can see that." Rhys lifted an eyebrow. "Is he a vampire? This place is putting me in mind of the broom closet."

She frowned at him and took his hand to lead him back to the doorway. Disturbing Mr. Mortimer wasn't a good idea. He'd never lost his temper, as far as Olivia could remember, but the steely glare in his faded blue eyes if his crossword puzzle was interrupted had always been enough to give her a chill.

She blinked as she glanced back at him, head bent over his neatly folded edition of the *New York Times*. He had it delivered daily, along with his groceries. Maybe he *was* a vampire. She couldn't remember the last time she'd seen him venture outside the building.

"Olivia?"

She glanced back at Rhys with an embarrassed smile. "Sorry. I hate to interrupt him. He usually spends part of every day in here, with the newspaper. He does the crossword."

"A pensioner, yeah?" Rhys raked a hand through his tousled hair, eyebrows raised. "I hope you don't have too many kiddies in the building, love. That lots scary."

"He's harmless," Olivia assured him. "He's been here . . . well, forever. I think . . ." She stopped as a half-forgotten bit of information surfaced and had to bite her lip to restrain a nervous laugh. "I think he used to be a funeral director."

"Please tell me you're kidding," Rhys said, and then took her arm and steered her toward the elevators. "Let's revisit the library another time, yeah?"

"Oh, but I wanted you to see the books," she said, glancing over her shoulder. "We have a whole set of vintage encyclopedias. And it's a lovely room, really. I spent a lot of time there when I was growing up."

"That was prior to the grim reaper moving in, I assume." Rhys punched the UP button, and the doors opened almost immediately. "Well, there's service," he said, ushering her inside.

"Aren't these nice?" she said as the doors shut behind him. She pushed the button for the fourth floor before running her hand over the smooth brass wall. "They're original."

"I guessed as much." He made a face and slouched against the rail as the car began its ascent.

She blinked. That reaction wasn't part of any fantasy she'd ever had. "What does that mean?"

He shrugged. "I can see they're original, love, but they're a bit creaky, yeah? In need of some polish? Or possibly replacement?"

"Replacement?" Gaping wasn't a pretty expression on

anybody, really, but she couldn't help it. "They're . . . *original!*"

His brow shot up again. She was beginning to want to rip it off and step on it. "Olivia, they're *old*."

"They're charming," she argued, folding her arms over her chest. "Vintage. Romantic!"

"They're a bit worse for the wear, old, and creaky," he said with a shrug as the doors opened on the fourth floor. "But if you like them . . ."

"Of course I like them," she said as she stepped off the elevator in front of him. "They're part of the hotel's history and appeal."

And she planned to illustrate just how charming Callender House was. That was the point of the tour, wasn't it? Showing off her home to someone who was actually interested in it—and her, if she wasn't mistaken. She didn't think she'd ever had a chance to do that before, not really.

And there was so much to show off! The rooms celebrities had stayed in over the years, the supposedly haunted pantry on the seventh floor, the room where Margaret Mitchell had once purportedly begun work on a second book. There were a million stories to tell before she even got around to her own memories of the place. Everyone always wanted to hear about the mess Picasso had made in the suite on the sixth floor.

But the elevators *were* a little creaky. Just a little. She'd allow that, she thought as she led him down the hall to Suite 406. Rhys was simply being honest, and she couldn't fault him for that.

"Wallpaper's peeling," he said, pointing to a curling seam.

She gritted her teeth. "Thank you. I'll get right on that."

"I'm just saying."

She resisted the impulse to smack him and fished in her

pocket for the master key. "This is one of our biggest suites," she said as she opened the door. "Greer Garson stayed here for a month in 1955 when she was filming an episode of *Star Stage*."

Rhys nodded as he walked in and ran his hand along the top of the walnut dresser. "Greer who now?"

She rolled her eyes. "Greer Garson. Film star of the 1940s? Had the lead in *Mrs. Miniver* and *Pride and Prejudice*?"

"Never saw 'em," he said with a cheery grin, and sat down on the bed, which he patted. "Well, the mattress is sound, at least. Join me?"

"I think not," she replied primly, but she had to bite back a smile as she turned toward the door. "Come on, there's more to see."

"And a dripping faucet, as well, love," Rhys pointed out as they passed the bathroom.

She restrained an irritable sigh. "I'll let Angel know."

"Building this size, this old, plumbing must be bloody difficult to maintain." Hands jammed in his pockets, head tilted to one side, he was the picture of innocence as she locked the door behind them. Down the hall, Katja, one of the housekeeping staff, pushed a cart out of a guest room and waved.

Olivia waved back, then steered Rhys firmly toward the elevator. He was just making conversation, after all. Not particularly tactful conversation, but he couldn't have any idea how much it stung for her to hear criticisms of the hotel. She'd take him to the seventh floor and tell him about the ghost. He couldn't criticize that, at least. Any hotel worth its salt had a ghost or two.

"How's the wiring, love?" he said as the elevator dinged to a stop and the doors opened. "It's been updated, yeah?"

Maybe the hard knot of frustration in her chest would

loosen if she pushed him into the elevator and kissed him senseless. At least then he'd stop talking.

The thought made her blush as she pressed the button for the seventh floor. How weird was it to want to hit him over the head with something—hard—and kiss him at the same time? It was worrisome enough that she was fantasizing about kissing him at all. He was a guest here, no matter how flirtatious he was, and getting involved was a bad idea.

Tempting, but bad.

"Olivia?"

She glanced up at him to find those gray eyes gone smoky and intense again beneath an unruly fringe of dark hair that had fallen over his forehead. "Sorry, just . . . thinking."

"You do that a lot, love," he said, and took her hand as the elevator bumped to a stop on the seventh floor. "Regular woolgatherer, you are."

"I'll take that as a compliment." Why was it so hard to think when he was touching her? She'd held hands with men before. She'd slept with men before! Not many, but she wasn't exactly a trembling virgin.

Until Rhys held her hand and she was suddenly sure that no one anywhere had linked fingers with such promise, such comfortable sensuality, such . . .

*Ding.* The elevator doors opened, and she cleared her throat as they stepped off the car together. Next lifetime, she was going to cure blushing, no question. If Rhys wanted an idea what she was gathering wool about, her cheeks were a dead giveaway.

"What's up here?" he asked. He ran his thumb over the back of her hand, and every nerve ending in her body reacted with a racy tingle.

"The lady in gray," she said, trying not to shiver when he let go of her hand and rested his against the small of her back. It was such a vulnerable place, so rarely touched unless someone touched it purposely. Her shirt suddenly felt very thin, an almost nonexistent barrier between her skin and his hand.

"Who's the lady in gray?"

"Our resident ghost," she answered, stopping in front of the door to the service pantry at the end of the hall.

When the hotel was built, the pantry had been used for the guests' personal staff, if they had one, to make tea or coffee or light meals—there was a pantry like it on floors five through eight, as well as very small guest rooms that had been reserved specifically for those servants, she explained to Rhys.

"And in 1916, one of the ladies' maids who was here with her employer took arsenic in this pantry," she said, opening the door. Inside, the tiny room was barely eight feet square, with a long counter on one side. The cupboards above were empty now, and the gas rings once used to boil water were long gone.

"Bit dusty, yeah?" Rhys said, squinting into the dim space.

"That's not the point," Olivia said carefully. Heavens, he was infuriating. "The room isn't used anymore, so of course it's dusty. The point is that for years guests and staff have reported seeing a crying young woman in a gray dress and white apron in this spot."

"Why'd she off herself, then?" This asked as casually as if inquiring what kind of jam was available for breakfast.

"There are a lot of different stories, but the most common one is that she was distraught because her employer claimed she was going to let her go without a reference after finding her talking to one of the grooms here at the hotel."

It was such a tragic story, really. She could imagine the poor girl, faced with the notion of being alone in a big city, without a reference or a position. Rumor had it that the girl's employer was a widower, visiting the city from somewhere upstate, who intended to leave her maid in New York to fend for herself. Her heart squeezed just thinking about it.

"Silly girl. That's no reason to do yourself in," Rhys said abruptly, interrupting her momentary reverie. She frowned. He wrenched open a cabinet door that was nearly stuck shut, and snorted. "Well, someone clearly uses this place, love. Look here."

He pointed, eyebrows raised, and she stretched up on tip-toe to find a handful of foil-wrapped condoms resting on the top shelf. Her gasp was equal parts surprise and out-rage.

"I hope your lady in gray isn't too modest," Rhys said with a horribly male smirk.

"That's not funny," she protested, shooing him out of the space and locking the door behind them. Firmly. Maybe for good. Ghost or no ghost.

"Where to next, love?" Rhys said, and she turned to find him standing much too close to her. God, he smelled as good as he looked. "Is there a rooftop pool? A skeleton in a closet? Wait, no more closets. I'm right off them at the moment."

"There are no skeletons anywhere," she hissed, and smacked him on the arm when a couple walked by on the way to their room. "Hush. I'm tempted to end the tour right now, you know. You're not taking it very seriously. Callender House really is a New York institution, you know."

"Your uncle doesn't come up here much, does he?" Rhys asked as if he hadn't heard a word she'd said. He was ex-amining a light fixture beside the elevator that just hap-pened to be flickering like a firefly at the moment. "Because I don't think you want him to start in on you about the wiring. You really should see to that, you know. Fire hazard and all."

He turned a bright, helpful smile on her, and her impulse to smack him melted. She could always tune him out and simply enjoy looking at him while he was here, she thought, and let him take her arm as they stepped onto the elevator again. It would be much more relaxing than actually listening to his litany of the hotel's faults.

She pushed the button for the eighth floor just as the light in the car sputtered and died.

"Wiring, see?" Rhys said, shaking his head sadly, those broad shoulders hunched in a shrug. "Don't say I didn't warn you."

She restrained another sigh. If she was lucky, there was a pair of earplugs somewhere on the eighth floor.

# Chapter 6

Alone in the Coach and Four's kitchen three days later, Rhys dipped a spoon into a saucepan bubbling with an orange cranberry glaze. It was perfect—sweet and tart at the same time.

Just like Olivia was turning out to be, he thought as he took a peek at the walnut-ginger risotto in another pot, which he'd borrowed from the restaurant's pantry—just as he'd "borrowed" the kitchen after the dinner service was over, despite Josef's disapproving scowl. Olivia was mostly sweet, no doubt about it, as delightful as a bit of candy floss at a carnival, but every once in a while the surprising bite of her tart tongue startled him.

When he had the chance to get close enough to her to hear it, that was. In the three days since she'd shown him around the hotel, he'd barely had a chance to speak to her, sod it all.

He dumped two generous handfuls of freshly cut green beans into yet another pot, and turned on the gas beneath it. Room service was the way to go, clearly. Olivia had managed to keep firmly out of kissing range the last few days, but if he showed up at her door with dinner, flowers, and his most charming attitude fixed in place, he could change that, yes sir.

He had to kiss her, that was the thing. Really kiss her. He'd landed in New York without a plan, without even a conscious thought about why he was coming, only to find himself literally on the sidewalk at her feet. And every minute since then, he'd been able to think of nothing but her. Nothing but that glossy cloud of hair that was always escaping its pins, flying around her face like a nimbus, and the dreamy look in her eyes when he found her humming to herself at the registration desk or straightening up the lobby.

Well, that wasn't entirely true, he reminded himself as he gave the glaze another stir. Now and then he found himself quite happily contemplating the sweet curve of her hips, and the way her breasts filled out the soft, all-too-touchable sweaters she wore.

He'd fallen for women before—far too many of them, by most accounts—but he was usually able to satisfy his interest pretty quickly. Unwrap the package, taste the goods, and be on his way, sated and perfectly content to search out his next flirtation.

Aside from Clodagh, he'd done pretty well till now. And despite what he'd learned from his mum and his gran, he'd fallen for more than Clodagh's pretty white blonde hair and butterfly mouth. He'd fallen for her lies.

Not this time, he thought. Olivia couldn't lie if her life depended on it.

No, the problem here was that he hadn't been close enough to touch her since Tuesday. She was like a magnet. A stubborn one, to be sure, one that had managed to stay just out of reach, but a magnet nonetheless. He'd been in New York five days now and hadn't done anything other than follow her around like a homeless puppy, eager for a scratch behind the ears.

And she wasn't even his type! Not that he had a type, per se, unless he defined it by women who were a little more forthright in their sexuality than Olivia was.

But that was precisely the reason she fascinated him, wasn't it? She was shy, she was old-fashioned, she was bizarrely committed to this falling down hotel, and she was most definitely not the type to fall into bed with a relative stranger.

And if he didn't at least kiss her soon, he was going to go mad as a bag of snakes.

A change in strategy was clearly called for. Especially since every attempt to search her out during the day had been thwarted.

And he'd had such plans! Wednesday he'd wanted to ask her to accompany him sightseeing, which he'd foreseen as a perfect opportunity for a bit of handholding in one of those big red tour buses, but the maintenance bloke had stopped him before he'd even had a chance to ask her.

"She's busy," he'd grunted, and folded his arms in front of his chest in a remarkable imitation of a man who'd spent some time as a bouncer at a biker bar. "In a meeting," he'd added before Rhys had even asked what exactly she was busy with. As he looked all too willing to cuff Rhys around the ears if he argued about it, he'd retreated. Sullenly, but he'd retreated nonetheless.

Thursday, he'd imagined lunch at a bistro downtown he'd read about. Just the two of them, a nice long cab ride between the hotel and the restaurant, and a delicious meal during which he would have plenty of time to charm her.

Except Roseanne had waylaid him in the lobby with a stern glare. "She's in the kitchen with Josef," she'd told him, hooking an ample arm around his shoulders. "The annual Manhattan Knitting Gild luncheon is this afternoon, and the old ladies love for Olivia to eat with them—she's got a collection of scarves or mittens from them going back twenty-five years, you know. She can't miss it, not even for lunch with a charmer like you."

Somehow "charmer" didn't sound like a compliment coming from the older woman. She'd steered him toward the bar, where he'd fumed for over an hour. At least Tommy the barkeep had been willing to share anecdotes about Olivia, one of which proved that she would undoubtedly love the Katharine Hepburn retrospective showing at a theater in the Village.

But when he'd scouted the hotel for her this morning, he'd found only traces of her perfume in the library she'd just left, a book she'd put down in the lobby, and Gus.

"It's Friday," the other man had said with a shrug. Beneath the brim of his ball cap, he had the sad, watchful eyes of a hound dog. "Always a busy day, getting ready for the weekend and all. And I think she said something about needing to do some shopping today."

Said something? To Gus? Hmmm. "So you saw her this morning?" Rhys asked, aiming for a casual tone.

"Sure." More shrugging, this time accompanied by a gentle smile. "We have breakfast together most Fridays."

A completely irrational spear of jealousy arrowed through Rhys. Breakfast? Alone together? He could have sworn Yelena said Olivia was too distracted to date . . .

But Gus had gone on while his mind was racing. "I like to pick up bagels on Friday mornings," he said, "and I always bring one to her in the office. Cinnamon raisin, toasted, with butter. It's kind of a tradition."

Ah. That kind of alone together. That was all right then. Rhys grinned. Gus might prove to know exactly the kinds of things about Olivia that Rhys wanted to know. "Care for some lunch, old man?" he said. "On me?"

A café cheeseburger was all it took to discover where Olivia was likely to be tonight, what number her apartment was, and what kind of food she especially liked. A good man was Gus. Especially when it was beginning to seem as if Olivia was the princess in the tower, surrounded by far too many overprotective guards.

Not that he believed in fairy tales, but he couldn't shake the feeling that he'd wound up in New York, outside Olivia's hotel, for a reason. That there was a reason a little voice in his head had begun to whisper "kiss the girl" every time he was within five feet of her. Which hadn't been often enough the past few days.

Thus, he was making her dinner. Idiotic of him not to think of cooking before now, really—it was what he did best, although he had to admit he was usually a lot smoother when it came to courting a pretty girl. Between the spilled latte and the strewn underwear, and finding himself stuck in a transom, he hadn't precisely shown Olivia his best side.

Tonight would be different.

A bottle of wine he'd bought this afternoon was already open and breathing on the counter, and dessert—a sinfully creamy white chocolate tart with a macadamia nut topping—was already plated and garnished with blackberries. He'd outdone himself, he had.

And he hadn't even resorted to oysters, much as he'd been tempted to.

All he wanted was a kiss, after all. Well, no, that was a lie. But he'd settle for that, wouldn't he? He'd have to, if Olivia wasn't interested, but that didn't bear consideration at the moment. No, at the moment he needed to concentrate on the green beans ready to come out of their pot, and then plating the risotto. Then the chicken, of course, as soon as the sauce had cooked down just a bit more. He wouldn't grill the breasts until everything else was done, so they'd be perfect and juicy.

He grinned as he sniffed the sauce. He was a dab hand when it came to food, that was certain. And if he couldn't woo the woman with a meal like this one, then chances were she couldn't be wooed at all.

He picked up the pot of beans and turned toward the sink, only to find the woman in question standing in the doorway to the kitchen, her brow furrowed in confusion.

And was so startled, he dropped the pot with a furious clatter into the sink, spraying water and beans all over the counter and his shirt.

"What are you doing?" Olivia asked, rushing forward to grab a paper towel. She was wearing an old, faded pair of jeans and another soft gray sweater, with her hair piled haphazardly on top of her head, wisps escaping to tickle her cheeks.

She was a vision, Rhys thought vaguely, before he realized that the hot water from the pan had soaked his shirtfront, and the green beans were a complete loss.

"I *was* making you dinner," he said with a bit of acid, and helped her scrape the exploded vegetable back into the pot. "Planned on it being a surprise, too. What are you doing down here?"

She raised one eyebrow, but she was trying not to smile, and a moment later she picked a stray bean off his sleeve. "It is my hotel, you know. I was looking for a snack, to be honest."

"A snack?" He waved away the notion, hoping he appeared casual, which was difficult with spilled vegetables all over him. Sod it all, why was it so hard to be charming in Olivia's presence? Tossing a pot of green beans like a scared schoolgirl? What the hell was wrong with him? "I've got a proper meal for you right here. Minus the veg, sadly."

"This is for me?" She took a step closer to the cook top and peered into the saucepan, then squinted up at him suspiciously. "What were you planning?"

He motioned to the metal trolley parked on the other side of the counter. "Room service, love."

Clearly, she was dreaming, Olivia thought as she spotted the cart laden with dishes and silverware. And a bud vase graced with a single red rose!

Rhys Spencer had to be a product of her imagination, if not her dreams. He was too charming, too sweet, too overwhelmingly sexy.

And too interested in her. Every time she turned around, someone was mentioning that he'd been looking for her, asking about her. And now he was cooking for her? And planning to deliver it right to her door?

The implications of that sank in as she gazed at the dessert waiting on its clean white plate. Room service meant her apartment. Where the two of them would have been all alone, with a romantic meal obviously meant to share, as the pairs of dessert plates and wineglasses proved.

Suddenly her pulse was ticking like an overwound clock. After Tuesday, and the patent failure of the hotel tour, she hadn't seen him face to face, and it had been so easy to dream of him. Call up that wicked grin, and the adorably restless spikes of his hair, the dark, musky scent of him. He'd begun to seem like something she'd fantasized, to tell the truth.

And fantasies were what she did best. They were certainly a lot easier to manage than real life, especially when real life meant an uncle who'd turned into Snidely Whiplash and a hotel that everyone she knew was determined to tell her was falling down around her ears. She'd overslept the past two days, and she was ashamed to admit that she hadn't felt guilty about it at all. Snuggling under the covers was a hell of a lot easier than facing Roseanne, and Angel, and Josie, and the specter of Stuart.

Not to mention Rhys. Who made her blush and tingle and imagine all kinds of things she had never even done before, especially when she was standing right next to him.

"Surprise is ruined, I suppose, but dinner isn't," he said now, stirring something that smelled absolutely sinful. "Except, you know, for the veg."

The sheepish look on his face was so at odds with that air of danger he wore like a second skin, she couldn't help laughing. "That's all right," she said, wiping up the last bit of spilled water on the counter. "I'm not very good about eating my vegetables anyway. I'm not very good at making dinner, either. If it involves more than opening a can or turning on the microwave, I'm out of my league."

"A can?" He stared at her as if she'd uttered the foulest curse word in history. "Please tell me different, love. Dinner from a tin is a sodding crime. Cooking's easy, anyway. I'll show you how."

She felt herself coloring again when he rested his hand on the small of her back, easing her toward the saucepan on the range. The weight of it there was comfortable, but somehow dangerous, too. It didn't make sense for something to feel so right and yet make her absolutely tingly with anticipation and nerves.

"You'll regret it," she said lightly, watching as he stirred some kind of sauce with a big wooden spoon. "I'm one of those types that burns water."

"Not possible," he scoffed, and handed her the spoon. "It's a glaze for the chicken breasts, which I need to get on the grill in a moment. Just some blood oranges and cranberries with brown sugar and a bit of cornstarch, and some spices and dry sherry. Nothing to it, you see?"

She managed a weak smile. Nothing to it. Right. Now if he would only tell her if the cranberries had to be peeled or otherwise dealt with, and where exactly one bought blood oranges . . .

He was grinning again, that lopsided smile that lit up his eyes. "Not convinced, yeah? Next time we'll do it together. Dead easy, I promise."

"What's that?" she said vaguely, concentrating on the spoon he'd left in her hand as he checked the contents of another pot. And trying not to focus on the "next time" he'd promised so casually. He wasn't going to be a guest forever, after all.

"Risotto." He spooned a bit from the pot and held it to her mouth. "Taste."

As if they'd known each other forever. As if they ate comfortably off the same spoon while making meals together on a regular basis. It was a silly little thing, but it was sexy, too.

Of course, that didn't stop her from sounding like a prim, humorless virgin. "Oh. Well, all right . . ." Then the smooth edge of the spoon touched her bottom lip, and she took in the creamy stuff with a little sigh.

"Good, yeah?" His thumb brushed a stray morsel from her lip before she could reply and she cursed her burning cheeks.

"Delicious," she breathed. The risotto, him, everything. She was standing in the hotel kitchen in her oldest jeans with a near stranger intent on teaching her to cook, and yet she felt as if she'd walked into some elaborate fantasy. Rhys was so easy, so effortlessly charming and sensual, and so very, very delicious himself, he had to be a dream. Things like this didn't happen to her. Things like refereeing a cat-fight between eighty-year-old knitters happened to her, but at least the Knitting Guild's annual luncheon was over for another year.

"Do you taste the walnut?" He took another spoonful from the pot and sniffed it deeply before tasting it himself. "I toasted them, to bring out all that rich nuttiness, and then I added a bit of nutmeg to deepen the flavor."

She blinked, watching as his mouth worked, the generous curve of his lips as he spoke, his tongue as he licked the spoon before tossing it into the sink. "Uh-huh."

Everything changed then. Rhys's glance flicked over to her face, and whatever he saw there made his eyes darker, smoky with awareness. Suddenly, electricity crackled in the air, a distant hum in the silence, and her heartbeat was a frantic drum in her chest.

Rhys was standing so close to her, she could feel the heat coming off him, sense the solidity of his body. Every nerve ending in her own body had gone on alert, and when he eased closer, she melted, just a little bit, backing into the counter to hold herself up.

"I can teach you how to cook the chicken now, if you like," he said softly. "We don't want this feast to go to waste, now do we?"

She shook her head, and watched as he slit a package of chicken breasts and placed them on a heated grill pan that looked as if it was coated with some kind of oil. The meat sizzled as he seasoned them, and she jumped at the unexpected noise.

"Nothing to worry about, love," Rhys murmured, and slid his hand up her back. "They like the heat, because it holds in the juices. We don't want to rush them, because we want them done, but still moist in the end. Still a bit tender, yeah? So it's just right on the tongue."

She couldn't help it—a shudder of pure need rippled

through her. She was pretty sure he wasn't really talking about chicken.

Swallowing hard, she looked up at him. Those gray eyes were shadowed beneath the hair falling over his forehead, but she could see the desire in them, a steady flame.

"How do you know when they're done?" she asked in a voice that was nowhere near as steady.

"You have to turn them first," he answered, showing her. "You want both sides to get equal time, yeah? Equal exposure to the heat."

*Heat.* Oh dear. It was hot in here, that was for sure. She took another shuddering breath as he inched even closer, his hip brushing against her. Oh yeah, it was hot.

"The risotto's all done," he explained, staring into her eyes as if what he was saying was incredibly private and important. "It simmers for a long time, you see, slowly building up heat, steaming, until it's creamy and soft and plump."

*Oh my.*

"And the glaze here, well, that's the sweet, yeah?" He dipped another spoon in the saucepan and held it up. "All the juices and the sugar running together in the heat, and just melting on your tongue . . ."

"It sounds . . . delicious," she managed, unable to tear her eyes away from his. And felt her heart stutter in surprise—or was that inevitability?—when he leaned in.

"I wager you taste even better."

And then he was kissing her, his mouth hot against her, a firm pressure that went on and on, until her lips parted and she tasted his tongue, as dark and wicked as he was, and just as tempting. The spoon he'd been holding clattered to the counter as he pulled her against his chest, and she let her arms snake around him, holding on for dear life.

She'd never been kissed so well before in her life. So deeply, so long, so relentlessly sensually as his mouth explored hers and his hands glided up her back and into her hair. The heat between them was dizzying.

And total, she realized, as she felt her bones begin to melt into the sensation, every part of her softening, giving, sliding against him. Another minute and she would be nothing but a puddle.

But Rhys held her up, his hands on her hips now, positioning her against him more firmly. And still he kissed her, on and on, until she was breathless and so full of need, she was one continuous tingle, a spark just waiting to burst into flame.

She was vaguely aware of the bright overhead lights, and the cold metal of the counter against the small of her back, of the gentle sizzle of the chicken in the pan, but none of it mattered. What mattered was Rhys, hot and hard and demanding against her, his hands and his mouth moving over her like a ribbon, binding her to him, tying her up in one big knot of . . .

"Shit!"

She stumbled when Rhys wrenched away from her, and realized the chicken in the pan was far past simmering and had caught flame. Smoke poured off the pan in a cloudy gray haze, bitter in the air, and then the smoke alarm went off.

God, the noise was horrible. Like an agonized robot wailing for its mother. She glanced around for a broom or something else to jab at it while Rhys put out the flames. She didn't even care about dinner—she wanted to go back to the kissing. If she could just get the damn alarm to shut up . . .

Or get the sprinklers to turn off, she realized a moment later. Rhys glanced up at the sudden shower, his face white, and sputtered, "The tart!" Flapping a sodden dishtowel over the smoking pan, he added, "Sod that, the wine!"

She grabbed the bottle and stuffed the wet cork inside, or tried to, but the heavy glass was slippery, and a moment later it slid out of her hands onto the floor, where it crashed with a spectacular spray.

"Oh, *bloody* hell," Rhys moaned.

She couldn't help it—they were both soaked, the kitchen was slick with spray, and the tart Rhys had made for dessert was going to float off its plate any second. Rhys had planned a romantic meal, all for her, and they'd somehow ended up in a Three Stooges movie.

So she laughed. There was no stopping it—it bubbled up from inside with such force, it nearly exploded from her throat.

And after a moment of what Olivia could only call shock and horror, Rhys broke down, too, until they were both helpless with it, sliding toward each other on the slippery floor and blinking water out of their eyes.

"Not what I . . . planned," Rhys gasped, brushing away the hair plastered to his forehead.

"I hope not!" Olivia answered with a giggle, and then turned at the sound of a new voice behind her.

"What on earth . . . ?" Hector asked, his mouth hanging open. He was one of the night maintenance staff, a sweet Puerto Rican man in his late fifties. Hesitating in the doorway to the kitchen, he regarded the busy sprinklers and the shrieking alarm with amazement.

"Little cooking accident," Rhys said, and bit back a grin.

"No one was hurt," Olivia added, squeezing water out of the hem of her sweater. "Well, except the chicken."

Rhys doubled over at that, and Hector's brow rose even higher.

"You two go on now," he said cautiously, clearly not sure if they were completely sane at the moment. "I turn it off and clean up. You go put on dry clothes, Miss Olivia. And . . . and you, sir."

"Thank you, Hector," Olivia said, trying to look dignified as she made her way across the slick floor, blinking droplets of water out of her eyes. "I'll take you up on that."

Rhys hesitated, surveying the mess, but Hector shooed him toward the door. Olivia held out her hand, and after a moment Rhys took it.

"Where are we going?"

"My place," she whispered, drawing him closer as they walked to the service elevator. "Just like you planned."

"I need some dry clothes," Rhys reminded her, but she hushed him with a pointed stare and reached up on tiptoe to kiss him just as the elevator bell dinged.

"Not for what I have planned."

# Chapter 7

If Olivia had ever said anything so blatantly suggestive before, she couldn't remember it. But there was no way she was going to let the sprinkler system put a damper on the heat she and Rhys had created in the kitchen.

A *damper*. Huh. She giggled as the elevator lurched upward, and Rhys leaned in to nuzzle her cheek.

"What's so funny, love?"

She colored, even though she was soaked to the skin and beginning to shiver. "Nothing. We're, um, dripping."

"I'll mop it up later," Rhys promised, and pushed her back against the wall, his arms braced on either side of her, and his wet lips surprisingly warm.

Oh, there it was again. That incredible heat, as if he'd lit a fire inside her that had only been banked for a moment. She'd never felt anything like it—and she was willing to bet the moment he touched her again, *really* touched her, the blaze was going to be magnificent. She shivered just thinking about it, and Rhys pulled her closer, until they were chest to chest. Amazing that they weren't giving off steam, she thought as his fingers combed through her wet hair and his tongue delved into her mouth, stroking hers.

The bell for her floor pinged, and Rhys pulled himself

away from her just as the doors slid open. "Lead the way, love."

*Lead the way.* She was doing just that, wasn't she? The unfortunate chicken fire and the surprise shower would have been a perfect opportunity to back away from Rhys, slow down, consider the wisdom of getting involved with a guest, but no. No way. Whatever this was between them, she wanted more of it. And if it did turn out to be some crazy dream, well, at least she would have enjoyed it, right?

Her hands shook, just a little bit, as she turned the key in the lock, and Rhys's steadying hand on her back only made her more nervous. She wanted this, yes, but now that they were here—almost inside, okay, inside now, he was shutting the door behind them, oh dear—it was impossible not to realize they were going to be naked together in a few minutes. That Rhys would see her naked.

She blinked, considering. That was what was going to happen, wasn't it?

"Now I'm dripping on your rug, love," Rhys pointed out as she hesitated in the small space that served as the foyer, so she led the way into the kitchen after kicking off her shoes. The bathroom was too small, too intimate, at least for now. Not that the kitchen was much bigger. It was sort of an ambitious closet.

And as they stood on the faded linoleum, it was suddenly much too quiet. The old-fashioned alarm clock on her bedside table across the room ticked in the silence, drawing attention to the bed. Which was right there, practically in the middle of the room, the comforter still rumpled. Waiting for them.

*Oh dear.*

"You're soaked through." Rhys stripped off the shirt he was wearing and shook his wet head over the sink. "You're going to catch your death, as mums everywhere say."

"I think I'll live," Olivia said, and then realized how ridiculous that sounded. She had to take off her wet clothes at some point. That was why they were up here, after all.

But it was very hard to concentrate with Rhys bare-chested, not more than a foot away, his wet skin still glistening.

"You may," he agreed, "but I'd feel better if you got out of those wet things." He leaned over to skim his lips over her damp cheek. "For a lot of reasons."

She shivered again, and this time she knew full well her wet skin had nothing to do with it.

But she couldn't help stalling, at least for another minute. "I'm sorry your lovely dinner was ruined."

"I'm not," he murmured, stepping closer and tugging up the hem of her sweater. She let him, raising her arms so he could pull it over head. Oh, hell, she was wearing her oldest bra.

"But you went to all that trouble," she protested, resisting the urge to fold her arms over the plain white cotton.

"No trouble at all." Rhys kissed the side of her face, then her neck and her throat, skimming his hands down her sides to the waistband of her jeans. "I'll make you another one tomorrow."

"Oh, that's not necessary." God, why was she still talking?

*To distract yourself from the fact that he's peeling off your jeans,* a voice in her head whispered with what sounded very much like a naughty smirk.

And he was—she lifted her legs when he nudged her, stepping out of the soaked denim and watching it fall to the floor.

Oh boy.

"Towels?" Rhys murmured, and disappeared into the bathroom, which was just across the tiny hall. Along the way, he shucked off his boots, then returned to dry her wet head.

"I can do that," she said, but he leaned down to look her in the eye with a wicked smile.

"It's more fun if I do it, yeah?"

*Oh yeah*. He was toweling off her back now, his hands amazingly firm through the thick terrycloth, then her shoulders and her chest . . .

"I think this better go," he whispered, and distracted her with another kiss as he unhooked her bra. "It's soaked through, as well."

"So are your jeans," she said when she found the willpower to drag her mouth away from his.

The gleam in his eyes was strangely satisfying. She drew in a shuddering breath as he stood back and peeled them off, leaving them in a wet heap next to hers. He was clad only in black boxer briefs that revealed the lean hardness of his hips and thighs now, and she bit back a whimper of excitement.

This was no dream. Rhys, out of nowhere, completely unexpected, was quite real, and right here in front of her, in her own little apartment, his damp, bare skin warm and his eyes burning into hers with desire.

He held out his hand, and she took it without thinking twice. When he hauled her against him, devouring her mouth in a hungry kiss, she held on tight, kissing him back, riding the wave of arousal in her belly, rippling down her thighs and deep in her core.

"I think we'll be more comfortable over there, yeah?" Rhys murmured, and hauled her up further, carrying her over to the bed.

"That's what it's for," she managed, flat on her back and staring up at him. He was so strangely beautiful, with that sharp jawline and those gray eyes, his hair falling in careless waves around his ears.

So beautiful . . . and probably so experienced. God, what was she doing with a man like him? What was he expecting?

And how on earth was she supposed to figure it out when he was lowering his mouth to her breasts, licking the nipples with teasing swipes of his tongue? She groaned and wriggled closer, clutching at his lean hips.

"Ah, yes, the bed was a proper choice," he murmured, pausing to glance up at her with another wicked grin. "All the better to eat you with."

*Oh God.*

His hands were busy, too, smoothing over her hips and down her thighs as he knelt above her. All she could do was run her hands over his chest and down his arms, corded with muscle. He was so hard everywhere, so warm, so alive— and just as talented with his mouth as he was with his hands. He was kissing her rib cage now, running his tongue along each curved bone as if he were tasting her.

Who would have guessed that it would feel so deliciously good?

But surely she should be doing something, too—something more than groaning with pleasure, at least. She wriggled just out of reach and waited until he looked up at her to speak.

"I can take my . . . panties off," she whispered, cursing the breathless hitch in her voice. "If you want to, you know . . ."

He shook his head with a fond scowl. "We're not even close, love. Remember what I said about slow cooking? We've got to warm you up right and proper." To prove it, he reached down and took a rigid nipple between his lips, licking it slowly before sucking it into his mouth.

*Oh God. Oh, that was . . .* She couldn't form words, and he hadn't even taken off her panties yet.

Still, it was worth another try. She didn't want to be selfish, even though nothing sounded better than lying back and letting him have his way with her for a few more hours. She had a feeling his "way" would probably be fabulous.

But she propped herself up on her elbows and nudged at him until he met her lips with his. "I don't want to be selfish . . ." she murmured against his mouth, which was so hot, so dark and rich with the taste of him. "I want to please you, too, you know . . ."

"Oh, you are, love," he assured her. "You are. This is about me, too, because nothing is more arousing than pleasing you." He kissed her firmly, then urged her onto her back. "Watching you melt. Feeling you heat up and shudder, and hearing you groan. Trust me."

There was no arguing with that, she decided, giving in and lying back against the pillow as he slid her panties off. The scrap of faded white cotton hit the floor somewhere beside the bed, but she didn't look up to see where—Rhys had parted her thighs gently, and his fingers were stroking through the wiry nest of curls between them.

"You're so lovely," he whispered, leaving a trail of light kisses down the smooth expanse of her belly, then lower. "So soft and lush and perfect." He kissed the curls, blowing into them teasingly, as one finger slid between the folds, stroking her.

She wasn't going to survive this. She was sure of it. It was too good, too overwhelming, too *much* . . .

His finger skimmed against her clitoris then, and she came without warning, an explosive ripple of sensation that made her cry out in surprise.

"Oh, love," Rhys whispered, cupping her gently as the ripples subsided, "that was bloody brilliant. And a bit of a surprise, yeah? We'll build the next one a bit slower, I think."

The next one? She opened her eyes and found him already bent to his work again, sliding his finger deep inside her, stroking the far wall in a slow, steady rhythm that made her groan all over again.

"Rhys, please . . ." she began, clutching at the comforter with both hands curled into fists. She didn't even know what she was asking for, but the words were out before she even knew she had opened her mouth.

"Patience, love," he murmured, and slid up beside her, one finger still buried deep, to take her nipple in his mouth again. "Slowly now. Make it last, yeah? Your body, your pleasure. I want you to have as much of it as you can take."

*Oh* . . .

Everything had receded. The room, the light on in the kitchen, the ticking clock, the feel of the wrinkled comforter beneath her. Nothing existed but her body, alive with sensation, and Rhys's hands and mouth and tongue, building the flame up again, stoking it with every caress, every slow, licking kiss, every . . .

Oh God, he was moving again. Sliding down the mattress to position himself between her legs, spreading her thighs even further, his chest hot and hard against her skin, his finger still moving inside her and his mouth joining it now, licking through the lush, wet folds to the sensitive flesh inside.

No one had ever done that before. Not to her, at least. It was so revealing, him tasting her there, his tongue lapping her up like some kind of delicious treat, but she found she didn't care. Who would? Who *could?* It felt so good, so very, very good, his tongue so wet and hot against her, the core of her slippery with desire and vibrating with pleasure . . .

When she came this time, she stiffened all over, the tightly wound coil of arousal springing fast and hard. She felt it everywhere, pleasure radiating out from that center point in hot, languid waves. And then Rhys was there, covering her from head to toe, kissing her throat, her breasts, his hands stroking her hips as she shuddered.

"Come inside me," she whispered. "Right now. Please."

"With pleasure, love." When he climbed off the bed and disappeared, she blinked in confusion, but he returned carrying a condom apparently retrieved from his jeans pocket.

And he'd shucked off his briefs in the process.

He was magnificently erect, and she sucked in a breath as he climbed onto the bed again. It was beautiful, she thought with a kind of wonder. She couldn't remember ever really looking at an erection before, but Rhys's was gorgeous, so proud, so hard, a dark blue vein running its length and pulsing with arousal.

Without thinking, she reached out to curl her fingers around it, and he groaned in approval. "Ah, God, love, I've been waiting for that."

She found his eyes darkened nearly to charcoal, smoky with need, but he stopped her when she began to stroke him. "But I can't wait to be inside you. No bloody way."

She took the condom before he could protest, and her hands shook only slightly as she unwrapped it and slid the slippery rubber over his erection. It fit snugly, and the moment it was on, he nudged her backward.

As if they'd known each other forever, she thought with a sudden spear of joy. So natural, so right, as if they were meant to be, just like in the fairy tales . . .

But there was no time to consider that possibility further. She opened her legs as he lowered himself toward her, and then he thrust inside in one smooth motion. Oh God, he'd gone so deep, filling her so totally, she groaned out loud and wrapped her legs around his waist.

He answered with an incoherent grunt, thrusting deeper, slowly, as if savoring each plunge inside.

She had to see his face, watch him as he'd watched her. Wriggling her arms free, she took his head between her hands, angling his face toward her, and found his eyes nearly black with pleasure.

He gazed at her for a long moment, then lowered his head to kiss her, hungry and hot and hard. She could live on his kisses, she thought, moving her mouth beneath his, tasting his tongue as it slid against hers. They were like . . . well, like life. Raw and passionate and real.

But then he was thrusting faster, even deeper, touching a place inside her she hadn't known existed. When he reared back, tearing his mouth away from hers, she was ready, thrusting up to meet him. With a strangled roar, he came, and a moment later buried his face in the hollow of her neck, raining kisses there.

The last electric ripples of sensation were still fading away when he finally raised his face to hers, and she smiled at him.

"I'll trade dinner for that any day," she whispered, and grinned when he threw his head back and laughed.

So much for getting Olivia out of his system, Rhys thought hours later. He was spooned against her back in her cozy bed, lazily stroking her breasts and belly as she dozed. Once hadn't been enough. Twice, it turned out, hadn't even been close. He was fairly certain three times would only be the beginning.

A bit scary, that. What was even scarier was that, if anything, the ruin of his surprise room service meal had probably seduced Olivia into his arms more quickly than sharing supper with her would have.

His groin tightened at the thought of her in the kitchen earlier, her mouth soft and sweet as he bent to kiss her the first time, her eyes gone dreamy and hot as he spoke to her.

And then that wet gray sweater, clinging to her torso, outlining the gorgeous shape of her breasts . . .

He grunted, shifting closer to her, stroking one swollen nipple with his thumb and breathing in the scent of her hair. Not enough, no. He wanted her again, right now.

She'd nearly passed out after the second go-round, limp with the force of an orgasm that had shuddered through her from head to toe, her brow damp and her cheeks flushed a brilliant rose. Asleep now, she looked like nothing so much as a princess, a cloud of hair spread on the pillowcase, her lips pink and plump from all of the kissing, her creamy skin smooth and bare beneath the sheet.

*A princess.* There he went again, spouting fairy tale nonsense like a sodding lunatic. What was with this bloody hotel? The place—or perhaps the woman—had cast some sort of spell on him.

No! No spells. Bollocks, he was going to be on the analyst's couch before this was over. If only to figure out how it was that he ended up on his bum or stuck in a closet or soaked to the skin whenever he was within five feet of Olivia. If he'd fancied himself as Superman, she was clearly his kryptonite. He'd never felt less suave in his life.

And yet, making love to her had been so bloody right. The taste of her on his tongue, the feel of her in his hands, the gorgeous little sighs she breathed when he was stroking her, kissing her, as if he'd given her a gift, woken her from some lush, drowsy daze. . . . There would never be enough of that, no sir. Not even close.

But sometime it would have to be enough, wouldn't it?

Running a hand through his hair, Rhys edged away from her, settling the sheet over her before climbing out of bed. He needed to pee. He needed to get a grip on himself, that was what he needed. He wasn't going to be in New York for more than a few weeks, and he wasn't the sort to make false promises. Honesty, that was his motto. It was just a bit of a shock that, honestly, he was no less fascinated by Olivia than he had been earlier tonight.

Striding across the apartment to the loo, he stopped for a moment to glance around him. She'd taken a studio efficiency, one generous room with the bath at the back and the kitchen along one wall. Compact and cozy, it somehow looked just like her.

The furniture was more old world than simply old, dark chestnut and walnut stuff that was quite clearly solid wood. Framed prints he thought were Maxfield Parrish's work were hung over a loveseat in one corner of the room, all dreamy blues and pale gold and pink light. More fairy tales, he thought with a rueful smile.

A cat he hadn't noticed before wound around his ankles, long pale fur like velvet. Without warning the beast leapt from the carpet to Olivia's small desk, where a very modern laptop looked out of place among the silver-framed photos and an antique lamp. Photos of the hotel, he saw when he inched closer and squinted in the darkness.

Everything in Olivia's life was about the hotel, wasn't it? Callender House as it had been in years past, and as she seemed determined to keep it even now. A shame that there wasn't more of "her" about the place, because beneath the cashmere sweater sets and sensible pearl earrings, she was a good deal more passionate and, hell, even a bit funkier than he'd expected.

But wait, there was some proof of it, he thought, crossing the room to the loveseat, where a beaded purple Indian pillow rested on the very proper Victorian settee. And there, on the wall leading to the bath, a very stark, elegant piece of black-and-white photography, which was unsigned. Olivia may have been a princess in a tower, but she was one who had access to the Internet and liked to look out the window once in a while.

He used the loo and came out to find her sitting up in the bed, her hair spilled over her shoulders and the cat busily washing her hindquarters from Rhys's side of the bed.

"Eloise will move," Olivia assured him as he approached, one eyebrow cocked at the feline. "I mean, you are coming back to bed, aren't you?"

"Where else would I go, love?" Eloise, all offended dignity, sprang off the bed as he climbed in and stalked toward the kitchen. "Just had to find the loo, that's all."

"Oh. Good."

Even in the dim light, Rhys could tell she was blushing. As if they hadn't just fucked each other into incoherence, bare-ass naked and groaning. What she had to be embarrassed or shy about now was anyone's guess.

But the fact that she was tentative with him now produced an unfamiliar stab of protectiveness. He didn't want her shy, not with him, and he certainly didn't want her embarrassed. Hell, at the moment he wanted everything she felt to be either sunshine and kittens or more of the lusty hunger he'd witnessed earlier.

"I'm not the type to fuck and run," he murmured, propped up on one elbow so he could kiss her bare shoulder.

She blushed deeper at the curse word—he could feel the heat in her cheeks—but she didn't protest.

Which was good. He wasn't about to change his stripes, and that included the ones on his tongue. And he wasn't about to lie, either. He swore like a sailor, but he *didn't* fuck and run, never had—he figured if he fancied a woman enough to crawl between her legs, spending the night in her bed, or his, was a given. Then again, he wasn't exactly the type to sign on for a committed relationship on day one, either.

But they weren't talking about that, were they? Not yet anyway.

She shifted closer to him, sliding down the pillows as he reached for her breasts. Soft everywhere, that was Olivia, soft and lush and ripe as a good peach. As she relaxed into his touch, he said idly, "I saw your laptop over there. A gift, was it?"

She snorted. "God, no. I picked it out myself. The computers in this place are . . . well, 'original' wouldn't really be the wrong word. I wanted something fast and something with a lot of memory."

Interesting. He toyed with a thick lock of hair that had fallen across her throat. "And the picture there in the hall? The photo? Is that a new artist?"

This time she laughed. "Only if you consider me to be an artist, which I certainly don't. I was just fooling around with the camera one day, and I liked the way that shot came out. It's from the Central Park carousel."

Huh. A quite adult shot of a childhood pleasure, then. He looped her hair over her ear and bent to kiss her cheek. "You're a fascinating woman, Olivia Callender."

That flustered her. "Am I?"

"You are indeed," he assured, gently angling her onto her back. "I think the world needs a bit more of you."

"The . . . world?" Her voice had gone breathless as he lowered his mouth to her breast, and his hand to the inside of one warm thigh.

"Certainly," he whispered, glancing up into her dark eyes with an honesty that was disconcertingly fierce, even for him. "The world, and me."

# Chapter 8

At ten minutes after six the next morning, Olivia was awake. Wide awake. So awake she wasn't even in a rush to make coffee, which was a little weird. She was actually impatient for the sun to rise.

She should have been unconscious. Possibly comatose. She'd never made love like that, so many times, in one night. Come to think of it, she'd never made love like that period. Not until she was limp and boneless, positively sated with pleasure and the new and delicious privilege of a man's body to explore any way she liked, for as long as she liked.

She definitely should have been comatose.

Instead, she was more awake than she ever had been in her life. Wide awake, as if every nerve ending and blood cell had been pumped full of caffeine. Not only that, but everything looked clearer, smelled sharper, sounded louder. The cat mewling for water, for instance. The ghost of perfume from the top of her dresser. The ratty old upholstery on the easy chair that faced the TV.

Hmmm. It was a strange feeling, unsettling, but . . . good. Of course, it would have been better if Rhys had been awake, since then they could make love again, but she had a feeling he wasn't a six A.M. kind of person. Actually, she'd bet folding money that he didn't even know six A.M. existed, being a chef and therefore probably a night person.

Wow. Her brain was wide awake, too. She didn't usually think this fast. If she'd been speaking out loud, she would have told herself to slow down.

She'd already gotten up to use the bathroom, brushing her teeth and her hair, and had taken her single sexy nightgown from the closet and put it on. Of course, sexy was relative. This one was knee length, with spaghetti straps and a kind of fitted bodice, in champagne silk. Actually, it looked more like a slip than something she would call "lingerie," but unless she wanted Rhys to see her in an ancient NYC Ballet T-shirt or the flannel pajamas she wore in the dead of winter, she was out of luck.

She leaned over the bed to peek at him—he was flat on his stomach, one arm buried beneath the pillow and the other flung out to one side. His back was smoothly muscled, and the knob of one hip was visible where the sheet had slid past his waist.

She sighed. The temptation to crawl back into bed beside him, run her fingers through that dark messy hair, stroke the firm flesh of his ass. . . . He grunted, startling her, and shifted into a new position. She backed away from the bed in a hurry. Probably better to let him sleep.

But she had nothing to do, that was the problem. What did other early risers do with these bonus hours? Since she'd never been one before, she had no idea. She'd been oversleeping since childhood, for heaven's sake.

Rhys had obviously found some secret "on" switch and flipped it, she thought as she wandered toward her desk, Eloise following, her rippling plume of a tail tickling Olivia's ankle. She wanted to *do* something, now. Anything, really, although there were clearly a few areas that deserved priority.

The hotel, for one. She'd been avoiding thinking about it all week, but the truth was that if Stuart was up to something, if he was planning to wrest this old place away from her, she needed to be ready. She needed to go on the offensive, in fact. She needed to beat him at his own game, whatever game that was.

He couldn't simply take it away from her—it was hers, legally and officially and in every other way that mattered to the law. But he could . . . bankrupt her. He could spread rumors about the hotel. It was possible that he could take her to court—Callender House was a kind of institution, after all, and his name was Callender. Maybe if he proved that she was making a mess of things, a judge would hand him the deed.

That didn't seem likely, really. But what Olivia knew about real estate law fit on the head of a pin, maybe two if she was lucky. The object was to beat Stuart before he beat her. Maybe to put Callender House in the public eye again, so Stuart couldn't pull any underhanded tricks.

But how to do that? How to make Callender House a success? Especially after all these years of simply hanging on, the city growing up and changing around the old building. Hanging on like one of those pathetic kittens in the posters elementary school teachers hung in their classrooms.

That's what she'd been doing, she realized. The staff, too. Hanging on, pretending the ship wasn't sinking and playing a merry little tune while they were at it to make the truth less painful.

"How absurd," she said aloud, and winced when Rhys snorted in his sleep. Holding her finger to her lips, she warned the cat to be quiet and took a pad and a pen from her desk. She sat down on the floor with her back to the loveseat, so she could spread out, even though she had no idea exactly what she'd be spreading out yet.

But that was all right. She needed a plan. She could plan. She could brainstorm. Heck, she could do whatever she wanted, couldn't she? She could . . . sell the place! That would teach Uncle Stuart.

She frowned at Eloise, who had come to sit smack in the middle of the legal tablet Olivia had laid on the carpet beside her. She couldn't sell the hotel any more than she could cut off her own arm. It was hers, her history and her childhood and her family all rolled into one. She had to save it, and right this moment she was beginning to feel a bit guilty that she hadn't thought harder about how to do that before now.

The sun was just beginning to streak the sky a soft sherbet pink when she picked up her pen and shooed the cat off her pad of paper. History and family aside, she didn't simply need to save the hotel—she wanted to. It was hers, thanks to her father, and if she hadn't realized until now that ownership meant she could run Callender House the way she liked, that was her fault. Traditions had been upheld for over a century, yes, but even her father had put his own stamp on the place. She could do the same thing. She was *going* to do the same thing, starting now. No one on earth but her wanted to remember the Callender House that had been—new guests needed reasons to visit that didn't revolve around her memories, and she was going to come up with those reasons. She bit the end of her pen thoughtfully. Callender House would be on the New York City map again, and she was going to put it there.

*    *    *

Rhys woke to the smell of coffee. For a moment, he had no idea where he was—he was snugged under a rather froufrou pink flowered blanket, with a thick pillow beneath his head, so he wasn't in his London flat. Or *Fork in the Road*'s dorm in L.A. Where the hell was he?

He sat up gingerly, squinting the sleep out of his eyes, and found a steaming mug of black coffee on the bedside table. There was service, but who . . . ? And then he saw Olivia on the floor across the room, and as the night came flooding back, his mouth widened in a satisfied grin. Olivia, that was it. Olivia and her lovely mouth and her sweet, funny shyness, her grand old bedraggled hotel, and her gorgeous sighing moans.

She was busy with something, so he took up the mug and sniffed it—Christ, she must have brewed it for an hour. Tasted like mud, too. He'd have to teach her the beauty of a French press and some decent beans.

But that was for later. Right now he wanted to know what the hell she was doing up and out of bed. At—he glanced at the bedside table clock, which was surprisingly shaped like a penguin—not even eight A.M.? She wasn't just awake, she was in the midst of what looked like an explosion at a paper factory—scraps of notepaper were strewn around her on the floor, and one had landed precariously atop her coffee mug. Her hair was screwed up on top of her head as if a blind woman had arranged it, and a pen was stuck through the back of it to hold it in place. A pencil was clenched between her teeth.

What the hell was she on about?

Last night, he'd imagined a lazy morning in bed, with her underneath him, or possibly above him, and then perhaps a shower, equally lazy, with lots of sexy soap suds and the feel of her slick skin under his hands.

Christ, he was getting a hard-on just thinking about it. He shifted onto his elbows and glared across the room at her. Instead of waking up to her naked body, he'd woken to Olivia . . . writing a novel? Writing letters to everyone she'd ever known? Plotting a bloody overthrow of the government? What the hell was she doing?

When he flicked off the comforter and swung his legs out of bed, she glanced up at him. Her cheeks were pink with excitement, and she scrambled up out of the tornado of paper to cross the room. A silky bit nightgown clung to her hips and her lovely full breasts, which appeased him a little bit.

"Morning, love," he said, holding out his hands until she took them. Without warning, he pulled her onto his lap. "What on earth are you doing there? And why at this god-forsaken hour?"

"Did the coffee wake you?" She frowned, sitting so primly in his lap he felt a bit like a dirty old man. "I was afraid of that. But I couldn't wait to make some for myself, and I thought it might be nice for you to wake up and find a cup right on the table, so I left it there, but I should have thought about the smell, since you are a chef, and your olfactory senses are probably extremely developed—"

He put his hand up to her mouth. Good lord, he'd broken her. She was wound up like a penny toy from the High Street. "Olivia, love? What did you put in the coffee? Airplane fuel?"

She rolled her eyes so dramatically he had to laugh. "Of course not. I'm just . . . Well, I'm strangely wide awake this morning." She looked up at him from under her lashes, a fetching combination of shy and flirtatious. "Maybe good sex will do that for me."

"Apparently." He pulled her closer and kissed her before he asked, "So it was good, yeah? You're telling me I was brilliant, and you just don't want to swell my head, I suppose. But you did say good—"

This time she put her hand to his mouth, but she was smiling just the same. "Drink your coffee. I was thinking of making you breakfast, but I wasn't sure what you'd like."

"You are wide awake, aren't you?" He frowned when she climbed off his lap, missing her warmth—and a bit apprehensive about her offer. "Weren't you telling me just last night that you were famous for burning water, love?"

"Well, to be honest, yes." She sniffed as she settled down in the storm of paper again. "But I thought I would give it a shot anyway."

"Looks like you were thinking about something else, as well," he pointed out, standing up to join her on the rug. She flushed a bit when she realized he was still naked, but at least she didn't protest. "What exactly are you doing here, Olivia?"

"Planning."

He waited, but she was already scowling at a list she'd written earlier and searching for the pencil she'd dropped. "Planning . . . ?"

"How to fix this." She gestured vaguely at the room. "How to beat him. How to win."

For someone who claimed to be wide awake, she sounded suspiciously as though she'd drifted into a fugue state. Still frowning, he glanced into the kitchen and found his jeans hanging off the counter. She'd smoothed them out, and they looked dry enough, so he tugged them on. This seemed like the kind of conversation that required pants.

"Olivia?"

She looked up and smiled at his jeans. "You found them! I put them in the oven for a little bit, since I don't have a washer or dryer up here."

In the . . . ? He shook the thought away and crouched beside her on the floor. "Winning what, love? Beating who? Not to put too fine a point on it, but what the bloody hell are you on about?"

"The hotel." If she'd added *duh* in punctuation, he wouldn't have been surprised. She stared at him as if this should have been obvious. "Uncle Stuart's threats. I can't let him get a hold of this place. I *won't* let him. So I'm throwing a party."

Hiring a hit man to dispatch Stuart, selling the place to the highest bidder, renovating the building from top to bottom—any of those plans he could have understood. But a party? What on earth would that accomplish?

She sifted through a pile of papers and waved a sheet at him in triumph. "It's all right here," she announced with a proud smile. "A Monsters' Ball."

He blinked. "A what now?"

"A Monsters' Ball. You know, a costume party for Halloween." She cocked her head to one side, regarding him thoughtfully. "Do you have Halloween in London? Are you from London originally? Or another part of England? I don't think I ever asked."

He blinked again. "Are you sure you didn't doctor up the coffee, love? Add a bit of Jolt Cola to the brew?"

"Rhys." She was really quite adorable when she rolled her eyes at him that way, like a schoolmarm secretly fond of her naughtiest charge. "Do you?"

"Do I what?"

Her shoulders slumped in defeat, and she leaned back against the loveseat, where Eloise regarded him with suspicion. "I think you need to drink that coffee. You're not really awake yet, are you?"

"Love, that coffee tastes a bit like you brewed it a week ago and added a dash of motor oil to it this morning." He shrugged when she glared at him, mouth open in outrage.

"I'm just being honest, Liv. And I'm quite awake now, thank you. I'm just having a bit of trouble following your train of thought. Which seems to be of the Silver Bullet variety."

She sighed. "I was asking about Halloween. Because the party I'm planning is to celebrate Halloween. It's huge here in the city, for adults as well as kids, and I thought it would be the perfect way to get the hotel back in the public eye."

"So who's invited?" he asked, settling back and picking up pieces of paper at random. Her neat, round hand was all over each one in black ink, lists and jotted ideas, menu items and bar needs. She really had been planning this morning. He was still unclear on the details, of course, but given her present mood he had no doubt she would fill him in.

"No one," she said absently.

No one. Right. He stared at her until she looked up.

"I mean, no one in particular. Although we could invite some celebrities, couldn't we? A few people guaranteed to come, and to draw a crowd!" She beamed. "Isn't that a good idea?"

"I don't know what the bloody hell you're talking about!" Crikey, he was going to have to drink the murk she was calling coffee just to keep up with her.

When she stopped cold and smiled at him, the same warm, sweet smile he'd begun to expect from her this week, he felt like an ass. She was altogether too forgiving.

"I'm going too fast, I know," she said, moving aside the piles of papers and her coffee mug to slide closer to him. She sat with her hands folded on her lap until he tugged her to his side and put his arm around her. "It's just that my brain is going so fast this morning. I woke up so early, and you were still sleeping, and then I realized that I should have been thinking about ways to save this place years ago—" She stopped short. "There I go again. Anyway, I thought a Halloween event would be something we could throw and open to the public. They would have to pay for tickets, of course, but I thought if we planned something really fabulous, and kept the tickets fairly cheap, we could attract a huge crowd, and get written up in the paper."

Huh. It was a workable plan at that. He rested his chin on the top of her head as he thought about it. "Or you could invite all the swankiest celebrities in town, gratis. Then you'd really make a splash in the papers."

"I don't think we can afford to do that." She rested her head against his shoulder. "I don't think those types would come anyway, you know? They've probably got much better things to do than show up here for a party."

"Hey now! Where's the Callender House cheerleader I met just this week?"

"She's gone into retirement." Her tone was laced with sadness, which hurt him to hear. "If I'm going to turn this hotel around I need to be more realistic, not blindly loyal."

She was right, of course. Still, it was a bit disappointing to find that dreamy fondness gone from her voice. "Probably, yeah."

Without warning, she wriggled away and stood up. "So here's what I'm going to do," she announced, and paced the length of the room with her hands squarely on her hips. "I'm going to enlist Josie and Roseanne and everyone else who wants to help, and we're going to brainstorm a budget. And a menu. Then decorations, of course, because we should probably have a theme more specific than simply Halloween. I'm thinking zombies, since this is all about bringing Callender House back from the dead. Plus, you can do a heck of a lot with cheesecloth and fake spider webs. Then we need to figure out where to advertise, and who the most likely attendees would be—the *Village Voice* or the *Times*? Then we have to think of our own costumes, of course . . ."

Rhys glanced longingly at the empty bed as Olivia barreled on. Somehow he didn't think she was quite in the mood for another lush, leisurely shag at the moment.

He sighed. He'd gone to bed with Sleeping Beauty and woken up with Wellington.

"They didn't."

"I'm telling you, they did."

"I don't believe it."

"Hector was there, he saw them!"

Josie narrowed her eyes at this piece of news, and leaned back in her chair. If Roseanne was right—and really, when wasn't she where this place was concerned?—Olivia was probably either having morning-after regrets or gearing up for another go at the horizontal mambo with Rhys Spencer.

Who had been, if Roseanne's account was accurate, making dinner for her in the hotel kitchen before something set off the fire alarm and the sprinklers.

Roseanne raised her eyebrows knowingly when Josie glanced up at her. She'd arrived just moments ago, straight from the kitchen, with a bagel in one hand and a mouthful of gossip, and parked her ample bottom in Josie's guest chair to spill the news.

"Still," Josie said carefully, "you don't know that they spent the night together. Just because they went upstairs together doesn't mean . . ."

Roseanne shook her head. "Rhys isn't in his room. Unless he sleeps like the dead, that is. Or *is* dead, I guess. I sent Katja to bang on the door, which she did, and he didn't answer."

"That was a risky thing to do," Josie chided her. "What if he had answered? What was Katja going to say?"

"That she had the wrong room, so sorry, sir." Roseanne waved the problem away with a hand adorned with at least eight silver rings. "Happens all the time."

Josie sighed. "Well, it shouldn't! It doesn't, in other hotels!"

"Focus, woman," Roseanne said, leaning closer and widening her eyes. "We're talking about Olivia and the British lothario, not what goes on in the Plaza."

"Lothario? Really?"

"You don't think he's a lothario?" Roseanne argued. "Have you read the papers? *People* magazine?"

Josie reached out to snatch half of Roseanne's bagel off the corner of her desk. "Of course I think he's a . . . lothario. It's just that no one but my grandmother uses that word. In fact, I think I heard my grandmother call George Clooney a player just the other day."

"Will you be serious, please?"

Josie shrugged. "It's never worked before, but I can try."

Roseanne glared at her and reached across the desk to snatch the bagel back before Josie took a bite. "He's too fast for her, is all. Too . . . worldly. I just don't want to see her heart broken. She's got enough problems already."

Yes, well, there was no denying that, Josie thought. She wasn't even supposed to be working on a Saturday, but Rob had called from the front desk at eight o'clock to say that his replacement had called in sick. No one treated Callender House as an actual place of employment. More like a halfway house where they could spend the day if they felt like it.

A halfway house for lunatics.

And she was one of them now, Josie realized. The truth was, she would rather be here than slouching around her messy little apartment waiting for the phone to ring or for something to happen. At least something was always happening here. Something interesting, too. Even if it was happening to someone else.

And when the someone else was Olivia, she couldn't help but be a little bit concerned. She'd never met anyone as purely innocent as Olivia. She didn't seem to exist in the same century, much less on the same planet. Chances were Olivia didn't even know who Britney Spears was, or that Red Bull existed, much less what the blogosphere had said about the newest cell phones.

Sinking back in her chair and eyeing Roseanne with sympathy, she sighed. Olivia was probably better off for it, too.

She was so insulated, and apparently so happy, here in her own little world. A strange, rundown world, of course, with a cast of characters that Josie had privately decided would be considered too weird even for reality TV, for that was beside the point. Olivia didn't know anything about men like Rhys Spencer.

Especially since Rhys Spencer in particular was a culinary nomad and hadn't stayed in one place longer than eight months in the last four years. He was due back in L.A. in three weeks, and who knew where he would go from there? Nope, he was not the sort of guy a girl should set her heart on, that was for sure.

And Josie was pretty sure Olivia didn't set her heart on anyone without picturing a happily ever after straight out of a fairy tale.

"Look, I agree Rhys is probably not really the right guy for her," she said finally. "But what are we supposed to do about it? Olivia was a grownup last time I checked. She's allowed to make her own decisions—and her own mistakes. Plus? There's something a little too weird about telling your boss, hey, you know that guy you probably slept with last night? Don't do that anymore."

Roseanne's face screwed up in thought at that, and she

lurched out of her chair to cross the room to the window. Resting her hands on the broad ledge, where Josie's various binders were stacked in dangerous piles, she addressed the bright fall morning outside when she said, "Then we'll have to hang back, keep an eye on them. See what develops."

If she'd added *constant vigilance* Josie wouldn't have been surprised. Roseanne looked as if she were ready to march into battle. With a frying pan for Rhys and a bottle of restorative smelling salts for Olivia.

It was probably much ado about nothing anyway, Josie thought as she stared into her empty coffee mug. Olivia was probably having the best time—and the best sex—of her life right now. Everyone needed a good old-fashioned fling with a bad boy once in a while. She wouldn't say no to one herself, come to think of it. Her social life, not to mention her sex life, had been sadly bad-boy free for much too long.

Oh, hell, her life in general had been free of any type of guy for much too long, she thought as she got up to wander into the minikitchen down the hall and find more coffee. If the perfect guy had dropped into Olivia's lap out of nowhere—even if he was only the perfect guy for right now—more power to her. Josie wouldn't object to a good man appearing out of nowhere in her life. No sir.

Which was when she opened the door to the hall and ran smack into Gus.

Fate, she decided as Gus gave her a shy smile from beneath the brim of his cap, was definitely trying to tell her something.

# Chapter 9

"Zombies? Really?"

"How about werewolves? Werewolves are much sexier than zombies."

"Zombies aren't sexy at all. Zombies eat brains."

"Vampires, now . . . vampires are sexy. I think we should do a Count Dracula thing."

"I don't see why it has to be scary. I hate scary. The monkeys in *The Wizard of Oz* scarred me for life."

"It's Halloween, that's why it has to be scary. Who wants to go to a Halloween party that's all rainbows and puppies?"

Olivia propped her chin in her hands and surveyed her staff down the polished expanse of the meeting room table. As meetings went, this one was typical, at least when it came to the general chaos and nearly a dozen voices all fighting to be heard at once.

When it came to the agenda, though, it was definitely different.

Her idea for a Halloween ball had been met, at least initially, with silence. Silence and blank faces, as if everyone in the room was waiting for the punch line to the joke. Callender House hadn't thrown an event like this in years—over a decade, probably. Not without someone else paying for it, at least.

And the Sons of the American Revolution reunion hadn't exactly been an unqualified success, what with the salmon being spoiled and two of the oldest members duking out a difference of opinion with their canes.

Maribel Clinton, the head of housekeeping, had finally broken the silence. "A ball? You want to throw a ball."

"A ball, a party, an event—we can call it whatever you want," Olivia had explained patiently. "I don't care. I just want to get people into the hotel, get some publicity, entice people to come back, or recommend the hotel to their friends."

"And you want to do that with zombies?" Roseanne had asked, her brow furrowed in confusion.

Josie gave Olivia a sympathetic shrug as the conversation devolved into the relative attractions of Halloween monsters, but she didn't chime in. She was still new, Olivia reminded herself. She probably still thought they were all crazy.

Which, actually, they were. Now that she thought about it, Callender House had to be a weird place to work after putting in time at the St. Regis. It had to make this place look like a meager step up from a mental asylum.

And that had to stop, she realized. Just because she'd always treated everyone on staff like family didn't mean they were allowed to bicker like children. This was a business, and zombies or not, it needed to be taken seriously.

She stood up, pushing her chair away from the table. At least she'd worn her red sweater this morning. That would get their attention. "Excuse me. *Excuse* me."

After a moment the room fell silent, and Olivia cleared her throat. Nine pairs of eyes stared up at her expectantly— and a little warily when it came to Josie.

"All right then," she said, surprised at how authoritative her voice sounded. "I want to make this happen, and we don't even have four weeks to get it done. That means decorations, food, drink, publicity, tickets, entertainment, all of it. And we *are* going to stick with the zombie theme."

From his perch on the radiator at the far end of the room, Stanley Whitehead, Roseanne's assistant, frowned. "Why?"

Why? What would be a good reason? Did she need a good reason, when it was her idea, and her hotel? She folded her arms across her chest. "Well, because I say so."

There was a heavy beat of silence, and Stanley said, "Oh."

"Zombies are good," Maribel said with a comforting pat on her arm. "Look what they did for Michael Jackson."

"Thank you," Olivia said, pretending she didn't notice Josie trying not to laugh. "I think."

"Is this why we were stripping the wallpaper in the ballroom yesterday?" Angel asked. He'd been checking his cell phone obsessively since the meeting began, and he'd done the same thing yesterday when Olivia had rounded up as many of the maintenance staff as she could find to attack the ballroom. Theresa, his wife, was due to have a baby any moment.

Rhys, on the other hand, had been having a cow since Saturday morning. It probably wasn't good form to kiss and run off to undertake renovations, but she couldn't help it. If she was going to throw this Monsters' Ball, she couldn't wait until the novelty of sleeping with Rhys had worn off.

She was pretty sure that would never happen in the first place.

"Where are you *going?*" he'd demanded Saturday at lunchtime, after persuading her into the shower.

"To the hardware store," she'd told him, pulling on clothes and watching as he strode through her very small, very feminine apartment in all his naked masculinity, a damp towel knotted at his waist. "I need to start looking at paint chips if I'm going to get the ballroom done in time for Halloween."

"Surely it can wait till tomorrow," he'd whispered, pulling her close and nuzzling her neck. "Or until after I've taken you out for a proper lunch."

She'd kissed him quickly and wiggled out of his arms. "It really can't, not if I want the maintenance guys to begin tomorrow. I bet you have a million things to do anyway."

His reply to that had been an arched eyebrow, but she couldn't help it if he was bored. Surely he could find something to do in a city the size of New York for one afternoon.

And she would be wise not to depend on him eager for her company every minute anyway.

According to the clippings Roseanne had left on her desk Saturday afternoon, Rhys had quite a reputation as a ladies' man. There was a whole column of gossip printed from the *L.A. Times* Web site devoted to his appearance on that cooking show, *Fork in the Road*, which was apparently a huge ratings success and the talk of the Internet. She really had to watch some TV filmed in the current decade sometime.

She was . . . lucky. That she'd knocked him over, instead of someone else. That he'd liked her enough to check into Callender House. Okay, that he'd liked her enough to want to make her dinner and, well, introduce her to the best sex of her life.

But he wasn't going to be around forever. That was a given. And somehow it wasn't as easy to fantasize a happy ending now that he'd woken her up so thoroughly. At least not a happy ending that was more than a very enjoyable fling.

And that was okay, she told herself, realizing with a jolt that she'd gone and done it again. She was standing in front of a roomful people, her employees, no less, daydreaming, just like she used to. And daydreaming about nakedness at that.

Well, no one changed completely overnight.

She cleared her throat again, fighting the blush on her cheeks, and announced, "Yes, we're going to start by painting the ballroom and attacking those floors and drapes. We want that room, at least, to look brand new for the event. We'll have to work on the second-floor restrooms, as well."

"And probably the lobby," Josie said quietly. "That's the first thing everyone sees."

"True." Olivia frowned. "Let me think about that. In the meantime, Angel, round up your crew. The paint and supplies were delivered this morning, and I'll be up to help as soon as I change my clothes."

"Miss Olivia!" Hector protested. He was wringing the hem of his flannel shirt as he spoke. "You don't have to do that! You were in there all day yesterday, Angel said."

And Rhys had been none too happy about that, either. "You're going to scrape woodwork? All day?"

"I want to supervise," she'd told him, pulling an ancient Oxford of her father's out of a storage bin and buttoning it over her oldest pair of jeans. "Anyway, I can use a little exercise."

"I know a million ways we can exercise together right here," he'd said, approaching like a tiger on the prowl, his eyes dark with desire.

How she'd walked away from that offer was still a mystery. What wasn't was her sore muscles, but she wasn't about to let that stop her from wielding a paintbrush today. The staff needed to know that she was serious about this—and other changes that kept springing to mind from out of nowhere—and that she wasn't asking them to do anything she wasn't willing to do herself.

Except for anything involving the sewage system. That was Angel's problem.

"I like to paint," she told Hector now, with a gentle smile. "And if someone brings a radio, it'll practically be a party."

"But no Randy Travis!" Angel and another of the maintenance guys shouted in unison. Hector sulked, but he slunk off to find a boom box anyway.

"Good luck." Roseanne patted her on the shoulder kindly as she picked up her coffee mug and left the room. Her eyes were twinkling when she said, "Wait until you hear what Angel and Mike like to listen to."

"I want one bourbon, one scotch, and one beer," Olivia muttered as she pushed the button for the elevator seven hours later. "Actually, just the bourbon will do."

George Thorogood. That's who Angel and Mike listened to. For hours. Same seven or eight songs over and over again. Next time she signed up for something like this, she was going to bring a Yanni tape and some earplugs and see how they liked it.

Her arms ached, and her legs weren't quite as steady as they should have been. Painting seemed like such a sedate activity, but when you were climbing ladders and wielding rollers for hours on end, it certainly took a toll. She hadn't eaten anything since a sandwich sometime around one, but she wasn't sure she had the strength to hold a fork at the moment. As long as she could manage to run herself the hottest, bubbliest bath in history, she'd survive.

She hoped.

The bell for the elevator dinged, and when the brass doors slid open she found Rhys smiling at her in surprise.

"Hello, love. I was just looking for you."

The smooth caress of his tone was enough to make her stumble against him in relief. When the doors closed behind her, she let him tug her close. "You have paint on your nose. It's quite fetching, actually."

"I probably have paint everywhere," she admitted, and looked down at her clothes. Splotches of sky blue and a creamy eggshell white dotted her jeans, her shirt, even the tops of her sneakers. Oops. "Is it in my hair?"

"Well, it's not in your eyelashes," Rhys said carefully, and ran his finger along the top curve of her cheek. "Oh, wait, I take that back."

"Gee, thanks."

"Were you painting all afternoon?" he asked as the elevator stopped at her floor. "I was waiting for you in the bar for a bit, talking to Tommy, and then I sweet-talked Josef into letting me into the kitchen."

She narrowed her eyes. "What for?"

"You'll see." His hand resting comfortably on the small of her back, he steered her down the hall, waving at Delancey Pruitt on the way.

"Well, hello there, Rhys," the other man said with a smile that bordered on a leer. Olivia might have pulled Rhys closer if she didn't know for a fact that Delancey had been living happily with his lover, Frankie Garson, for fifteen years. "Olivia, honey, you look awful! Let the nice man fix you up."

Her mouth dropped open in outrage, but Rhys propelled her smoothly down the hall and stopped at her apartment— where he produced a key and proceeded to open the door.

"Hey!" she protested. "Where did you get that?"

"It wasn't easy," Rhys grumbled as they went inside. "Roseanne actually asked for my birth certificate."

"She didn't!"

Rhys laughed. "Well, no, she didn't, but she came close. I had to promise I would return it tonight, no exceptions. And she only agreed after I told her why I needed it."

Something smelled delicious. Olivia sniffed the air with a smile. "And why was that?"

"So I could make up for the dinner I ruined the other night." He had begun peeling her clothes off as he spoke, unbuttoning her shirt and unhooking the barrette that held her hair, sort of, in place.

"You didn't ruin it," she murmured, enjoying the feel of his hands as he smoothed them over her back in search of the clasp on her bra. "The sprinklers did."

"Semantics." He opened the button on her jeans as he ran his tongue lightly over her aching shoulder and across her collarbone. "You've got shrimp and crab bisque, parmesan crisps, and a piece of gorgeous rare filet with roasted potatoes waiting for you."

So much for not being hungry. Her mouth was watering already. "Am I eating naked?" she managed, melting into him as he pushed her jeans over her hips.

"Maybe later." He helped her step out of the pants and then turned her toward the bathroom. "I think what you need is a long, hot bath first."

"But your dinner will be ruined," she protested. Weakly, but still. The idea of hot, bubbly water was too good to pass up at the moment—and when she walked into the bathroom, she saw that the tub had already been run. The steamy water had left a film on the mirror, and candles were lit on the back of the toilet and the edge of the sink.

"Are you psychic?" she said as Rhys tugged off her panties and left a naughty kiss on her backside.

"Not quite, love." He grinned. "Roseanne said you were a bit worse for the wear when I called downstairs looking for you."

"But dinner . . ."

"Will heat up good and proper when the time comes." His tone was firm. As she sank into the hot bubbles, she groaned a little bit, and looked up to find his eyes smoky with appreciation.

"Feels good, does it?" he said.

"So good. You have no idea."

"I haven't taken a bath in years," he admitted, and took a step closer to the tub, inhaling the scent of the bubbles. He was dressed in his usual uniform, a pair of jeans that looked to be about twenty years old and hung just right on his narrow hips and a long-sleeved black T-shirt that fit snugly across his chest. "I'm strictly a shower man after all those years in the tub as a lad. We never had enough hot water."

She sat up in the water, batting bubbles away as she tried to hold back a smile. He wasn't very sly about hinting. "You can join me if you like."

"Oh, well, it's your bath, love . . ."

She shrugged and closed her eyes, sliding into the steam once more and heard a blurted, "But if you insist."

His boots hit the floor with twin thumps, then his jeans, the belt buckle pinging against the tile. She opened her eyes to find him gloriously naked in the candlelight, the gentle flames casting a warm glow on his skin.

"Slide forward?" he asked, and when she did he climbed in behind her. A moment later he pulled her between his legs, and she rested her head against his chest. The water was still blissfully hot, the bubbles were her favorite Night Garden mix, and the solid feel of his body behind her was a surprising comfort.

"I should have asked if you wanted a drink," Rhys murmured into her hair.

"I think I've had quite enough bourbon, scotch, and beer for one day, thank you," she said with a laugh.

"You've *what* now?"

She twisted her head to look back at him. "I was just kidding. This is plenty relaxing, believe me."

"Relaxing is what you need, love." He kissed the top of her head. "All that painting. You must be exhausted. I should have helped."

"There weren't enough rollers." Even to her own ears, her voice sounded drowsy and faraway. He was rubbing her shoulders just hard enough to ease out the kinks, and the soapy water made the sensation of his fingers on her skin hypnotic. "And anyway, I keep telling you, you're a—"

"Guest. Right. I know, love."

She twisted around to look at him again. "Don't be mad. I can't imagine checking into a hotel and then being handed a paint roller."

He leaned down to give her a lingering kiss, and she melted just a little bit more at the heat of his mouth. "No worries, love," he said when he dragged his lips away. "Just lie back and relax."

"I'm not sure I *can* relax if you keep doing that." His arms had come around her waist, and his hands had found her breasts, caressing them lazily in the soapy water.

"Try," he murmured, and rubbed his thumbs across her nipples.

She wasn't sure she could relax anyway. Aside from the urgent flicker of arousal, her brain was hissing warnings every few seconds. *It won't last. He's leaving in three weeks. How many other women has he bathed with?!*

She wasn't used to this. She wasn't used to a man who rode in to her rescue out of the blue, even when she didn't know she needed rescuing. She'd never dated a man who cooked, or who had such a wicked grin and an even wickeder sense of humor, or who apparently liked her enough to sit and listen to her babble incoherently about a work problem she'd only just figured out.

She'd never ever dated a man who could make her insides melt with just one knowing look, and who seemed to consider it a personal challenge to make sure she had so many orgasms she lost count.

But she had dreamed. She'd spent years dreaming, she realized now, holed up in her own little castle here in the middle of the city. Dreaming of the past and the people she missed, and sometimes, at night, in bed, dreaming of the future.

Dating hadn't ever been her strong suit, but it didn't mean she didn't want a relationship. Okay, a husband. Someone who knew her inside and out, who loved her, someone she could love completely, someone she could share her life with, good and bad.

And she'd dreamed of someone like Rhys so often, his unexpected arrival in her life was a little disconcerting. Okay, not exactly like Rhys, because who could have imagined someone so unique and fascinating and, frankly, gorgeous? But she'd thought about meeting a man who worked for himself—an architect maybe, or a photographer, or even a chef. Someone who would appreciate the hotel, who could work from the hotel, who would live here with her, in one of the bigger residential apartments, becoming a part of the place, making himself a home here and loving it as she did.

And Rhys fit that bill so well. On the surface, at least.

Well, he didn't really appreciate the hotel—yet—but that could change.

It was the rest of it that was so dangerous. Fantasizing about having him here at the hotel every day, sharing lunch with him or stealing off to a midday movie when it was slow. Coming home to him, to his smile, his touch, his slow, sensuous kisses, forever . . .

Even if she hadn't already known that Rhys was scheduled to fly back to L.A. in a few weeks, he didn't stick around. She'd gathered that much from the little she had asked him, and from the hints Roseanne and Josie and even Gus seemed determined to drop, even if Gus seemed to share them reluctantly. As far as she knew, this was just a fling for Rhys. An enjoyable one, she didn't doubt that, but a fling nonetheless.

She wanted to enjoy herself, too. Give herself up the fun of Rhys's company and the novelty of having a lover and the sheer oh-my-goodness of the sex. But it was so hard, too, because every time Rhys was kind, and generous, and heartbreakingly good to her, and she let herself revel in it, she knew that the day he left would be that much more difficult.

"Are you asleep?" he whispered now, nuzzling the top of her head as his hands slid lower, stroking across her belly and down to her thighs.

"Not yet." She let him part her legs and groaned when his fingers slid into her folds, combing through the wet hair teasingly. "Nope, I don't think I'm going to nod off now."

His erection was pressed against her behind, and she wriggled backward experimentally. "You're clearly not sleepy, either," she added.

"Not a bit." His words were a rough growl against the back of her neck, and he pushed his erection against her bottom.

Once, it would have been so easy to disappear into the fantasy, let him thrust inside her without thinking about the consequences. Of course, once, this sensual little interlude would have been nothing more than a fantasy as she lay in bed dreaming.

Not now, though.

"You don't have a condom in here, do you?" she whispered.

For a moment, he paused so completely that the room rang with the silence. Then he sighed, his breath tickling her nape.

"Nope, no condom, love." He licked water off her shoulder, and his tongue felt cool and slick in comparison to the heated water. "But that doesn't mean you can't have a bit of pleasure, yeah?"

Her "yeah" emerged on the heels of a groan as he thrust his fingers inside her, pumping in rhythm. Oh, God, it felt so good.

Seize the moment. That was what everyone said, wasn't it? Well, she was going to seize every moment she had with Rhys—even if there would never be as many as she wanted.

# Chapter 10

"Kidnapping," Rhys said gloomily, staring into the gin and tonic Tommy had poured for him days later. "It's the only way."

Beside him, Gus shrugged and nodded. "Looks like it, my friend."

"She's become the blasted Energizer Bunny," Rhys said, smacking his hand on the top of the bar. "I can't turn the woman off for love nor money."

"She is kind of hopped up about this ball," Gus agreed, and rattled the ice cubes in his glass at Tommy. The bar was deserted, as usual on a late Friday afternoon. "I'll take another Coke."

"Hopped up? The woman is obsessed!" Rhys slugged back the rest of his drink and then reconsidered his words. "Not that she shouldn't be, yeah? It's her hotel, and it could certainly use a bit of spiffing up, and some decent publicity. But I'd like to spend at least a moment with her alone with no mention of zombies, the relative merits of crepe paper, and dry ice for the sodding punch!"

In the days since he'd cornered her in the elevator, he'd spent approximately thirty-eight minutes alone with her.

Well, that wasn't entirely true. They'd spent evenings together, in her bed usually, but that was just sex.

Just sex. He shook his head in disbelief, ignoring Gus's glance. Once upon a time "just sex" would have been fine with him. The ultimate in a relationship, in fact. No strings, no bloody requests to "talk," nothing but two naked bodies and all the many ways they could find pleasure together.

Now he wanted to talk to Olivia, damn it. Not that he didn't appreciate making love to her—appreciate was far too weak a word, in fact. Bloody hell. When had he begun to think of it as making love, anyway? Shagging, fucking, those were his words, his terms.

And even when they were definitely shagging, like they had been up against the wall in the entryway of her little flat the other night, it wasn't *just* shagging, was it?

Not for him, anyway.

And the way she'd stopped him the other night in the tub—that had hit home. He hadn't been thinking beyond the wet, slippery pleasure of their skin sliding together in the water, and if Liv hadn't said anything he would have thrust inside her in a heartbeat. But she had—she'd been the one to remind him that a condom was necessary if they didn't want to be surprised a few weeks down the line.

Unlike Clodagh.

"I'm out of sorts myself," he said aloud, in an effort to derail his uncomfortable train of thought. "I've not been cooking, and I miss it. I've got that final competition hanging over my head, and no way to prepare for it. And God only knows what I'll do after that's over."

Gus nodded thoughtfully. They'd spent so many afternoons together recently, just like this, that Rhys had eventually filled him in about *Fork in the Road*. After a moment, he said, "What about opening a restaurant of your own?"

"It's a possibility—but not a good one unless I win that

bloody competition." Even to his own ears Rhys sounded like a pouting child.

"Well, why not ask Josef to let you mess around in the kitchen this afternoon, maybe help with dinner?"

Rhys had been asking himself the same question for days. The answer was really quite simple, frightening as it was. "Because I want to be snogging Olivia somewhere, that's why. Because I can't think about anything but her, if you want the truth. Haven't been able to since she knocked me down on the sidewalk that first day."

Gus considered this for a moment, then took a cocktail napkin from the pile on the bar and retrieved a pen from his pocket. "Well then, buddy, it looks like we're back to kidnapping."

Standing in the center of the ballroom, Olivia whirled around and clapped her hands. "It looks gorgeous. If I do say so myself."

Two weeks and approximately a thousand cans of paint and paint stripper and rollers and floor wax and pieces of sandpaper, and the room was finally done. The walls were a rich sky blue, and the woodwork and moldings were all creamy eggshell. With the old drapes torn down and fresh new ones hung—fresh new cheaply made ones, thanks to some plain muslin on sale and the talents of Maribel's mother—the whole room was as light and airy as it had once been dull and tattered. Even the ladders and scaffolding and drop cloths had finally been cleared away.

Plus, a friend of Declan the doorman was an artist who had very generously agreed to paint a mural on the ceiling for a song. Which was fortunate, since Olivia's personal credit cards had been getting quite a workout ever since she had decided to undertake Callender House's new image. For a mere $500, plus generous credit in conspicuous places, the grand domed ceiling of the ballroom now sported pale drifts of clouds, and trios of very baroque angels in flight, each with a particular New York theme—one was eating a bagel and carrying a cup of coffee, another was a cabdriver, a third was draped in Liberty-like robes.

"It's genius, I have to say," Josie told her, nudging Olivia with a friendly elbow and tipping back her head to admire the artwork. "It's a whole other room now."

"It is, isn't it?" Olivia said with a happy grin. "Although now that I think about it, we probably should have redone the lobby first and saved the doom and gloom in here for the party. It doesn't look very spooky now, does it?"

"Fake cobwebs are preferable to real ones, if you ask me." Josie nudged her again. "We have company."

Olivia glanced at the door to find Rhys slouched there, head tilted to one side as he looked at her, his hands jammed in his jeans pockets. He winked at her, and she blushed.

"Oh, for God's sake," Josie muttered. "Get a room." She was out the door, ponytail bouncing after her, before Olivia could protest.

"What do you think?" she asked Rhys instead, spreading her arms to encompass the whole room. "Do you like it?"

"It's brilliant."

"You're not even looking."

"I've seen the whole thing in progress, remember?"

"Humor me." She gave him a sad puppy dog look, and he groaned in defeat. Walking into the room, he turned in a circle, eyes on the ceiling.

"Brilliant. Just like I said."

"You're being stubborn," she said as he caught her up in his arms and turned her around the floor in an impromptu waltz. Their footfalls echoed in the huge, empty room, a strange staccato rhythm.

"Not stubborn, just determined," he answered. His gray

eyes gleamed with mischief. "I have something to show you."

"What is it?" God, if he kept feeding her, she was going to gain a thousand pounds. One more chocolate torte and none of her pants would fit right.

"I'd be telling you then, wouldn't I? I want to *show* you." He danced them toward the door, but she dug her heels in.

She had to stall, if nothing else. Rhys was far too persuasive when he got his hands on her, and it was only five o'clock. She still had a list of things she wanted to check on before clocking out for the day.

*Think of something quick.* "Where did you learn to waltz like that?"

"I was born to dance," he said dryly. "No stalling. I'm hardly Michael Flatley."

Damn it. "Can you dip me?"

He smirked. "Like this, you mean?"

Before she knew it, she was bent back over his arm, and he was lowering his mouth to hers in a hot, lingering kiss that was so dark and spicy she could hardly breathe.

"Um, yes . . . like that," she managed when he had her upright again. "That was wonderful. Do it again."

"You're going to be over my shoulder in a minute," he warned, and steered her toward the door. "I have something to show you and I'm not taking no for an answer."

"The caveman in you is hardly appealing," she said waspishly, but she let him lead her out the door and downstairs. In the lobby, though, she wriggled out of reach when he headed for the revolving door.

"Rhys, just tell me," she pleaded. "I shouldn't take off without a word to anyone, you know."

"Already taken care of." He hooked his arm around her shoulder and cocked his head at the registration desk, where Roseanne stood grinning at her. She waggled her fingers and mouthed, " 'Bye-bye."

"It's a conspiracy," Olivia protested when she turned to see Gus waving from the door to the bar. Josie was beside him, looking a bit confused but waving nonetheless.

"A happy one," Rhys promised as he propelled her outside. "I'm not whisking you off to a torture chamber, yeah?"

"How am I supposed to know?" she replied, simply to be argumentative. The man got his own way so often, he'd probably forgotten the world didn't always bend to his wishes. She bent to his wishes all too often, in fact. Even if most of them were designed for her enjoyment, if not toe-curling physical pleasure.

"Because this is what I wanted to show you." He spread one arm toward the curb as they stood outside on the windy sidewalk, and in the gathering dusk she saw a horse-drawn carriage.

It was white, and looked freshly washed, with gleaming black-painted wheels and two glowing carriage lamps already lit against the darkness. A garland of fall flowers lay along the back of the seat, and the horse was adorned with a wreath, the purple and yellow mums rich against his thick white mane.

Oh, Rhys. He had no idea what he was doing to her.

"This is for me?" she said, turning her face up to his. "For us?"

"All ours, love, for as long as we want it." He flicked a glance at the driver, who was bundled into a heavy corduroy coat under his black top hat. "That right, Pete?"

"Yes, sir." The man grinned and let go of the reins to hop down and offer his arm. "My lady?"

Well, there was no way on earth to deny Rhys the pleasure of arranging this surprise. And there was, honestly, no way she was going to miss out on it. She climbed up the hanging steps with Pete's help, and turned to Rhys when he joined her.

"This is lovely. I'm sorry I was being difficult."

"No worries, love." He was practically beaming now that he had her in the carriage, and before she had decided how to mention that the October air was really kind of chilly, he'd presented her jacket and a snug lap blanket.

God, she was going to cry if she wasn't careful. "You thought of everything."

"I try, I try." He rummaged at his feet and came up with a thermos. "Thirsty? I've got hot tea here, just the way you like it, and there's a bit of a snack for later, as well."

"Why are you doing all this?" She whispered the words, not trusting her voice to remain steady, as he snugged her up against him and put his arm around her shoulders.

"What a nonsensical question, Liv." He kissed the top of her head as the carriage pulled away from the curb, heading uptown. "Because I want to. Because it makes me happy. Because I hoped it would make you happy. And truly? Because I wanted a chance to spend a few minutes with you away from the hotel."

He was the only person who'd ever called her Liv—even her father had only ever called her Olivia, since his pet name for her had been, inexplicably, Button. But Liv seemed right on Rhys's tongue, and the intimacy of a name only he used gave her a little thrill whenever she heard it.

She hid her face against his coat and snuggled closer. The horse's shoes made a soothing clopping noise on the pavement. "Why? I mean, why away from the hotel? At the hotel we can . . . you know."

He set her away from him so abruptly, she was startled. His dark eyes blazed with outrage. "Do you think that's the only reason I want to spend time with you? Because it's certainly not. Not that I object to the way we spend time in your bed, you see, not at all, but really, Olivia. That's a bit unflattering."

Oh my goodness. He was so incensed, she didn't quite know what to say. The sex was wonderful—it was amazing, transporting, and amazingly addictive—but it wasn't the only reason she was attracted to him, either.

But . . . if it wasn't just sex for him, what was it? Because the minute she began to believe that it might be more, that it might be forever, she was going to get her heart broken. She knew it. He was leaving in just a few weeks, and he'd never said a word about coming back after he was finished with the show.

But she couldn't say that, not here. Not now. Not at all, probably, because he'd never made one promise that involved more than a few hours together.

She put her hands on his cheeks and drew his head closer, so she could look him in the eye. "I'm sorry. That was horrible of me to say."

He let the silence linger a moment in the crisp night air. Somewhere a cabbie was leaning on his horn, and the noise cut through the background hum of traffic rushing by on Madison. "Forgiven," he said finally. "Or you will be if you let me grope you under the blanket."

She smacked his hand away with a laugh. "I am sorry," she repeated. "It's just that everything sort of happened at once. You showing up the day that Uncle Stuart made those awful threats, and then I had the idea about the Monsters' Ball. I've probably been insufferably self-absorbed, huh?"

"Let's say understandably distracted." He smiled and pulled her into the circle of his arm again.

"It's just that I can't help feeling responsible for everything that goes on there," she said, enjoying the cool air on her cheeks. "I mean, I am responsible. It's my hotel, after all. And if this ball fails . . ."

"It won't," Rhys assured her. "Haven't you already had a bit of good press? The preparations are coming along just fine, the menu's all been sorted, and Roseanne said you've already sold dozens and dozens of tickets."

"That's true," she admitted. Maybe she should let him reassure her on a daily basis. Everything sounded sensible and under control in his crisp British accent.

"You know the staff is all pulling for you, too, yeah? They're going to do their damnedest to make the thing work brilliantly. Look at Angel, asking his brother-in-law's band to play. Free publicity for the band, free entertainment for you."

"Also true," she said and watched as Pete pulled the carriage onto Fifty-Ninth Street. "Are we going to the park?"

"Where else?" Rhys tipped her chin up to kiss her. "Just for a little while. So we can enjoy a bit of privacy and talk to each other, away from it all. The hotel's in good hands, love."

He was right, of course. She settled into him and closed her eyes as the horse clopped into the park proper. She deserved to get away for a little while now and then. After all, what could happen?

Stuart Callender's office was as gloomy and gray as he was, Marty Kinsella thought as he and Davey O'Brian stood waiting for the big man himself to end his phone call. It was tonight, because it was already dark and the man had only turned on the desk lamp, but it always felt like a frigging cave to Marty.

Or it would have, if it weren't for the sweep of windows behind Callender's desk. He and Davey were reflected in them now, and Davey was rummaging in the pocket of his khakis. Dress pants, according to Davey. Someone really needed to smack some sense, or at least some taste, into him.

"Stop fidgeting," he hissed at Davey. Whenever Mr. Callender wanted them for one of his special "assignments," the pay rocked. The work wasn't always steady, but there were creative ways to make funds last, and anyway, it beat slinging burgers somewhere on the Jersey Turnpike. Or, God forbid, riding the back of a sanitation truck with his uncle Lou.

"I'm not fidgeting!" Davey protested—too loud, because Callender looked up and glared at them both.

"You fuck this up for me, and you're gonna regret it," Marty whispered in Davey's direction. "I promised Shelley I'd get her an iPod for Christmas, one of the big video ones, and I need the money."

"Don't worry," Davey whispered back, but not before rolling his eyes. His eyebrows looked like rusty beetles crawling across his forehead, Marty thought. That Brillo hair had to be the reason he never got laid.

Callender hung up the phone with a distinct thud, and sat back in his chair. It was one of those snazzy black leather jobs, of course.

"Two people on the maintenance staff of Callender House are quitting without notice, thanks to me," he said without preliminaries. Figured. "I've managed to plant a seed, through mutual acquaintances who have assured me my name will be kept out of it, that you two are the perfect replacements."

Maintenance? What the hell? He didn't want to push a fucking broom, not even for whatever Stuart Callender was willing to pay. But he kept his mouth shut, waiting for the other shoe to drop. There was always another shoe with Callender.

"All you two have to do is show up at the hotel tomorrow

and ask for Angel Dorsey. The rest should be as simple as adding two plus two."

The rest? What did that mean? Getting the jobs, or whatever extras Callender wanted them to perform? Davey was already scratching his head thoughtfully, and Marty resisted the urge to elbow him in the ribs. Hard.

Too late. Davey said, "And then what?" God, he was a moron.

Callender rolled his eyes as he folded his arms across his chest. The glare he directed at Davey was lethal. "And then you take every opportunity you find to cause trouble. On the sly, of course. Think sabotage, secret and subtle, not wrecking balls. Can you handle that?"

Sabotage? That was more like it. Marty straightened up, and decided to lob a ball back to the big man, just to be sure they were playing the same game. "Screwing with the plumbing, maybe. Stuff like that."

Callender's smile was as cold as midwinter day. "Exactly."

"No problem, sir," Marty said proudly, before something confusing occurred to him. He should probably keep his mouth shut, but maybe it was better to be sure. . . . "Can I ask . . . why? Don't you want the hotel for yourself, sir? Why do you want us to ruin stuff?"

"I don't want that falling down pile of bricks," Callender scoffed. "I want the property, which is worth far more. And I'm going to have it one way or another."

# Chapter 11

"Good afternoon, Mrs. Gilchrist," Olivia said on Saturday morning as one of their permanent residents ventured carefully into the lobby. Olivia couldn't blame her for the caution—it looked as if a bomb had gone off, with buckets for tile cleaning in one corner, the brass on the reception desk being polished, and Olivia herself kneeling in front of the red velvet banquette, an upholstery knife in hand and torn red velvet splashed like blood on the floor.

"What on earth are you doing, dear?" The old woman squinted through the bright red frames of her glasses. "Oh, are you re-covering this old thing? It's about time, you know. That old velvet has seen better days. You should try the new microsuede everyone talks about!"

"Um, good," Olivia said as Louise Gilchrist crossed the room to the revolving door, her customary flowered tote bag over one arm. If it was Saturday, Louise ventured out to buy her groceries, just as surely as the sun rose and set.

But Olivia never would have guessed that Louise was tired of the banquette—she had lived at Callender House for eighteen years, taking over her sister Adele's apartment when she passed away unexpectedly. Louise was close to seventy, Olivia was pretty sure, and her usual fashion statement was something in polyester with matching plastic beads. She would have thought the red velvet was right up her generation's alley.

But what did she know? She hadn't been in Louise's apartment in years. It could be all chrome and black lights, although she kind of doubted it. Still, microsuede? God, maybe Louise was even hooked up to the Internet.

"Well, at least she's honest," Josie said as she crouched beside Olivia with a steaming cup of coffee. She was wearing an old pair of denim overalls with a black turtleneck beneath them, and her traditional ponytail had been wrapped around its base into a bun. Ready for painting, she'd said with a marked lack of enthusiasm when she showed up this morning, although Olivia wasn't really sure why she'd come. She didn't work Saturdays.

"You know, if you're such a nonfan of painting, what are you doing here?" she asked now, setting down her knife and picking up her own coffee, which had gone cold. "You could be out doing a million things today. Seeing a movie. Antiquing. Shopping. *Sleeping*."

"Haven't gotten much of that yourself, huh?" Josie winked at her, but she settled on the floor and crossed her legs like a child waiting for storytime. "I'm only here because I'm running the pool on how much paint you get in your hair by the end of the day." She laughed when Olivia rolled her eyes. "Okay, I admit it. My social life is a disaster. Being here is more fun than sitting home and wondering if I should get a cat."

"I have a cat!"

Josie patted her head fondly. "At least you don't have seven. Or seventeen."

"Hey."

Josie threw her hands up, smirking. "I'm the last one to make fun, believe me. At least you have a sex life. And it seems to be a good one."

Hot color flooded Olivia's cheeks. "It's not half bad at that."

"You're a queen of understatement," Josie said wryly and got to her feet. "Now, what should I do? Stand aside and supervise? Make droll comments on the proceedings?"

"Funny." Olivia pointed to Gus, who was off in the corner near the bar, sanding woodwork. "Help him out. We should be ready to paint in a little while."

Josie sighed. "Okay, okay. Is it a fun color at least? Something outrageous and unexpected?"

Olivia waved the color chip at her.

"It's . . . green."

"It's Velvet Leaf," Olivia said primly, which was hard to do when she was sprawled on the bare floor with her hair bundled into a bandana and her old sweatpants on. "And it's a very Bohemian color."

Josie perked up at that. "Bohemian? We're going Bohemian?"

"Well, funky. Funky Bohemian." Olivia shrugged. "I'm not sure, exactly. Bohemian actually works with some of the things I can't change right now, in terms of the era. And it's much more colorful. And funky."

"You said that." Josie grinned. "I think it'll be great. I like funky. You can't have 'funky' without fun, right?"

Olivia giggled. "Right."

Of course, it wasn't going to be quite that easy, she thought, surveying the chaos around her. She'd never reupholstered anything before, for one thing, although Roseanne had promised to help. She had years of sewing Renaissance Faire costumes under her belt. The question was what the lobby was going to look like when it was all done. A silk purse hung from a sow's ear? A string of pearls over jeans and a ratty old T-shirt?

She wanted to be honest with herself, that was the thing.

It had gotten much easier since her weird wake-up call two weeks ago, but it hadn't been very pleasant. Suddenly the things that had always been happily familiar and nostalgic just looked . . . old. Worn out. Broken, in some cases. She didn't want to fool herself into believing that a little paint and some new drapes were going to change the world. Or at least the fate of the hotel.

She was trying to ignore the fact that the brass polish she'd ordered was only making the pitted trim on the reception desk look worse. And that in removing the banquette's ancient red velvet, she'd accidentally torn a few of the cushions.

"You're going to exhaust yourself, love."

She looked up to find Rhys standing over her, his hands in his pockets and his brow furrowed into a concerned frown. She smiled up at him. "The only thing I'm exhausting so far is my credit card."

He was incredulous. "You're using your own dosh for this?"

"Well, spontaneous renovation isn't exactly in the budget," she admitted, and took his hand when he offered it to help her off the floor. "But I want to. It's okay, really."

He shook his head, his loose, tousled hair swinging against his face. "You're a wonder, Liv."

She let him pull her close and hid her face against his T-shirt, breathing him in. She wasn't a wonder. Not the way he meant. Not unless he'd intended to say "wondrously idiotic." She could blather to herself all day long about honesty, but she was certainly having a hard time being honest with herself when it came to Rhys. Every day he was still at the hotel, still in her bed, was another gift—and another wrench she would feel, painfully, in awful, secret places, when he moved on.

If she was going to embrace reality at this late date, she should at least ask Rhys if this relationship was going to last after he left for L.A. Or simply push him away and save herself a little bit of heartbreak later.

But she couldn't. She was too good at fantasies and daydreams. And Rhys was, so far, a daydream come to life. Wasn't he here this morning, helping to scrape and sand when the hotel wasn't his problem? Hadn't he brought her coffee and breakfast this morning before she was even out of bed? He was Prince Charming, for heaven's sake.

"You've made a right mess of that banquette," he said now, and she sighed.

An honest Prince Charming, but still.

"Roseanne is going to help me on Monday," she explained. "I was just . . . getting it started."

"Looks like you nearly ended it instead," he pointed out, toeing up a piece of the old upholstery that still had ancient stuffing attached.

Maybe "charming" wasn't the right word, either.

"Are you quite through?" she said, pushing away from him.

"Don't you sound like a British schoolmarm when you're narked." He gave her a quick, smacking kiss and patted her rear end in punctuation. "Sorry, love. Do you have any gas masks, by the way? This place is probably crawling with asbestos, you know."

When he walked away, she smacked his rear, hard, but she couldn't help laughing. Sheer willpower had to count for something, didn't it? No matter how much or how little she could change this old place, at least she would have tried. And that was a success in itself.

She took a deep breath and turned to attack the banquette once more, full of confidence and hope.

Until Angel walked into the lobby with two strange men and announced with a helpless shrug, "The sign outside's fallen down again."

Three hours later, Rhys stood up and stretched. He'd been sanding woodwork for far too long, in far too uncomfortable a position. If anyone had told him a few weeks ago he'd be holed up in a one-star hotel working his arse off for free, he'd have laughed and ordered another pint or two.

There were easily a dozen things he would rather be doing at the moment, chief among them stripping Olivia's clothes off and taking her in a hot, pulsing shower, but that would have to wait until later. If she was so determined to get this lobby redone today, then he was going to help. Whether he liked it or not.

Didn't mean it wasn't time to break for a few cold drinks and a bit of lunch, though. And, God or Olivia willing, a nap.

She was busy trying to cram exploded upholstery stuffing back into the banquette, and drifts of yellowed cotton had stuck to her hair and her shirt. She looked up at him when he stood over her and offered a weak smile.

"I feel like I walked into an *I Love Lucy* episode," she said.

"A what now?"

"Didn't you ever watch TV as a kid?" She let him pull her to her feet and picked a bit of cotton from the front of her shirt.

"I watched *EastEnders*, love," he said, "just like all proper Londoners. Time for a break, yeah? You look done in."

"Well, everyone else is still working," she said doubtfully. Gus and Josie were still working on the east wall of the lobby, and Angel had given the two new guys the job of cleaning the tile floor near the elevators, which they didn't seem well pleased about. Two girls from Maribel's house-keeping staff were still working on the reception desk, which unfortunately looked worse now than it had before.

But the minute Olivia glanced about the room, heads came up automatically. "I could use a break," Josie said, and Lindy put down her polish and rag. "Me, too. I'm starved."

"Lunch for everyone then," Rhys announced, and steered Olivia into the empty bar and then into a chair. "I'll pop into the shop and order some sandwiches, yeah? Tommy can pour some cold drinks all around."

"I don't think Tommy's here today." Olivia's shoulders had begun to sag, and she leaned back in the chair grate-fully.

"I'll pour." Josie had followed them into the bar with Gus on her heels and was already behind the counter. "I'm parched. And hungry. And tired. Am I getting overtime for this? Where are those nice home improvement people from all the TV shows when you need them?"

She squirted diet soda into a glass with ice and handed across the counter to Rhys. "Give that to Olivia. First drink's on the house."

"I heard that," Olivia muttered, but she accepted the glass and took a long drink. "Oh, caffeine. How I love you."

Rhys snickered and kissed the top of her head. "Well, the nosh is on me, love. I'll be back in a bit."

"Want some help?" Gus said, his eyes pleading with Rhys from beneath his Yankees cap. He'd come into the bar with Josie, sanding dust and primer all over his sweatshirt.

Looked as if he wanted to talk. The bloke's expression bordered on desperate, and when Rhys saw him glance over at Josie, busy gulping down a glass of water herself, he thought he knew why.

"Sure, mate," he said easily. "You can point me in the direction of the best sandwich shop."

They set off, skirting the housekeeping girls, who had claimed a corner of the lobby floor and were already busy on their cell phones. The new maintenance blokes had disappeared, which was a bad sign, but Angel would have to deal with that himself, Rhys thought. He was already in over his head when it came to Olivia, much less the blasted hotel.

As was Gus, apparently. Because the moment they were through the revolving door and out on the pavement in the crisp October sunshine, he said, "You have to help me."

Bloody hell. Did he look like the sodding answer man? All he wanted was a roast beef on rye, and the chance to hijack Olivia into bed sooner rather than later. But the look on Gus's face was too pathetic to ignore. "Help you with what, mate?"

"Josie." He spread his hands helplessly as they turned onto Fiftieth Street and headed east. "I'm in love with her. I'm so in love with her I can't think straight. I'm pretty sure I sanded the same piece of woodwork about fifteen times this morning. And then primed a strip I hadn't sanded at all."

Rhys restrained a snort of amusement. Poor fellow.

Not that he had any right to laugh, he realized with a jolt a moment later. He was in the same bloody boat. He and Gus were probably sharing a single oar.

Not that he was in love with Olivia. He didn't fall in love, as a rule. He was a bit obsessed at the moment. That was all. It would pass. Had to, didn't it? He was leaving for L.A. shortly after the Halloween ball, and after that he was going to have decisions to make. He should have been giving them some consideration before now, truth to tell. What he would do with the contest money if he won. What he would do with himself if he didn't.

And he would think about it, he promised himself. Later today even. After he took Olivia to bed.

"Ever since Josie started work at the hotel," Gus had continued, padding alongside Rhys with his hands in his jeans pockets and his ball cap casting a shadow over his face. "I mean, from the first day. I took one look at her and almost tripped over my own feet."

"I did trip," Rhys muttered. "At least you didn't end up on your arse."

Gus smiled a little bit at that, but as they stopped at the light at Park Avenue, he turned to Rhys. "I mean it. I don't know what to do. When she came over to help me this morning, I almost threw up."

"Crikey, man," Rhys protested, hands in the air. "Too much information."

"I said almost." Gus sighed. "I just don't know what to do. I can't think about anything but her, but I don't even know how to talk to her. I haven't . . . been in many . . . relationships."

"Yeah?" Rhys frowned and nodded his head as the light changed. "Come on. What do you mean by not many, exactly?"

"Um, three," Gus admitted, his eyes on his worn-out Adidas. "And one of them was in high school."

Rhys narrowed his eyes. This didn't sound promising. "What about the other two?"

"One was in college. And one was . . . while I was in Riverside, writing *The Other Side of the Moon*." He looked so sheepish, Rhys half expected him to *baaaah*.

"You had a relationship in a *mental hospital?*" he said incredulously.

"With a nurse," Gus was quick to point out, even though

his cheeks had flamed with color. "But she was a little upset to discover that I wasn't, you know, a patient after all."

Rhys nearly tripped over the curb as they crossed onto Lexington. "That's what she *wanted?*"

"Well, no, not exactly." Hunching his shoulders, Gus risked a sidelong glance. "She wasn't happy about the lying."

"But the fact that you weren't insane wasn't a bonus?"

"Look, that's not the point," Gus insisted, and waved an arm at the entrance to the Hello Market. "The point is that I don't have a lot of experience at this, and I can't get Josie off my mind. For one thing, she's always there, you know? I see her every day! There's no escaping her!"

"She's not the plague, mate, she's a pretty woman," Rhys said, eyebrow raised at the slightly hysterical tone in Gus's voice. "Why get her off your mind at all? Or, to be more specific, why not get her somewhere else? Ask her out. Ask her to lunch, or dinner, or a movie. Something."

Gus turned wild eyes on him. "Then what?"

"If you don't know *that,* better not ask her out at all, mate." Rhys folded his arms over his chest as they moved up in the line at the deli counter. "I mean, I'm not going to come with you, yeah?"

"No, I meant . . . well, what if she says no?"

"World won't stop turning, Gus," Rhys said kindly. "But you'll never know unless you ask, yeah? And if you want my opinion on the matter, she worked right alongside you all morning quite happily. I'm thinking she won't say no."

A tentative smile lit up Gus's face, and Rhys turned to look at the menu board with a sinking heart. Bloody hell. If the woman refused Gus now, he'd be forced to have a bit of chat with her.

As if he needed to be Gus's knight in shining armor now. Bloody hell. How did he get himself into these things? Before he'd come to New York he'd been quite satisfied to look out for number one, no strings attached to anyone else, no promises made.

Promises got a bloke in trouble. And believing in promises made was even worse. The great majority of people on the planet couldn't be trusted—he'd figured that out long ago, thanks to his mum.

But he believed Olivia. Believed in her, as well. Had since the moment he'd met her. She was true, all the way down to her bones, he was sure of it.

The kid behind the counter barked, "Next?" and Rhys stepped aside to let Gus order.

Not that it meant anything, he told himself as Gus reeled off a list of sandwiches to carry back to the others. He'd always prided himself on his honesty, hadn't he? Well, the honest truth was he wished he could hang about Callender House a while longer. With Olivia. That was all. There was nothing serious about it. Nothing permanent, for God's sake. He was sure she knew it, too. Nothing to worry about on that front. Anyway, it wasn't going to happen. He had his flight to L.A. already booked, and it wasn't as if Olivia expected him to come straight back to her once the competition was over.

But as he and Gus moved aside to wait for their order, he ignored the spike of unease in his chest. He wasn't lying to himself. He didn't do that, never had.

He glanced out the broad window to look at the sky. Still a clear, crisp blue, which meant no chance of lightning today.

God, he was a lucky man.

# Chapter 12

Sometimes, Olivia decided two days later as she stood in the restaurant kitchen with Josef, it might have been better to stay asleep.

She'd come to think of her life pre-Rhys that way. It was amazing, really, how much she had missed, just drifting through every day here at the hotel like some sort of ghost, not quite real, not quite touching anything—or letting anything touch her.

With Rhys, of course, there was a lot of touching. The nice kind, too. But now everything seemed to slap at her—she couldn't help but notice how awful the carpets upstairs really were when she wasn't looking at them through the rose-colored glasses of childhood nostalgia. She hadn't realized that Josef's Swedish meatballs and veal croquettes were stuck in the fifties like stubborn spinsters until Rhys introduced her to the glories of a good seviche and even simpler things like chiles, freshly made salsa, and artisanal cheeses. She hadn't even considered how close the hotel had skated to the edge of disaster.

But daydreaming her life away also meant that she wasn't faced with a furious chef, who was at the moment slamming pots and pans around the kitchen as if he had a personal beef with each and every one of them.

She took a deep breath and stood back as Josef crashed a saucepan onto the range with a ringing bang.

He wasn't happy about the Monsters' Ball. Or the new sous chef, as it turned out.

The line chefs and the other kitchen staff had fled to the pantry and the walk-in when he started ranting. It was a good thing the lunch service was over, Olivia thought, watching as he inexplicably picked up the same saucepan and hung it from its hook above the counter, where it clanged into the others.

"I will not do this!" he shouted at her, turning with his hands on his hips, his chef's whites as pristine as they must have been first thing in the morning. Josef was nothing if not fastidious. "I do not like this . . . this . . . Rusty you hire!"

Rusty was pronounced a bit like "roosty," which Olivia couldn't imagine the new sous chef appreciated. Of course, he probably appreciated Josef's veiled threats even less. He'd only been working at the Coach and Four for a week, and even though Josef had given his approval when Olivia hired him, Rusty's skills, his recipes, and even the sneakers he wore in the kitchen had all come under fire. If she didn't know better, she would have guessed that his eyebrows had been singed in the latest battle—the Great Turkey Roulade Debate.

"Josef, you know you need a sous chef," she reminded him gently. "You haven't worked the breakfast service for years—Rick always did that. And you gave me the go-ahead when I narrowed down the candidates."

"Turkey roulade," he scoffed, and suddenly stopped short and began taking off his apron.

The beginnings of panic rippled through her. Why was he doing that? Josef was never in the kitchen without it, and the prep for the dinner service needed to begin any time now.

"We don't have to serve turkey roulade," Olivia told him, rushing around the counter to follow him when he tilted his head to one side, as if in thought, and started for the pantry. "I'll talk to Rusty about it, I promise. Josef?"

He'd hung up his apron and taken his knife case from its place on the shelf. "Is not my problem anymore," he said softly, and then allowed himself to glance at her. "Olivia, I work here for how many years? I love your family, your father, you, but I am tired. I have no more time for turkey roulade, or for silly parties with too many finger foods. I talk to my sister in Hamburg this week, and I think . . . yes, I think it is time to go home."

"Home?" she echoed, which was a miracle, since speaking when her heart had dropped into her stomach had to be impossible. "As in, *Germany* home?"

"Yes, Germany home." He put down his knife case and reached out to pat her shoulder. "You let Rusty make his . . . dishes. And you remember Josef Vollner fondly, yes?"

"Remember . . . ?" He was leaving? Now? Today?

"I buy plane ticket tomorrow. Today I think I pack and relax for awhile." Without warning, he beamed at her, this man who had been almost a grandparent, his pale, wrinkled face as familiar as her father's. "I deserve it, yes? Maybe my sister will cook for *me*. I will go call her now."

Her mouth was actually hanging open, she realized, as he strolled out of the kitchen, looking lighter and happier than he had in weeks. Hanging open like an oven door. She shut it with effort and turned to see the staff trickling into the room.

"He . . . quit?" Rusty said. "Because of me?" He looked about twelve in his white apron and hat, and all the color had drained out of his face.

"No, no, not because of you," she assured him, offering the room at large a weak smile. "Because of . . . Well, I guess because it was time."

"Now?" Jesus said incredulously. "With the party coming up?"

"I don't think he liked the idea of the Monsters' Ball much," Olivia told him and turned back to Rusty, who was still white as a starched shirt, and beginning to look a little wobbly.

"What about . . . dinner?" he asked her and fumbled blindly behind him for one of the stools that were kept at the end of the counter.

"You'll make it," she told him with what she hoped sounded like confidence. "You and everyone else here. You can do it. Regular menu, no surprises. I have faith," she added with a smile.

She also had the beginning of a fierce headache, but no one else had to know that.

What on earth was she going to do? She'd finally pulled Callender House out of its decades-long torpor, and sold tickets to their first ever house-sponsored event, and her chef had just quit. Leaving her with a sous chef just barely out of culinary school and with only two years of professional restaurant experience.

She sighed as the staff started throwing out assignments and ideas for the dinner service. Why had she hired Rusty again?

Oh right. Because he was cheap. Suddenly her own knees felt a little wobbly. How was she going to pull money out of the budget to hire a new chef, when Josef hadn't asked for a raise in more than ten years?

"Olivia?" Josie poked her head in from the hallway, her brow creased in a frown. "Can I see you for a minute?"

"Don't tell me the sign fell down again," Olivia said, her shoulders slumping.

"No, not that," Josie said. "Not yet anyway."

Olivia glared at her before she turned to the kitchen staff. "I know you've got this under control, right? Jesus, you help Rusty with where things are, and Willie, maybe you could go over the menu with him, okay?"

She was met with blank stares.

"Okay then," she said brightly, and fled to the hallway where Josie was waiting.

"Josef just told me to wish him luck in Hamburg," she said darkly. "Why is Josef going to Hamburg?"

"Because he's retiring," Olivia told her, and slumped against the wall after waving to one of the new guys Angel had hired. Marty, she thought. Unless he was Davey. Well, he was one of them. He smiled back before pushing a broom past her into the pantry. "Right now. Today."

"*What?*"

"Don't ask." Olivia shook her head. "I don't think he's going to change his mind. But someone is going to have to pull a chef out of a top hat. Aside from the ball, we've got three meals a day to serve."

Josie shrugged. "Well, you've got yours. Whip him out."

"My what?"

"Your chef!" Josie raised her eyebrows. "Rhys, remember? Professional chef, currently doing nothing more than cooking up a little good loving for you?"

"Hey!"

"Excuse me," Josie said with exaggerated courtesy. "Great loving."

"Josie, I can't ask Rhys!" Olivia protested, lowering her voice to a stage whisper when Hector walked by with a broom in his hand. "He's a guest!"

"Oh, come on," Josie drawled. "He's your boyfriend and you know it."

"He is not my . . . boyfriend," Olivia hissed, glancing around to make sure they were alone.

"Well, you could have fooled me, what with the hand-holding and the public kissing and the romantic carriage rides." She sidled closer to Olivia and said without even a trace of sarcasm, "Seriously, Olivia, he's crazy about you. Have you seen how he looks at you? If you asked him to re-tar the roof he'd do it with a smile on his face. I mean, hell, I don't think sanding the woodwork in the lobby is exactly one of his favorite things to do, you know?"

Josie was probably right about that, Olivia mused as Josie hooked an arm through hers and they walked out to the lobby. Rhys wasn't the home improvement type, no. The first time she'd given him a paintbrush he'd looked about the way she thought she would if someone handed her a blowtorch.

But he was there helping, all the time, and without her even asking him. She didn't really understand it, not that she'd ever met a man like him before, but as far as she knew a fling meant a week or two of fun and laughs and good sex. Not scraping woodwork and painting walls. Oh, and fixing the broken handle on the broom closet door. He'd in-sisted on that one. That didn't sound like a fling to her, even though they were certainly fulfilling the requirement of lots of delicious sex.

"I can't ask him," she said to Josie now, and tugged her down on the banquette, newly re-covered in a Bohemian silk print. "No way. He's . . . we're . . . it would be taking advantage. Three meals a day is a lot of work."

"But he wouldn't have to do breakfast," Josie argued. "And it wouldn't be forever. I mean, he's leaving in two weeks anyway. So it would be just long enough to get us through the ball successfully and put out feelers for a new chef. A cheap one. With probably very little experience. Or a wanted poster at the Department of Health."

Olivia elbowed her. "Not funny."

"I know." Josie sighed and slouched against the back rest, her ponytail flipped over its top. "But not exactly untrue. Anyway, like I said, it wouldn't be forever. Just ask Rhys, will you?"

It wouldn't be forever. That's what she needed to remember about Rhys. Especially in moments like these, when her first instinct was to run and find him and spill everything.

"Ask me what?"

She looked up to find the man in question walking over from the elevator, his wicked grin in place and his eyes twinkling with a now familiar mix of desire, interest, and fondness. *Not forever*, she reminded herself as she stood up to meet him. *Because that would be like a fairy tale coming true. And everyone knows that never happens.*

She didn't want him to feel obligated. She really didn't want him to resent her. Anyway, he'd done enough rescuing. This was her problem, and she would fix it. Somehow.

"What you think of . . . the new upholstery," she began, when she had found her voice, and shrugged helplessly.

He cocked one dark eyebrow and put his arms around her. "It's lovely? I thought I told you that."

"Josef quit," Josie said without warning and folded her arms over her chest. "He's leaving tomorrow. We have no chef, as of now."

Olivia twisted around to smack Josie's arm even as she protested, "But I'm going to fix it. I'm going to . . . make some calls. And in the meantime Rusty is going to get some valuable experience."

"Rusty?" Rhys snorted. "He's a kid, Liv. I can take over the kitchen for a bit."

When she shook her head, he put his arm around her. Confusion and something that looked like surprise flickered across his face. "Don't be ridiculous, love. Let me help you out, yeah?"

One day, she thought as she let him steer her into the bar, she was going to rescue herself. Right and proper, as Rhys would say. But in the meantime . . .

She glanced up at him with a little smile. "So, have you ever made Chicken Veronique?"

With one last look in the mirror, Gus took a deep breath and straightened the brim of his cap. Okay. He was ready. For sure this time.

His heart stuttered wildly when he took a step toward the door.

All right. That was okay. In one more minute, he would definitely be ready. Definitely. He was pretty sure.

Maybe his red sweater would be better, he thought, staring at his reflection in the cloudy glass on the back of the bathroom door. Red was a confident color, wasn't it? Not that there was anything wrong with blue. And blue went with jeans. Although maybe jeans weren't serious enough. Maybe the khakis were a better idea. More formal.

Oh God, he was sweating. "Stop that," he said out loud, shaking his finger at himself in the mirror. Great. Now he looked like a mental patient. Yeah, Josie would really jump at the chance to go out with him.

"Stop that," he said again, and took a deep breath. He could do this. He *had* done this before, just not often. And if Josie said no . . . well, it wouldn't be the end of the world, although he might want it to be. And there was no way to find out without asking.

He adjusted his cap again, checked his teeth and his breath, and straightened his spine—mentally as well as physically. It was late afternoon, so Josie should still be around, but if she said no to a date, at least she would be leaving soon.

Which would give him time to pack his bags and check into another hotel before morning.

Not that he would do that, he admonished himself as he got on the elevator. Callender House had become home, in a weirdly comfortable way. He'd wanted somewhere discreet and out of the way when *The Other Side of the Moon* hit the best-seller list, and although he'd never said as much to Olivia, this place had struck him as the perfect solution. He hadn't wanted to leave New York, but he really hadn't wanted to find an apartment at first—too much solitude after all those months at Riverside, where the company had been constant if a little unbalanced.

Not unlike the hotel, actually.

The bell dinged and the doors groaned open when the elevator reached the first floor. Now to find Josie. Her office was the sensible place to look, and he'd already taken the risk of going there once, just a few weeks ago, although he'd been able to fib and say he was looking for Roseanne when he found her in Josie's office. One look at her face and he'd forgotten whatever ruse he'd planned for showing up in the first place.

But that wasn't going to happen now, he told himself firmly. He had it all planned, what he would say, how he would say it.

*How she would respond.* He hoped. As long as his heart didn't gallop off like a racehorse, he'd be fine.

He hoped.

The sound of voices from the bar caught his attention the minute he stepped into the lobby. Sounded like Rhys—there was no mistaking that British tone. And if Rhys was there, surely Olivia was, too. He hesitated outside the archway, in a corner where he hoped he couldn't be seen. Yup, there was Olivia's voice—and Josie's.

Okay, show time. He swallowed hard and walked in. There was safety in numbers, wasn't there? Maybe it would be easier to ask her out with Olivia and Rhys present.

Inspiration struck. Maybe she would be too polite to say no in front of them!

*Stop it*, he warned himself, pulling up a smile as he approached the bar. *Confident. Think confident.*

"You *cannot* change the whole menu tonight, Rhys, you know that," Olivia was saying, shaking her head in dismay. "They're already prepping for dinner!"

"We could throw in a special, yeah?" he argued, and scribbled something furiously on a cocktail napkin.

"Ooh, make bangers and mash!" Josie chimed in from a barstool. God, look at her. She was perfect. He couldn't even have described what she was wearing, but the sound of her voice, the full curve of her mouth, that bouncing ponytail. . . . He melted a little bit and felt his resolve melting with it. He couldn't ask her. She would never say yes. Not to him . . .

"Gus, hi!" Olivia said brightly. Or was that a note of desperation in her voice? "Come save me from the marauding chef. Please?"

Josie whirled around her stool, and the smile she flashed at him was so genuine, so dazzling, a flicker of hope sparked. "Hey, Gus! Don't you think bangers and mash is a great idea? I don't even know what it is, really, but it sounds cool, doesn't it?"

"It's sausage and potatoes, for Christ's sake," Rhys grumbled, flipping through what looked to be a stack of cocktail napkins. "I am not putting bangers and mash on the menu here."

"Rhys . . ." Olivia sent Gus a pleading glance, but he wasn't interested in whatever scheme Rhys had come up with now.

"I'm not going to cause chaos, love, don't worry," Rhys reassured Olivia. "But I am going to have to have another glance at that party menu. I'm thinking a whole new assortment of appetizers." He glanced up when Olivia whimpered. "No worries, love, it'll be brilliant."

This time Olivia groaned, and Josie reached over to pat her hand in comfort.

"He's the chef," she said with a shrug.

Olivia glared back in reply. "This was all your idea."

"But the ball was yours," Josie pointed out, and tried to hide the mischief in her grin.

"You know, I do know what I'm doing," Rhys protested with a grunt. "I'm a finalist in a sodding cooking competition, if you'll recall. I've cooked all over the bloody world."

"The world?" Olivia asked with a dubious expression.

Rhys's glare was much more threatening than Olivia's. "All right, Europe. Happy now?"

Josie snickered, but she looked up at Gus and waved him over. "Come on," she said. "Have a drink. Watch the lovebirds peck at each other."

Olivia blushed fiercely, but Rhys didn't appear to have heard Josie's remark—he was fumbling with makeshift notes and muttering something about lamb shanks.

"I'd love a beer," Gus said after he took the stool Josie patted. Right beside her. Oh boy.

"Rhys, get Gus a beer?" Olivia said, tapping the bar. "Sorry, he gets a little distracted when he's thinking food," she said in apology.

"Where's Tommy anyway?" Josie asked. When she swiveled on her stool, her thigh brushed against Gus's, and he started at the electric thrill of it. "Is he coming in to-night? We're going to need to hire another bartender for the Halloween ball, aren't we?"

"We'll need more than one in any event," Rhys said absently and looked up from whatever it was he was doing. "Judging by ticket sales, we're bound to have quite a crowd. Guinness, Gus? Or something domestic?"

Gus only vaguely heard Rhys's words—Josie had turned to look at him, and staring into her eyes all he could think of was the question he wanted to ask her.

It came out in a rush without any warning or lead-up. "Will you go to the Monsters' Ball with me?"

He felt rather than saw Olivia and Rhys, eyes wide, backing off, but that was all right. Josie had blinked in surprise at his offer, her bright blue eyes startled for a moment, but then she smiled.

A real smile, a warm, pleased smile aimed at him like a sunbeam, and he knew what her answer was going to be before she even opened her mouth. He was already singing inside, turning cartwheels, kicking up his heels like a six-year-old with all of Santa's booty laid out before him.

It didn't make her answer any less satisfying to hear out loud, though. "Yes," she said, and reached out to touch his hand. "Yes, I really would."

# Chapter 13

"Rhys, this package came for you," Roseanne said as Rhys passed through the lobby from the kitchen on the afternoon of the Monsters' Ball.

The lobby looked smashing, he thought. For amateur decorators, Olivia and Josie had done a bang-up job. Pots of dry ice had been hidden behind the ferns and wafted up a spooky, smoky ambience. The lights had been dimmed, and an entire day spent carving pumpkins of all sizes had resulted in a veritable army of jack-o'-lanterns, their unearthly grins glowing already. Old gilt picture frames had been hauled up from the basement to present eerily lettered signs pointing the way up to the ballroom and into the bar. The final touches were spiders, bones, bundles of dried herbs, and spell books—all the ingredients used in true voodoo.

Not half bad for weeks of effort, he thought, and crossed the space to take the oblong package from Roseanne.

"My costume," he said when he'd read the return address. "I was getting a bit worried when it didn't arrive yesterday."

"What is it?" Roseanne asked, craning her neck to peek

at the label as if it might reveal the nature of the box's contents.

"Never you mind," Rhys said with a smirk. He hadn't even told Olivia what he planned to wear, and he was looking forward to the moment when he would walk into the ballroom and surprise her.

"It's a big box." Roseanne trailed a finger over it in curiosity, and Rhys snatched it out of reach.

"Hands off, you." He laughed, but as he turned toward the elevator he couldn't help wondering why it was so big. Packing materials, most likely. It was a rental—but then again it was only fabric. Odd.

"Rhys!" Olivia caught him as he pushed the button for the lift, slightly out of breath, roses in her cheeks. She was still wearing the jeans and warm brown sweater she'd put on first thing this morning, and her hair was doing its usual crazy thing, escaping the loose knot she'd made in a cloud of tendrils around her face. "The food looks wonderful. You outdid yourself. What's that?"

"You'll see," he said, pulling the box out of her reach, as well. "Rusty and the others still hard at work in the kitchen then?"

"Everything looks pretty much good to go." She leaned against him when they stepped into the lift. "It looks delicious, I can tell you that. Of course, I'm so starved I would probably eat a piece of cardboard. Without salt, even. I forgot to have lunch."

"Can't have you wasting away to nothing," he said and kissed the top of her head. She smelled wonderful, as usual, like the pear-scented shampoo she used and something sweeter, richer, a particular Olivia scent that was purely her. He breathed deep as she leaned into him, riding beside him silently as the car climbed to the ninth floor.

"You're going . . . to your room?" she said as the doors opened.

*Home.* She'd almost said home, he knew it.

And why shouldn't she think of it that way? He'd been at Callender House for nearly a month, and in all that time he'd rarely left the building unless it was with her. He was running the restaurant, for God's sake, even if it was just temporarily.

Of course, he slept in her bed more often than his own downstairs. And that comfortable habit had created a kind of intimacy he knew Olivia adored.

Bloody hell. Who was he kidding? He adored it, too.

For something he'd believed would be a careless affair, it was beginning to feel a bit like a marriage—in the best possible way. He knew what kind of toothpaste Olivia used, and which underwear she considered everyday rather than special occasion. He'd learned that she liked a cup of tea before bed, and that she would rather watch old Bette Davis movies than anything from the current decade. The syrupy advertisements for greeting cards and children's charities made her sniffle from time to time, and she could tell stories about nearly every corner of the hotel.

That hardly said careless affair, did it?

She was watching his face, waiting for him to answer. He put his foot in front of the lift door to stop it from closing, and leaned over to give her a kiss. He let it linger, tasting the wistfulness on her lips, the banked heat just inside.

"I told you my costume was meant to be a surprise, yeah?" he said.

"Ah, yes, the famous costume." She narrowed her eyes at him, but she smiled just the same and pushed the button for the tenth floor. "I'll see you at the party, then?"

"Eight o'clock sharp, love, in the lobby." He stepped

back and let the door begin to close just as she called, "How will I know you?"

He grinned. "Oh, you'll know, Liv. You'll know."

The doors slid closed on her rolling her eyes, and he turned down the hall to his room, whistling. Yelena tottered toward him from the end of the corridor, her usual heels wobbling beneath her.

"Ah, Rhys, my love"—this was pronounced *luff*—"there you are. You haven't taken me to lunch in two weeks, you know. A girl gets heartbroken so easily . . ." She batted her eyes at him, shaded in a spectacular purple today, and adjusted the fit of her turban with one careful hand.

"I'm making lunch most days now, you know," he said, leaning down to give her proffered cheek the expected kiss. In an effort to change the subject, and hopefully prevent her from inviting herself into his room, which she had done a few too many times for comfort, he said, "Aren't you coming to the costume ball?"

"But of course," she said with an airy lift of her shoulders. "Is not time to dress yet, of course."

"Can I ask about your costume?" He gave her a friendly wink, and she answered with something remarkably close to a giggle for a woman her age.

"Is a surprise." She wobbled off, trailing perfume, with a wave. "But is *not* a zombie."

Not yet, he thought with an uncharitable chuckle. Still, Yelena was a surprisingly adept chess player and was not so secretly addicted to action flicks. He'd watched a double bill of Bruce Willis films with her just a week ago, before he'd taken over at the Coach and Four.

Imagine her not wanting to ask him to step in, he thought. Another surprise, courtesy of Olivia Callender. The woman was determined to squash his white knight act. But he'd been the obvious solution, with Josef deciding to retire on the dime, and he'd convinced her he was itching to get into the kitchen anyway. Outside of the occasional meal for Olivia, he hadn't had a chance to cook for far too long, and he was grateful for the chance to experiment, especially with the *Fork in the Road* finale coming up.

"It's only temporary, obviously," Olivia had said, all seriousness and more than a bit embarrassed. "You don't really have to do more than supervise dinner, to tell the truth. I think Rusty can handle breakfast and lunch on his own."

"That's three meals, love," he'd scoffed. "Boy's going to need a break once in a while, yeah? Or he'll go stark raving mad."

"But it's not your problem," she'd begun, worry shadowing those big brown eyes. He'd silenced her with a firm kiss and the murmured words, "I don't do anything I don't want to, love. No worries there."

Of course, that wasn't exactly true, he mused as he unlocked the door to his room and stepped inside. It smelled a bit mustier than usual, but he spent so little time in it, he wasn't surprised.

He hadn't wanted to spend the better part of a week painting woodwork. He wouldn't have chosen to carve faces into pumpkins for a whole bloody afternoon, given his way.

But he had done those things, hadn't he, and happily, too. Because they mattered to Olivia. Because doing them made her happy, and took a bit of the load off her narrow shoulders. Because she never asked, never assumed, even when it would have been easy to do both.

And because, in all honesty, he couldn't think of anywhere he wanted to be but here at Callender House.

*For now*, he told himself with a frown, tossing the brown carton on the bed and reaching into his jeans pocket for the utility knife he always carried. *Just for now*.

And right now he desperately needed to shower off the long day of kitchen prep for the party's array of appetizers and entrées, call downstairs to make sure everything was under control, and then get into his costume.

His cell phone shrilled from his pocket, and without thinking he flipped it open and pushed the button. " 'lo?"

"Rhys, lovey, it's Mum!"

He stifled a groan and sank onto the bed. His mother. Crikey, she was the last person he wanted to talk to today. Most days, actually.

"Rhys, are you there? *'elloooo?*"

"I'm here, Janet," he grumbled. "How are you?"

"Well, wondering how you are, love," she said with an audible sniff. "You haven't called Gram or me in weeks, and now you're on break from that show on telly. I know, because I called the producers."

Oh, bloody hell. He dropped onto his back, the phone still held to his ear, and stared at the ceiling. Huh. If he'd shagged Olivia here more often, he might have noticed the lightning-shaped crack in the plaster.

"Rhys?"

Had her voice always been so shrill? he wondered idly. He'd be the last to know, of course. He'd blocked out so much of his life with her, it was hard to remember the color of her eyes.

"I'm here," he said. "Just a bit busy at the moment."

"Where is here, Rhys?" She coughed, a rattling bark, and he pictured her blowing one of her perfect smoke rings in the sitting room of her latest flat. "You never tell me when you're off to the next place, you know. If it weren't for your mobile phone I sometimes think I'd never be able to track you down."

"I'm in New York for the moment," he said dutifully, his

gaze wandering around the room as he spoke. Before he checked out, he'd have to remember to tell Olivia about the clatter that radiator made, too. "But I'm heading back to L.A. in two days for the finale of the *Fork in the Road* competition. Or did the producers tell you that much already?"

It was all too believable that she'd rung them, more was the pity. The woman had no sense of boundaries, especially now that he wasn't just an obligation, but a successful chef, and one appearing on telly.

"Well, they did mention it," she confided in a raspy whisper. "And everyone here believes you're a shoe-in for the win, love. Imagine all that money! What do you think you'll do with it?"

There it was, the locus of nearly every one of their conversations these days. How much money he made—and how much he might see his way clear to spending on her. It never failed. At least she was consistent.

"I've no clue." He didn't bother to disguise the edge in his tone. Janet didn't deserve the courtesy. "And I have to ring off now. I've got an engagement tonight." He shut the phone without a second thought and threw it down on the mattress as he sat up, the box beside him a much more tempting task than thinking about his mother.

Olivia was going to squeal when she saw his costume, he thought with a grin, slicing open one end of the box. She'd decided nearly from the start to dress as a medieval princess, which hadn't surprised him in the least. Despite his inclination to rent a tux, go as Bond and be done with it, he'd ordered a Galahad costume to surprise her. It was perfect—the fair princess and her knight, even if his behavior certainly didn't qualify him for comparison to Galahad's purity.

She would love it, and that was worth dressing up in a

tunic and leggings. It was just for one evening, anyway. One very special evening, before he left for L.A., a day that had begun to loom in his mind the way a dark shadow might.

Not that it was going to change, he told himself with a shake of his head. He was in the running for two hundred grand American, and a nice bit of prestige. That was nothing to sneeze at.

Even if it would have been lovely to bring Olivia with him.

"Stop it, man," he warned himself and opened the flap of the box. But when he reached inside to take a look, he came away with his hands full of brown fur.

"No," he said aloud, snatching the thing out of the box and holding it up to the mirror. "Oh bloody hell, no."

The costume shop had delivered a gorilla suit.

"It's wonderful, isn't it?" Olivia whispered to Josie shortly after eight. They were standing just outside the doors to the ballroom, and guests in costumes of all kinds had begun to file in fifteen minutes ago.

"So far so good." Josie touched her hair cautiously. "As long as my wig stays on, I'll be happy."

She and Gus had decided to dress as Zelda and F. Scott Fitzgerald, and Josie's wealth of hair had been piled under a short brunette wig, complete with finger waves. Gus had found a beige tweed suit in a shop downtown, and Josie had even convinced him that his Yankees cap wasn't exactly appropriate for the evening. She'd parted his hair in the middle and applied a generous dollop of gel to keep it in place.

"You both look great," Olivia told her. "And Gus actually looks happy."

"Gus is . . . happy, yeah," Josie said with a little smirk. "It's good for my ego, I'll tell you that."

The Monsters' Ball was doing wonders for Olivia's ego, although she didn't have to tell anyone that. Even as late as this morning she'd been worried that the whole thing would fall apart, that no one would show up, that the decorations would fall down or catch fire or something equally disastrous. But so far everything was perfect.

Or it would be when Rhys finally showed up.

And tonight was . . . well, a little like the prom, wasn't it? Their big dress-up date, even if the dressing up didn't mean an evening gown and tuxedo. And it was most likely going to be their last date, too. Two days from now Rhys would board a plane for L.A.—and neither one of them had said a word about what would happen after that.

She scanned the wide staircase that led up from the lobby, looking for him. He'd said she would recognize him, but as the crowd grew, so did the variety of costumes. Napoleon and Josephine had walked by earlier, followed by a pirate, a Greek goddess, a football player, Marilyn Monroe, an army of zombies who had clearly taken the theme to heart, a bloody bride, and President Nixon.

No Rhys, though.

But the ballroom looked fabulous—the lights were low, groups of tables covered in black cloths and adorned with flickering gourds were set off in the corners, with the bar at one end. Angel had rigged a canopy above the bar, and more dried herbs, bones, gourds, and spiders hung from the tattered muslin. It was all fairly creepy, if you asked her, which meant it was just right.

"Are you Olivia Callender?" a man dressed as a prisoner, complete with ball and chain, asked. He was holding a notebook and a pencil.

"Yes?" she said, confused. Josie lifted an eyebrow and wandered away to find Gus. "I mean, yes, I am. And you are?"

"Rich Petrillo, with the *Village Voice*." He held out a press ID and shook her hand. "I got a press release and thought I would write up the event for the paper."

"Oh!" *Publicity.* There was one goal down. She flushed with pleasure and led him off to one side of the hallway to talk, scooping up her voluminous purple satin skirts with one hand. "Well, fire away. I'll be glad to tell you all about it."

He'd brought along a photographer who was already out in the crowd taking pictures. "Are you planning more events like this? And how do your guests feel about it?"

"Oh, we're definitely going to hold a few more events," Olivia said carefully. She wasn't sure exactly what they would be yet, but that would come in time. "And our guests are all invited to the ball, free of charge. We thought it would be a nice perk for out-of-towners, and so far everyone seems pretty happy about it. At least our guests don't have to worry about getting home afterward."

"True." The reporter winked at her. "Are other changes in store for Callender House, too?"

"Some, yes," Olivia told him, distracted by the person in the gorilla costume who had walked up beside her. "We have a lot of ideas about how to upgrade service and make some changes without losing the traditions Callender House is proud of. . . . Can I help you?" she said to the gorilla, who had moved even closer as the corridor grew more crowded.

"It's me."

The voice was muffled through the heavy gorilla mask, but there was a distinct hint of the British to it. Her eyes widened. *"Rhys?"*

It was impossible for the gorilla's face to change expression, but Olivia was somehow certain it looked more sour than it had a minute ago. "Yeah, it's me."

She couldn't help it—she clapped a hand to her mouth to prevent a shriek of laugher. "You're a . . . gorilla."

"Well, I wasn't meant to be, was I? I was meant to be Galahad, to match your outfit there. Very fetching, by the way. You look brilliant." He shrugged beneath the heavy brown fur, and Olivia bit back a grin.

"I'm sorry," she said to the reporter, who had watched their exchange with interest. "This is a friend of mine, Rhys Spencer. Rhys, meet Rich Petrillo from the *Village Voice*."

"A pleasure," Rhys grunted. "I'm going to check in on the kitchen staff, yeah? Make sure they've got the food coming out in the right order." He stalked off, a very unhappy gorilla, and Olivia choked back another giggle.

"Rhys Spencer?" the reporter asked. New interest lit up his eyes. "The same Rhys Spencer who cooked at Blue Door in London and Ferris Grill in Chicago, and is a contestant on *Fork in the Road?*"

"Well, yes," Olivia said. A warning bell went off in her head, distant but demanding. "He's a guest here."

"Really?" Petrillo scribbled notes on his pad, flipping to a new page when he ran out of room. "Can I ask you a few questions?"

"Of course," she said, although she would have much rather stuck to the subject of the hotel than to the subject of Rhys. Her mistake, of course, but how was she supposed to know some random feature writer would know who Rhys was? Apparently everyone in the world watched more TV than she did.

"So what does Mr. Spencer think of the Coach and Four?" he asked.

Well, he thought the menu was as outdated as the décor, and that the kitchen needed renovation, and their sous chef was, in his words, "green as a blade of spring grass," but she wasn't going to tell this man any of that. Rhys's life was his business, even his thoughts on her restaurant. "You'd have to ask him," she said carefully, and moved toward the door to the ballroom. "Can I show you what we did to emphasize our zombie theme? It was really a lot of fun to brainstorm with the staff, most of whom have worked here for years—"

"So Mr. Spencer didn't have anything to do with the menu for tonight's party?" Petrillo asked, scribbling again. He had followed her without once looking up from his little notepad. "No culinary tidbits to share at all?"

"Mr. Spencer is a guest," she repeated evenly. At least she hoped her voice sounded even. She wouldn't do it, she wouldn't throw his name around simply to ensure this piece made it into the paper. And it was infuriating that the only thing the man seemed interested in was Rhys. The ball had been her idea, after all.

"As one of *Fork in the Road*'s final three competitors, Mr. Spencer should be expected back in L.A. anytime for the finale, right?" Petrillo stared at her, pen poised over his pad.

As if she needed another reminder that Rhys was leaving. Damn it, tonight was supposed to be fun. The big payoff after all the weeks of work. The first step toward putting Callender House back on the map. She was dressed as a princess—couldn't she wave a scepter and have some courtier deal with this guy?

He was still waiting for her answer, but before she opened her mouth she saw a pair of zombies loitering at the bottom of the staircase. "Excuse me," she said to Petrillo. "Why don't you enjoy yourself for awhile and we can talk some more later?"

She took off before he had a chance to protest and scooped up her skirts to run down the steps. The zombies were Marty and Davey, the new guys—at least she was pretty sure they were. But they'd both said they weren't coming tonight, hadn't they?

She waved at Roseanne, who was dressed in her usual wenchy barmaid Renaissance Faire costume, as she made her way over to the guys. Yup, it was definitely them. Not that it mattered, of course, because everyone on staff was welcome, but it was probably better to have them upstairs with the others instead of hanging around the lobby like . . . well, like a couple of zombies.

"Marty?" she said tentatively.

He turned around, blinking. His gray makeup had been caked on with a heavy hand, but he'd certainly gone lighter on the blood than Davey had.

"Miss Olivia," he said, and cleared his throat. "Hey."

"It's just Olivia," she told him in a confidential whisper. "Really. So you two decided to come?"

"Angel called, ma'am," Davey said. He flicked a tattered piece of cheesecloth away from his face. "His wife is in labor, so he asked if we could fill in for him. Keep an eye out. In case you needed anything."

"Theresa's in labor?" She glanced over at Roseanne, who was busy checking IDs and fastening armbands on the latest arrivals. A baby! She'd forgotten all about the impending birth in the last few days, but she was confused, too. Angel wasn't supposed to be working tonight. He and Theresa were planning to come as a mouse dressed in footman's gear and Cinderella's magic coach—after it was turned back into a pumpkin, of course.

"Yeah, um, labor," Marty said, but not before he elbowed Davey in the ribs.

Okay. Either way, they needed to be up in the ballroom with everyone else. "Well, why don't the two of you head upstairs and have some fun," she said. "Angel wasn't really supposed to be working tonight, and I'm sure everything's under control. Go on, go upstairs, have some food, dance with a pretty . . . zombie girl." She laughed, and quickly shook it off when Marty and Davey stared at her blankly. "Okay, then."

From behind her she heard, "Everything all right?"

And there was her . . . gorilla. She smiled again, a happy warmth lighting her up from inside. "Everything's fine. How about in the kitchen?"

"Right on schedule," Rhys murmured, pulling her close with one leathery gorilla paw. "Care to dance, princess?"

"I'm beginning to regret that fact that I never saw *Planet of the Apes*," she said, but she let him lead her up the stairs. It was their night together, gorilla mask or not.

And upstairs in the ballroom, with the lights low and the band playing, it was their night, she thought. Rhys took off the gorilla mask and turned her around the floor when the song was a slow one, and when it wasn't he filled a plate with food for them to share off in one of the dim corners of the room.

He'd outdone himself, as always. There were pumpkin ravioli and garlic gougeres and tiny cranberry-walnut turkey sausages, parmesan crisps and tempura-fried sweet potato slices, and tiny crab tarts. Later there was going to be pork tenderloin glazed with wine and grapes, and roasted vegetable stew, with pecan caramel tarts and chocolate cupcakes for dessert.

She had no doubt that he was going to win the cooking competition, she thought as he crossed the room with fresh drinks for them both, the heavy brown fur of his costume sagging in some strange places. She just wished he'd won it already, or that the finale was being held in New York.

Or that she could get her hands on that time machine she'd been daydreaming about all those weeks ago, and she could fast forward through the next few weeks without him. He was leaving in two days and they still hadn't talked about what would happen when the competition was over. She couldn't bring herself to ask, and she wasn't even sure he'd thought about it.

Rhys was famous for saying whatever was on his mind, after all. Hadn't he told Angel just the other day that Theresa looked like a beached whale? A pretty one, he'd been quick to add, a glowing one to be sure, but that hadn't exactly mitigated Angel's outrage.

So it stood to reason that if Rhys had decided one way or another what he planned to do when the competition was over, he would have told her. Except . . . he hadn't. And she was too much of a chicken to ask him. At least for now.

Tonight was about magic, made-up or otherwise. And Rhys was the only one she wanted to share it with.

"Prosecco," he said and handed her a long-stemmed glass. "I ordered it just for you, for tonight. Go on, try it. Bellinis are made with Prosecco."

"What is it?" she said, sniffing the inside of the glass with pleasure.

"A sparkling wine," he said, coming closer. "To match your eyes."

She smiled up at him, blushing. "And just how much have you had to drink so far?"

"Not much." His lips brushed her cheek, then the tip of her nose. "I'm not drunk, love. Nothing but the truth from me."

Without warning, her eyes welled with tears. If only the truth was that he loved her. That he was never leaving. She could do without sparkling eyes then. Hell, she'd be happy to be blind.

She swallowed back the sudden lump in her throat and looked up at him through a faint haze of tears. If he saw them, he was kind enough not to say so, and instead put his arms around her, gorilla fur and all.

"Dance with me," he whispered and swayed against her as he lowered his mouth to hers in a kiss.

He tasted so good, so dark and hot and rich it was dizzying. She closed her eyes and kissed him back, letting him make love to her mouth, pouring everything she felt for him into the way she kissed him back.

And for a moment, everything went away. The ballroom, the music, the laughter a few feet away, the clink of glasses and the rhythmic thud of feet on the dance floor. There was nothing left but her and Rhys, here together, connected so deeply that she could feel his pulse thrumming in time with her own.

Naturally, that was when the lights went out, something crashed to the floor, and someone started to scream.

She and Rhys jumped apart so quickly, their teeth knocked together.

"What the bloody hell . . . ?" he muttered, pushing her behind him.

The music had stopped when the electricity went off, but there were enough candles lit to provide a slight glow in the darkness. Which was obviously a mistake, Olivia saw with horror, because everyone was panicking and shoving toward the doors, making the flames flicker dangerously.

"Stop!" she shouted, struggling to get around Rhys, the big gorilla, who seemed set on protecting her from the chaos. "Everyone calm down, please!"

"They can't hear you, love," Rhys grunted. "And why did the sodding power go out?"

"We need to get to the basement." She grabbed his arm. "Maybe it's just a fuse or a circuit breaker or whatever those things are."

"Needs to be faster than that, yeah?" He gestured toward the room. Half of the guests had crowded into the hall already, and it was now clear that the crash she'd heard earlier had been Willie and Helen, dropping trays of food in their surprise. Perfect.

It was turning into the kind of romantic evening only Stephen King would imagine, and there was nothing to do about it but wait for someone to dump a bucket of fake Halloween blood over her head.

Until Rhys grabbed up his gorilla mask and shoved it back on his head. She blinked, watching as he jumped up onto the nearest table and bellowed out a roar worthy of Tarzan.

And once again, everything—and everyone—stopped, turning to the gorilla at the far end of the room.

"Oi!" he yelled.

His British was coming on strong, she thought, and bit back a hysterical giggle. But he had the room's attention, and for that he could have been shouting obscenities and she would have kissed him.

"It's just the lights, yeah?" he went on, finally taking off the mask so his face was visible. "No one's hurt, nothing's on fire. Everyone needs to take a breath and relax until we can get the breaker fixed. That's it," he added as a crowd of the partygoers moved back into the room. "Brilliant. It's dark, so kiss your lasses and finish your drinks. We'll get this bloody party going again in just a moment."

A roar of laughter met his last remark, and Olivia sighed in relief.

Maybe it was a blessing in disguise, she thought as Rhys jumped off the table and grabbed her hand. And if nothing else, at least they could make out in the basement for awhile.

# Chapter 14

It was brilliant to know he could find work as an emergency electrician if he fouled up his cooking career, Rhys reflected sometime around three A.M. They'd rummaged flashlights out of her office, with the help of a candle, and made their way down to the basement, where someone had very obviously been messing with the circuit breakers.

And that was troubling, but at the moment he was too damn exhausted to think about it. Salvaging the party hadn't been quite as easy as flicking on the lights, in the end, despite the chance to grope Olivia in the darkness for a few minutes.

Several good trays of food had been ruined, and some wanker had also found the leftover paint tins in a closet on the second floor—and proceeded to tip them all over the lobby floor, which made a slimy, slippery green mess all over the newly polished tile.

Trying to sabotage the Monsters' Ball, he knew. The question was who.

Olivia hadn't wanted to address the issue, at least not right away. They'd got the guests fairly well sorted and had pooled credit cards to order a few pizzas since some of the food in the kitchen had been ruined by the time he got the electricity on again. In the end, a good time was had by all, despite the chaos. It had been a strange mix—lots of college students on shoestring budgets and out-of-towners, one gay and lesbian club whose venue had closed without warning, a handful of adventurous seniors, and locals who had seen the thing advertised in the neighborhood. The band's music and the flowing alcohol had overshadowed the few glitches, he thought. Yeah, a very good time had been had by all.

Including him, he thought as he stretched his legs out in front of him. The last of the guests, one of whom had been Yelena in a rather horrifying lavender tutu, had been shepherded out a half hour ago, and he and Olivia, Josie, and Gus were sitting at one of the tables in the ballroom. A bit stunned, more than a bit exhausted, but well pleased, he thought.

"It's over," Olivia said with a weary sigh. "It is over, right? I can sleep now?"

"I'm sleeping right here." Josie tugged off her wig and shook out her hair before putting her head down on her arms. "That's not a problem, right?"

"Not for me," Olivia said with a laugh. "I think you might be a little stiff in the morning, though."

She was tired, Rhys could tell, but more than that she looked exhilarated. Her cheeks were still flushed with the heat and excitement of the party, the dancing, the extra Prosecco she'd drunk somewhere near midnight. Despite the disaster, she'd come through with her head high, and then proceeded to enjoy herself. With him.

He smiled, watching as she rolled her shoulders back, easing out kinks, the fitted bodice of her gown stretching across her chest. She truly looked like a princess, didn't she? She'd left her hair down but threaded it with ribbons, and the thick length of it waved down her back in soft ripples.

The purple gown set off her eyes and her pink cheeks, and the softness of the dress suited her. She looked a bit dreamy again, otherwordly . . . although that might have been the exhaustion, he told himself.

Poor thing needed to be taken up to bed. And he was the man to take her.

"I believe it's time to call it a night, yeah?" he said. Even if he hadn't been about to pass out, he needed out of the damn gorilla costume. He'd started itching four hours ago, and he was sweating like a pig besides.

"Looks like it." Gus poked Josie's arm gently. "Uh-oh. I think she actually dozed off."

"I'm awake," Josie said blearily. "But I can't remember which room Roseanne put me in for the night."

"I've got your key." Gus stood up and took her arm to help her to her feet. He was blushing fiercely, and Rhys wondered if he was going to make a move or bolt once he got Josie upstairs. "'Night, Olivia, Rhys. Great party."

"'Night, F. Scott." Olivia waved with a dreamy smile. "Don't forget, breakfast for everyone in the conference room tomorrow at ten."

"We'll be there," Josie called as she picked up her shoes and followed Gus out of the ballroom, clinging to his arm. "I hope."

Gus shot Rhys an expression of pure terror over his shoulder. There was no proper response to that but for a quick thumbs-up, and a laugh after Gus had turned the corner.

"I'm not sure I can feel my feet," Olivia said absently. "I haven't danced like that in . . . well, ever."

"You were a lovely partner." Rhys heaved himself out of the chair and walked around the table to pull her to her feet. "In fact, dancing with you was my favorite part of the evening."

"Better than making out in the basement?" she said, turning her face up to him with a tired smile.

"Even better than that," he murmured and leaned in to kiss her. . . .

Just as she pulled back and said, "You know, my body is exhausted, but I can't seem to shut off my brain. All these new ideas for the hotel occurred to me tonight, and I'm tempted to go upstairs and write everything down before I forget."

"You are barking mad, you know that?" he whispered and tugged her close again. "Upstairs, woman. I want to see what a princess wears under her gown."

But even after they'd made it up to her apartment, and he'd skinned off the sodding gorilla suit and started on the buttons of her dress, she couldn't stop musing out loud.

"I think I want to redecorate the bar next," she said, letting him slide the gown off her shoulders. "I mean, it's a bar. There are never enough bars in New York. We should be doing better business."

He ignored her, stepping back to admire the lacy lavender bra and panties she'd worn underneath her costume. The sheer material clung to the gentle swells of her breasts, and the panties teasingly outlined the dark triangle between her legs. He grunted as his cock leapt to attention.

"Then there are all those meeting rooms on the second floor," she said, absently leaning into his hands as he ran them over her shoulders and down the silky expanse of her back. "I don't know what we can do with them, but they shouldn't be sitting empty all the time."

He steered her backward toward the bed and popped the clasp on her bra. Her breasts sprang free, the nipples rosy and coming erect in the cool breath of air. Or was it his gaze that aroused her? He didn't care particularly—he simply wanted them in his mouth, luscious and firm, salty-sweet.

She shivered with anticipation when he laid her back, raising her hips obediently as he tugged down the scrap of lace between her legs. Her thighs were so creamy, soft and slender and sensitive, especially on the inside. An incoherent noise of pleasure escaped her throat when he bent down and trailed his tongue up the gentle curve of one thigh and pressed a kiss to the curls above it.

She groaned when he spread her lush lips and slid his tongue between them, teasing wetness from her core, and his cock twitched in answer. He didn't want to talk about the hotel, he didn't want to listen to her talk about the hotel. He wanted all of her attention on him, on them. He wanted all of her, right now. He was leaving too soon to hear another word about Callender House.

"Rhys . . ." she began, her voice soft and hot with need.

"No more talking," he murmured, crawling up the bed on top of her. "Shhh." And with that he took her mouth roughly, plunging his tongue inside as his cock thrust into her dark heat.

*Oh God* . . . Olivia couldn't even think when he was inside her. Especially not when he was thrusting so deep, braced above her with his arms locked in place, touching something so deep inside her, it echoed with startled pleasure.

She hung on to him, wrapping her legs around his waist, her fingers digging into the lean muscle of his back. The sudden fierceness of his lovemaking was startling, as if he wanted to drive everything but the feel of him, the taste of him, out of her head.

That way lay danger, though. Every day he'd been at the hotel, every night he came to her room, every moment he looked at her with those smoky eyes full of mischief and desire, she'd gotten a little bit more lost. A little bit surer that when he left, she would be nothing more than a splattered puddle of hopelessness on a sidewalk somewhere.

Every day, she was a little bit more in love.

After years of drifting through her life, dating once in a while, ensconced on Memory Lane with the hotel and blissfully unaware of all the changes she needed to make, Rhys had woken her up. With a siren, clanging bells, and a fire alarm instead of a whispered greeting, but that didn't matter. She was awake now, and life was better than ever, because she was living it instead of dreaming it.

But she would be a fool to believe that she would get to live it with Rhys forever. Rhys, who was leaving for L.A. much too soon.

His tongue stroked inside of her mouth hungrily as he thrust even deeper, but more slowly now, drawing out each slide until she wanted to sob with the aching pleasure of it.

It wasn't fair—it was so good between them, not just in bed, but always, and she couldn't help wanting to hold on just a little longer. But he was the one who had walked into her life out of nowhere, into a life she was committed to. And he would walk out of it, whether she wanted him to or not.

But she wanted him to know that she cared. She wanted him to know that she'd changed, that she'd woken up . . .

She wrenched her mouth away from his and wriggled her arms between them, pushing hard. His grunt of surprise turned into a growl when she twisted, rolling them over until she straddled him.

"My turn," she said, and the gleam of approval in his eyes flicked her arousal higher.

Digging her knees into the bed on either side of him, she planted her palms on his chest and sat up so she could take him as deep as he would go. He thrust upward, his eyes never leaving her face as he did, and she answered by leaning forward to lick each of the flat, masculine discs of his nipples in turn.

Oh, he liked that. His throat vibrated with the same purring growl as she kissed it, but he pushed her away a second later, grabbing her around the waist to capture one of her nipples in his mouth. As he suckled, his hands moved down to her bottom, palms firm against each cheek, seating her deeper as he plunged, again and again . . .

She was strung so tight now, every nerve ending pulsing with sensation, with heat, with the glorious slide of him inside her and below her, with the look in his eyes as she wrestled away from him, stretching backward to plant her hands on his thighs. She was so close now, but she wanted this to last, she wanted to keep him right where he was . . .

He stretched up with her, his hands finding her breasts, rolling the rigid nipples with his thumbs—and then he pushed up, all the way up, grabbing her around the waist and launching them both off the bed. She clung to him, gasping in surprise and a shock of fresh arousal. Suddenly it was a competition, but that didn't matter. They were both going to win, weren't they?

At least here, in this bed, they were.

He twisted around and dumped her unceremoniously on the side of the mattress, but instead of climbing on top of her, he kept his feet on the floor, holding onto her hips as he thrust inside her.

It was almost savage, this new ferocity—he was sweating, and his eyes glittered with need. All she could do was hang on, groaning with each fierce plunge, until the heat was too bright, too sharp, and it broke over her in a million shimmering pieces.

Rhys roared his release a moment later, shuddering with the pleasure. When he collapsed on top of her, he pressed a hard kiss to her lips, and she wrapped her arms around him.

Sweaty, still shaking, they stared at one another. Rhys was still buried inside her, and she felt his heart pounding against her breast—hers answered back in kind. For a long, breath-held moment, she could almost see the words neither of them had spoken floating the air, and the room hummed with the electric force of their gaze.

And then he kissed her again, slow and deep and quiet, and she closed her eyes, pouring everything she felt into the kiss. She was trembling inside, as if she were teetering on the edge of some great height, but when he pulled her up into the bed and under the covers, he put his arms around her, resting his head on top of hers. It was a good place to be, she thought drowsily, letting the tension ebb out of her body as she dozed off. Even if it was just for tonight.

# Chapter 15

"Rhys, your car is here."

He looked up from the luggage he'd piled on the lobby floor and caught Roseanne pointing out the window at the street. Even her heavy gray braid seemed subdued today, tied with a neat black ribbon and hanging straight down her back as if in defeat.

*Defeat.* Oh, bollocks. It was just this place, making him metaphorical and more than a bit sappy again.

But he couldn't help reading disappointment on the faces of those who had come to see him off. To a person, they seemed a bit let down, as if he'd decided to head off and fight an unpopular war, or sign up for the Hanging Puppies Brigade or something. Roseanne, Josie, even Gus and Angel, who had his burly arms crossed over his chest and a scowl etched deep in his forehead.

He hitched up his backpack and slung it over his shoulder, saving the suitcase for the time being. To a person was wrong. Olivia didn't look disappointed, did she? Olivia, in his favorite deep pink sweater, the one that made her look a bit like a ripe, full-blown rose, seemed . . . hopeful.

If only he knew what she was hoping for.

He stared into her eyes, bigger than ever this morning

and a bit tired. They'd been up late last night, though. Saying good-bye to each other privately, physically, since they hadn't said so aloud.

And it had turned out their bodies had quite a bit to express, hadn't it?

"You need to remind Rusty that the eggs should be room temperature before the breakfast service," he told her without preamble. "And that he's overdipping the French toast. I've told him a million times, but he keeps forgetting."

She nodded, eyes fixed on his face, as if she were memorizing him. She stood so close, he caught the scent of her hair, and for one wild moment he was tempted to bury his face in it and breathe deep.

"I told Jesus to go easy on the dishwasher, too—the beast is on its last legs, Liv."

"I know. Thank you." Her voice was little more than a husky whisper, but the faint trace of a smile played around her lips.

He took a step closer, meaning to kiss her good-bye and said instead, "I told you about the crack in my ceiling, yeah? It's not an emergency, but I wanted you to know it was there." He reached out to tuck a stray curl behind her ear. Touching her seemed incredibly important at the moment.

"As long as the ceiling's not falling down, I think it'll be all right." She had turned her cheek into his hand, and he brushed his thumb over its soft curve.

"Okay, then." He needed to kiss her good-bye and get on with this. The car was waiting, but the plane wouldn't. So he'd say good-bye. Kiss her. Walk out the door.

Christ, it sounded so easy, but his feet wouldn't seem to move.

"You know you've got to figure out who pulled that stunt at the ball," he said suddenly. "Especially if it's some-

one on staff. Can't stand for that type of mischief, Liv. Someone could've been hurt, and it's a wonder no one was."

"I know, Rhys." She covered his hand with her own and
gently lifted it away from her face. "The car was late, you
know. And now you're going to be later. I don't want you to
miss your flight."

"I won't." He leaned down and pulled her close with one
arm, and she settled against him with a little sigh.

He'd never felt this before—the idea of leaving here, leaving *her*, was a bit like walking away without his right hand.
Something in him had broken the day he'd kissed her. He'd
always moved on, once his physical curiosity was satisfied
and the novelty of a new body had worn off. Even with
Clodagh, he'd been itchy, and then the only reason he'd
stayed hadn't been his interest in her, but an obligation—
one he'd discovered was unnecessary, since she would have
lied about the color of the sky and where the sun set if the
situation had called for it.

But Olivia . . . If anything, he was itchy to touch her
again, to throw down his bags and take her upstairs, just as
if he hadn't explored every facet of her face and form the
night before. He was addicted to her.

He was going, of course. No way around that. Two hundred thousand dollars was up for grabs if he could wow the
judges in the final competition, plus the perks of new
kitchen equipment, a feature in the best international cooking magazine, and a brilliant shot of prestige.

And then?

He still hadn't thought that far ahead. But he knew, no
matter what Olivia was hoping for, that when the competition was over, he would . . . call her. At least.

Her eyes shone with questions when he tipped her chin
up to kiss her, but she wouldn't ask them. He knew that
much. And for that moment, it was better that way.

She tasted like her morning coffee and the blueberry scones she'd eaten while he finished packing. With his arms around her, he pulled her up on her toes until she was crushed against his chest and deepened the kiss. Her hands were fisted in his coat, and he could feel the frantic stutter of her pulse in her throat.

He could also feel too many pairs of eyes trained on them. The lobby was electric with tension. But before he could break away, Olivia did, pulling back with another little sigh.

"You're really going to miss that flight," she murmured. She was examining the toe of his boot as if she'd never seen anything so mesmerizing.

"I'm going," he said softly and grabbed her chin to angle her mouth up for one more kiss. "When it's over," he added, "I'll ring you, yeah?"

Surprise and relief flickered across her face as she nodded. "Yeah."

When he looked up, the others pretended to be busy with other things, Josie biting her thumbnail and Roseanne flipping through a stack of paper attached to a clipboard. Even Angel had taken a hammer out of his tool belt and was actually polishing the head of it against his pants. Gus was staring at the floor, his hands stuffed in his jeans pockets.

Bad liars, all of them, pretending that they weren't watching him and Olivia kiss good-bye. Bad liars who loved Olivia and hated the fact that he was leaving, if not him.

Bad liars he considered his friends now. It had been a long time since he'd had many of those.

"Rhys, the car," Olivia murmured and gave him a little push toward the door.

He nodded and collected his suitcase, but when he turned

to Olivia again, her spine was straight and her jaw was set when she said, "Good-bye, Rhys. Good luck."

Right. He was leaving.

"I'll ring you," he repeated and pushed through the revolving door without a backward glance.

"Come on," Roseanne said when the hired car was long gone, its red taillights disappearing into the traffic turning onto Madison Avenue in the morning's gray drizzle. She put an arm around Olivia's shoulder, warm and heavy and familiar, and steered her back through the revolving doors into the lobby.

Olivia let her do it without protest. She couldn't very well stand on the sidewalk all day moping, and she knew it.

Even though she wanted to. Even though going upstairs and crawling into bed for the next week or so actually sounded even better.

"Do you want a cup of tea?" Roseanne asked when she'd led Olivia to the banquette. "Or, um, a tissue?"

Angel, Josie, and Gus, as well as Anna, who was pretending to be busy with nonexistent work at the reception desk, had fixed their gazes elsewhere when Olivia looked up. It was sweet, if a little unnecessary. She wasn't crying. She wasn't going to fall apart.

She *wasn't*.

So she said, "I'm not crying," and managed a smile for Roseanne, who had sat down beside her in a cloud of musk and a clatter of silver bangles.

"Oh, I know!" Roseanne actually flushed and appealed for help to Josie with a quick glance.

Letting go of Gus's hand, Josie crossed the lobby to sit on Olivia's other side. "Any plans for today?" she said softly. Her blue eyes, always so sharp, so cynical, were full of concern.

"I'm fine. Really." Olivia stood up and shook her head. "Look, I knew he was leaving when we . . . got involved. He didn't make any promises to me." She frowned, suddenly irritated. "And I didn't make any to him. It was . . . fun. It was a fling. For now, it's over. And I'm not going to fall apart." She glared at Josie and Roseanne in turn. "Okay?"

Cowed, they said in unison, "Okay."

It was the truth, kind of. She wasn't going to fall apart, even if it was tempting. She was awake now, thanks to Rhys. She wasn't hiding behind daydreams and memories anymore. She had a hotel to save, damn it, and that hadn't changed simply because they'd gotten through the Halloween ball. And today, especially, it was going to be important to remember that.

But she couldn't deny that today, especially, she wanted out of the hotel. Everywhere she turned, she would see Rhys, lounging in a doorway, wicked grin beckoning her closer for a kiss, those smoky, laughing eyes gazing at her.

Tugging her sweater into place and pushing her hair out of her eyes, she faced her friends. "I'm going out," she said resolutely.

Why were they staring at her as if she'd announced she was going to storm a battlement or join the circus? "I'm going shopping," she amended, lowering her voice.

"For what?" Josie said in confusion.

Right. For what? She glanced at the desk, where Angel was showing Anna and Gus a picture of the new baby. He and Theresa had named her Isabella, and he'd promised to bring her in to visit sometime soon.

"For a baby gift," she whispered, cocking her head at Angel. "And some . . . cookies. Or something. For Theresa."

"That's a good idea," Roseanne said, approval shining on her face. "Can I come?"

"You bet." Olivia took her arm as she stood up, feeling better already. Maybe the party was over, but her life wasn't.

In a perfect world, she would have been wearing the little black pencil skirt that made her legs look longer, Josie thought two hours later. Of course, in a perfect world she would have had a body that didn't embrace every carbohydrate she put into her mouth by happily adding another pound, or five.

But that didn't matter, she told herself firmly, reaching up to straighten her ponytail in the mirror on the back of her office door. World wasn't perfect. It wasn't a surprise.

And for what she had in mind, clothes were the least of her problems.

Courage, now that was a different story.

Gus hadn't even kissed her the night of the ball. He'd danced with her, he'd brought her drinks, he'd helped her up to her room, but he hadn't kissed her. He hadn't so much as touched her the two evenings they'd spent planning their costumes, not even when they'd taken the subway down to the Village to scout out thrift shops and secondhand stores.

But the way he looked at her . . . If an expression was worth a thousand words, she was pretty sure Gus could write his next book about wanting to kiss her, if not actually doing so.

He was a gentleman, she decided as she marched into the lobby and pushed the button for the elevator. A gentleman who was painfully, cripplingly shy, unfortunately. When she'd said she would go to the Monsters' Ball with him, he'd almost fallen off his bar stool.

But once she got him talking, the way she had on the subway that night, coming back from downtown, he was smart and funny and so very sweet, she wanted to climb into his lap and hug him.

And do a few other things, too.

She stepped onto the elevator when it came and took a deep breath as she pressed the button for the eighth floor. Well, today she was going to do those things. If Gus let her, of course. Because she was going to seduce him.

Watching Olivia and Rhys say good-bye in the lobby this morning, her knees had practically buckled. Some part of her—some dormant, well-hidden part of her that hadn't succumbed to cynicism way back in high school—had actually believed that he might stay, she realized. That two people so passionate about each other would get their happy ending, no matter what.

Maybe they would, in the end. Rhys could come back or Olivia could fly to L.A.—a million different things could still happen. Either way, they'd seized the chance to be together, hadn't they, at least for awhile?

Well, today she was going to seize Gus, before she died of waiting for him to work up the courage to make a move.

He looked startled when he opened the door, and she was charmed to see that his cap was on backward. He looked about ten when he wore it that way.

"Um, hi," she said, scrambling as he moved to let her inside. Shit. She'd had a whole script planned, and the ride up in the elevator had sucked it right out of her head.

"Is anything wrong?" Gus asked, shutting the door. "Is Olivia okay?"

She'd never been in his suite before, she realized, glancing around the room. He'd made himself at home, though, with his laptop set up on the desk, and piles of books on the rug and the table, and an ancient Yankees souvenir pennant taped to the mirror. In the far room, the bed was unmade, a rumpled nest of sheets and comforter tangled together. Well, good.

"Olivia's fine." She turned around and took a deep

breath as he walked closer, those hound dog eyes fixed on her in confusion. "But I'm . . . not."

Oh yeah. Real seductive.

But maybe it didn't matter. Gus was near enough to touch now, and an amazing array of thoughts flashed in his eyes as Josie watched.

"You're not?" He took her hand, and she was astounded to realize how big his hand felt, how warm and solid it was as it surrounded her fingers.

"No." She turned her face up to him, and took another deep breath. "I . . . want to kiss you."

His fingers tightened around hers. "You do?"

She nodded and took a step closer to him. "Uh-huh. In fact, I'm going to kiss you. Right now."

Instead of the "You are?" she had expected, a slow, pleased smile lit his face as he murmured, "Oh good," and put his arms around her.

She had to stretch up a little bit to reach him—he was taller than he seemed, especially when they were standing nose to nose. But he lowered his head to help her, and then they were kissing, his lips warm and firm against her, his arms holding her in place.

She'd worried that it might be weird. Unfamiliar, or awkward, at any rate. She didn't go around kissing men out of the blue as a rule, even men she liked as much as she liked Gus. Kissing was usually an end-of-the-date thing, lubricated with a little wine and a few hours of working up to it.

But kissing Gus wasn't weird—he tasted exactly the way she might have expected, if she'd thought about it beforehand. Warm and comfortable, and absolutely right.

Like coming home, she thought absently, as his hands slid up her back and his tongue licked sweetly at her bottom lip. Just exactly like coming home.

"I guess I should tell you that I've wanted to kiss you for

a long time, too," he murmured, and trailed feathery kisses over her cheek and jaw. "You should get extra points for doing it first."

"Yup," she agreed with a smile, pulling away from him to take his hand and lead him into the bedroom. She stopped at the foot of the bed and kicked off her shoes. "I win."

"You think?" He swallowed as he watched her unzip her skirt, but he toed off his sneakers and reached for his belt buckle. "We'll see, huh?"

Naked but for her bra and panties, she climbed onto the bed and reached for him. "Yeah," she said, grinning as he tugged his shirt over his head. She couldn't wait to run her hands over his bare chest, and when he knelt on the bed in front of her, his fingers busy with the clasp of her bra, she whispered, "Kiss me again and we'll call it a draw."

# Chapter 16

Bloody sunshine, Rhys thought four days later as he paced the roof of the L.A. building where the *Fork in the Road* finale had been filmed. The sun was relentless, hot and bright and so sodding cheerful he was becoming a bit homicidal. Maybe he really was a true Londoner at heart. He would have given his left arm for a bit of drizzle.

Across the roof, his competitors, a San Francisco native named Marco and a very young woman from somewhere in the south named Elyse, were smoking cigarettes and leaning on the lip of the roof, watching the street below. It was just gone five, and the competition was finally over—the judges were downstairs deliberating even now.

At the moment, Rhys couldn't be arsed to care who won the bloody thing. Much as he loved food, spending nine hours in the kitchen after three of the longest days of his life had about done him in. If someone asked him to choose an apple from among a pile of oranges right now he'd probably come up wrong.

His back ached, he'd burnt one hand on the handle of a hot pan, and a headache had lodged between his eyes, a dull, heavy pressure.

And the only thing he wanted by way of relief was a

night in Olivia's bed, with her stretched out beside him. No, that was bollocks. Just a moment to kiss her, feel her cool, smooth hand on his cheek and the soft give of her body against his, that was the cure.

Simple fact was, he missed her. Had missed her from the moment he tore down the gangway onto the plane four days ago, ignoring the irritation on the flight attendants' faces. Kept waking up alone in his narrow dorm bed, wondering why she wasn't there beside him. Kept picturing her face as he sliced peaches and chopped garlic.

Kept trying to ignore the ache in his chest when he thought of her, three thousand miles away from him.

As they had during the beginning of the competition, the contestants had been sequestered. That meant that calling anyone was off limits, but had that made it easier? Crikey, no.

Maybe because this time, as opposed to the first eight weeks of the show, he'd had someone he wanted to talk to.

In a few hours, this would all be over at any rate, he thought as he leaned back in the lounge chair he'd snagged. The judges—a renowned New York chef, a food writer, and a restaurateur with a dozen successful eateries to his name— would decide who had won, and the production crew would film the announcement and the contestants' reaction.

Sneaking a glance across the roof, Rhys couldn't imagine it would be Elyse. She was talented, yeah, but so young. Not innocent, though—she'd wielded her knives like a warrior all through the competition, talking trash about some of the others, making herself look good on camera whenever possible, and flipping her blond hair over her shoulders as if she were in a beauty pageant instead of a cookery competition.

Marco was far more experienced, and a bit easier going, but the man was all about the chile pepper. Rhys wouldn't have been surprised if they'd turned up in one of his desserts. His culinary mantra seemed to be the hotter the better, and damn the poor fool who wasn't ready for the heat.

"How do you think you did?" Marco called now, another cigarette lit, a pale stream of smoke issuing from it like a tail. His red-gold hair was spiked up like a parrot's plumes.

"He'll never tell," Elyse laughed. Crikey, there she went with the famous hair flip. "He's the original tight-lipped Brit."

"It only matters what the judges think now, yeah?" Rhys said evenly. "But for the record, I was bloody brilliant."

Marco snorted in surprise, but Elyse's smile was patently false. She'd come on to him repeatedly since the competition started, long before he met Olivia, but he'd turned her down every time. There was no sense tangling up work and play, and *Fork in the Road* was very much work to Rhys.

That hadn't mattered with Olivia, though, had it? He let his head fall back on the lounge chair, cursing the sun's early evening warmth on his face. He'd worked the kitchen of the Coach and Four with hardly a word from her. And despite living right there in the building, at least for the duration, he'd never felt the need to escape at day's end, had he?

His escape had been Olivia. Her soft voice, her warm brown eyes, her sweet, lush kisses, her hands on his skin . . .

His groin tightened uncomfortably at the thought, and he shifted in the chair, lowering his sunglasses into place over his closed eyes. Sod it all, he needed to concentrate. Any time now the judges were going to call them in and grill them about the choices they'd made in this final competition, and he needed to be ready.

The challenge had been what he'd expected—his vision for a restaurant of his own, accompanied by a five-course signature meal. Without meaning to, he'd pictured the inside of the Coach and Four, the way he would redesign it if given the chance, and the menu he would introduce there, featuring some of the things he'd made for the Halloween ball. It was American through and through, but with a funky twist, and with every course he'd heard Olivia's sighing breaths of satisfaction as she tasted it.

A muse, he thought now. He'd gone and found himself a muse. At least he hoped that's what she'd become. If he couldn't drive her out of his head, using her for inspiration seemed only fitting.

He and Marco and Elyse had been given different areas of the enormous kitchen during the competition today, but he couldn't have said what kind of food either of them had prepared. He hated comparison, at any rate—he wanted to win or lose on his own merits.

No, sod that. He wanted to win.

A door opened at the far end of the roof, and Julie, one of the production assistants, called, "Okay, guys. Time to face the music. Come on in."

Marco stood and brushed off his chef's jacket, grinding his cigarette under the heel of his shoe. Elyse ran a hand through her hair, passing Rhys without a word as she followed Julie through the door.

"Luck," Marco said and extended a hand.

"And to you, mate," Rhys agreed. It wasn't a lie, precisely. He hadn't said what kind.

Down in the dining room, the remains of the contestants' meals had been cleared away. The judges sat at a long table, their wineglasses still half full beside them, and smiled as the three chefs walked in.

"Good work, everyone," Paula Chase said. "Congratulations for making it to this point in the competition."

Richard Gorder and Jeff Felicia joined her in a round of applause, and they all bowed.

*Get on with it, yeah?* Rhys kept his smile in place as the judges began with a rundown of Marco's meal, but he couldn't concentrate on the details. Something about a Southwestern theme—what a shocker, Rhys thought with an inward roll of his eyes—and one miss with a rice dish that had been too soupy for their taste. When they moved on to Elyse's fare, Rhys only kept from gritting his teeth with effort. She'd gone new-wave French, apparently, and fouled up her pastry course as well as the Provençale chicken entrée.

Bloody hell, he just didn't care. He wanted to win, yeah, but he wanted to win and then fish his mobile phone out of his luggage and call Olivia.

"Rhys," Paula said with a slow, satisfied smile. "Your take on modern American was really well done—maybe especially given the fact that you hail from the United Kingdom."

Hail from the United Kingdom? Did she think that would sound sophisticated for the viewing audience? *Doesn't matter*, he reminded himself, fixing his own smile firmly in place as she continued.

"The pork tenderloin with the roasted vegetables was absolutely my favorite," she said, and turned to look at Richard. "It was moist, full of flavor, and perfectly plated. But I know the others have their own preferences."

"I could eat the pumpkin ravioli every day," Jeff told him, grinning over his folded hands, his gold watch flashing in the camera lights. "That and the turkey sausage were perfect beginnings to the meal."

"I agree," Richard chimed in, his neat goatee bobbing as he nodded. "And the dessert was the finishing touch. Showcasing all those American flavors with the pecans and the peaches, you really pulled out a showstopper for the finale."

Without realizing it, Rhys's pulse had kicked up. They liked his meal, all right. They'd fucking loved it, in fact. He fisted his hands behind his back, strung taut with anticipation.

"After much deliberation, we'd like to announce that *Fork in the Road* has a winner," Paula said her gaze traveling over each of the contestants. "And the winner is . . . Rhys Spencer."

He heard the words, recognized the sound of applause as the judges stood and clapped, but the truth hadn't quite sunk in yet. He'd won, he told himself as Marco gave him a hug. He'd won. But as a grin spread over his face and he accepted the congratulations, he realized with a start that his only thought was, *Wait until I tell Olivia.*

"Are you telling me that the only thing you managed to do was cut the electricity and spill some paint?"

Seated at his desk, his chair turned toward the window, Stuart Callender addressed Marty and Davey in a tone Marty hadn't heard before.

It sounded a little bit like a snake might, if snakes could talk, he thought, uncomfortably aware of a bead of sweat on his brow. Kind of a hiss.

He didn't like it. But then, it was pretty clear Mr. Callender didn't like them at the moment.

"We busted the dishwasher," Davey said. Christ, he sounded like a pouting kid, Marty thought. "Fucked up dinner pretty good."

After a moment's silence, the chair swiveled toward them and Callender narrowed his eyes. "Fucked up dinner pretty good? Did you drop out of school in the eighth grade, Mr. O'Brian?"

Davey blinked, just like the asshole he was. "Ninth grade," he muttered.

For a moment, Marty thought Callender was going to bust a vein screaming at them, but instead he smiled. A snake's smile, Marty thought, swallowing hard. Vicious and thin.

"Well, think back to those glorious days, will you?" Standing up, Callender leaned over his desk, his fists planted on its smooth, shiny surface. "Think about all the trouble you might have caused, if you'd had the chance. Then take it a step further, yes? I want Olivia thwarted at *every turn*. I want her to give up, to give in. I want that place to be constant chaos. Do you understand me?"

Davey answered with a sullen nod, but Marty made sure to say, "Yes, sir."

Callender was the boss, after all, and Marty knew in his bones the man liked to hear the proof of it out loud.

What sucked was working for him, this time around. The cash was great, sure, but every day he and Davey clocked in at the hotel, guilt crept over him like a rash. He liked Angel, and even more, he liked Olivia. He even liked the damn hotel.

He'd never worked in a place where you got treated like family right from the start. Hell, he'd never worked in a place like that at all. But Olivia was always checking in, handing out bottles of water or a tray of snacks from the kitchen, making sure they had their breaks and they knew to ask Angel for help if they needed it.

If he had his way, he'd quit Stuart Callender and keep his job at the hotel. Mopping floors and repairing molding and leaky faucets would be worth it if he didn't have to think about Olivia's face every time something went wrong.

Davey hadn't mentioned the other afternoon, when they'd overflowed the toilets in the lobby rest room, or the day after the Halloween party when they'd trashed three guest rooms while the others were cleaning up from the ball.

Of course, neither of them mentioned that in each case, they'd been the ones cleaning up the mess, too, which kind of sucked.

The whole deal sucked, Marty thought as they walked out of Callender's office and got into the elevator. And he didn't feel even a twinge of remorse when he realized that he was rooting for Olivia to knock Callender off his high horse and stomp on him.

Ringing. Something was ringing, Olivia thought blearily, coming awake in the dark quiet of her apartment. She hit out for the alarm clock without thinking, and then realized it was the phone.

The phone? It was almost one in the morning, she saw when she blinked at the clock.

*Oh God.* As long as it wasn't Angel or one of his crew reporting another disaster, she didn't care who it was. She grabbed the receiver and mumbled, "Hello?"

"Liv?"

*Liv?* Her heart pounded in answer. No one called her Liv but Rhys, and unless she was dreaming that was his crisp British voice on the other end. Oh God. He'd called. He'd *called.*

"Liv? Are you there, love?"

Oh. Shoot. "I'm here," she said, a ridiculous grin stretched across her face. "I'm . . . Wait, where are you? Are you still in L.A.?"

He chuckled, and she could picture the wicked curve of his lips as he did. "Yeah. Sorry, love. It must be—Oh, bloody hell, I didn't look at the time. You were asleep, yeah?"

"That's okay." She hoped he couldn't hear her yawning.

And she wished she knew what to say. *I love you? Come back, please?* She could have described the last few days in detail, of course, but that would have involved little more than saying, "I missed you. And then I missed you some more. And then the toilets got backed up, and I missed you. And then I made more plans for the hotel and missed you . . ."

Silence.

She froze, blinking in the darkness, suddenly aware that the room was freezing, too. What happened to the heat? It definitely hadn't been this cold when she went to bed. She shivered, holding her breath, waiting, scrambling for something to say . . .

And Rhys said softly, "Liv? I won."

"You won?" God, she'd actually squealed, she thought, sitting up straight. "You won! I knew it! I knew you would win!"

He laughed again, his voice low and husky, as if he'd been talking all night. "Well, it's brilliant to hear you had faith in me. I wasn't so sure there for awhile. It's a secret, though—I'm not supposed to tell anyone, so the finale won't get spoiled."

God, he sounded so familiar, so close, she couldn't quite believe he was all the way across the country. And he'd won! He'd *won*.

But . . . what did that mean?

"I'm so proud of you," she said softly and tried to ignore the way her heart was fluttering. He'd won, and he'd called to share the news with her. She was thrilled for him, but more than anything else she wondered what this unexpected conversation meant.

He was silent for another moment, and when he spoke again his voice was even huskier. "Proud of me? That's . . . Well, that's a brilliant thing to hear, Liv. Thank you."

"I mean it," she said, and frowned when she saw Eloise

hop onto the bedside table. "This is huge. You must be . . . Well, you must be absolutely over the moon."

He laughed. "Over the moon? Yeah, there and back again."

She swatted a hand at Eloise, who was nosing delicately around the glass of water Olivia had left on the table before she went to sleep. "Stop that," she mouthed at the cat and shifted closer to the edge of the bed. Wow, it really was freezing. Her bare arm had goose bumps already, and she couldn't imagine how chilly the floor was going to be. "So tell me about it," she said to Rhys. "What did you make?"

He described the final challenge, with wickedly pointed comments about his competitors, while she listened, swatting at the cat all the while. The stupid beast! What was wrong with her tonight? She'd never done anything remotely like this before, and now instead of jumping down and trotting off the way Olivia had imagined, she'd simply backed up, knocking a picture frame off the table.

Letting the covers fall back, and shivering in the chilly air, Olivia leaned over farther, waving her arm at the cat as Rhys finished his story.

"And that's all she wrote, as they say." He paused to clear his throat. "I am sorry it's so late, love. As soon as we were through filming, I wanted to call, but the producers had a whole celebration planned, as well as taping a reunion with the other contestants, and well . . . I couldn't get away till now."

She paused midswat, biting her bottom lip. He'd wanted to call her right away? There went her heart again, thumping in excitement. If he'd been standing in front of her, she would have leaped into his arms, and damn the consequences. As it was, she was grinning like an idiot—and still swiping at the cat, who was going to be renamed Beast the minute she hung up the phone.

God, the stupid thing was actually dipping her paw into the glass. What was she *doing?* Testing the water temperature? Fishing out a bug?

"Liv?"

The sound of her nickname was so sweet. "Yes?"

"I do have one question for you."

"Of course," she said, leaning over as far as she could and grabbing for the cat. "Anything."

"I wanted to know if my room was still available," he said softly.

Which was precisely when she tumbled out of bed and hit the floor with a thud.

# Chapter 17

Wrapped in an old cardigan she'd piled on over a heavy sweater the next morning, Olivia found Josie in the lobby. She was glowing—even her ponytail had more bounce these days. Of course, her nose was glowing because it was so cold in the hotel, but still, it gave Olivia a little rush of satisfaction to see her so happy. She wasn't exactly sure what had happened between Josie and Gus, but she could guess.

Especially since Gus had been walking around the building with a goofy grin since the day Rhys had left.

"Got a minute?"

Josie sniffed and wound her scarf tighter around her throat. "Sure. I hear freezing to death takes a while."

Olivia made a face at her but dragged her into the bar anyway, rubbing her sore hip. She'd landed on the floor pretty hard last night, not that anyone but her would ever know about it. "He called." She sounded like a teenager and she knew it, but she didn't care.

Josie pounced, understanding immediately. "Rhys?"

Olivia nodded, and then had the air smooshed out of her lungs when Josie enveloped her in a hard hug. "He wanted to know if his room was still available," she said when she could breathe again.

"And you told him no, I guess." Josie stood back, her usual wry smile in place now.

Olivia elbowed her, but she was grinning, too. "He's coming in a couple days, after he ties up some loose ends in L.A."

"Well, at least you'll have heat," Josie said, waggling her eyebrows. "If you know what I mean."

"Look who's talking," Olivia pointed out as they walked back into the lobby. "And speaking of heat, what's the verdict?"

"We need some," Josie grumbled. "It's only November, and this place is already like a meat locker."

Yelena had come downstairs, wrapped in an ancient fur coat, and with her were Delancey and Frank, as well as several of the out-of-town guests. All of whom were jabbering to poor Rob, on front desk duty this morning and staring in wide-eyed despair at the crowd.

"Oh, Olivia, there you are," Frank said, sighing. "What's going on? It's cold in here, my dear. My toes were blue this morning, and that's not a good look for anyone."

"Cold? Is frigid," Yelena announced, wrinkling her nose in disgust. She hadn't even bothered with her usual eye shadow this morning, and despite her imperious attitude, she looked old and dangerously fragile to Olivia. "Good thing I have fur. Others not so lucky."

"I know, it's freezing, but . . . Angel's working on it." Olivia said, looking to Josie for confirmation.

She nodded, and settled against Gus when he walked into the lobby, his only concession to the cold a striped scarf knotted around his neck.

Herding the out-of-town guests toward the dining room, Olivia told them, "Hot tea and coffee on the house, everyone. It's an old building, and every once in a while it decides to remind us about that. Of course, last night's room charges will be waived, as well."

This drew appreciative noises even as Josie glared at her, but Olivia shrugged. It hardly mattered, in the big picture. When she wasn't putting out fires or trying to numb the ache of missing Rhys with ice cream, she'd spent the last few days holed up in her office, making plans.

And a few nights' empty guest rooms wasn't going to break Callender House, that was for sure. It was already broken, when it came to that. No, what they needed was something new, something fresh, ways to generate income that her father and her grandfather had never thought of.

Selling off some of the residential places as condos had occurred to her, but when she looked at Yelena, and thought of Mr. Mortimer, and Mrs. Gilchrist with her neat little grocery bag and her Social Security check, she didn't know what to do. Callender House was home to them, and even if Frank and Delancey could afford to find another place in the city, it was home to them, too. A falling down home, perhaps, but home nevertheless.

There was no magic answer, no one thing that would solve all of her problems.

Just like Rhys coming back to New York, to the hotel, didn't mean that a happy ending would unfurl like some sparkly banner at the end of a fairy tale. She knew better than to expect it now. If she was going to be realistic about the hotel, she figured it made sense to be realistic about her life, too.

But it didn't mean she couldn't grab a little happiness where she could. She knew exactly where she wanted to grab Rhys when he walked through the door, too, but the people who had stood by her and Callender House for so long deserved some happiness as well.

Just a slightly different kind.

Yelena had parked herself on the banquette and was blowing her nose as if pneumonia was setting in at that very moment. Olivia sat down next to her and wound an arm around her birdlike shoulders.

"I have an announcement," she said, waiting until Frank and Delancey and the others turned to look at her. "We're having Thanksgiving dinner here, just us."

An array of blank faces met this pronouncement. She blinked.

"On me," she added quickly. "I mean, on the hotel. I'm thinking a big family feast for the residents and the staff, right here in the dining room, on Thanksgiving Day. To celebrate," she said when brows began to wrinkle in thought, "the hotel's new beginning and its history. Its family."

Well, so much for spontaneity, she thought when no one spoke. But then Frank and Delancey and Yelena surprised her with applause, and everyone else joined in with hoots of approval.

"That's not exactly a moneymaker, you know," Josie said when everyone had finally wandered off to find hot coffee. Gus frowned at her, but he didn't disagree.

"I know." Olivia leaned on the reception desk and rubbed her hands together. Her fingertips were pink with cold. "But it's worth doing anyway. And you've already sent out the press releases about renovating the restaurant and the Christmas bazaar."

Josie rolled her eyes. The idea for the Christmas bazaar had been born at two in the morning the other night, when Olivia couldn't sleep, but she'd handed a list of ideas for it to Josie the minute she walked in the door the next day. Olivia wanted to showcase local artisans and then give half of the proceeds to charity, which would create a newsworthy event as well as good will. Josie couldn't argue with that,

exactly, but she was still looking for ways to get more paying guests into rooms.

"I want to draw the line at selling tube sock snowmen,"
she'd said, but she'd typed up a press release all the same.

Olivia grinned at her now, bundled into her scarf with
Gus's arm around her. "It's harder to be a Scrooge these
days, isn't it?" she whispered.

Josie responded by sticking her tongue out.

Just then, Angel came up from the basement, rubbing his
hands together. He looked exhausted, which probably had
as much to do with the new baby at home as it did with the
boiler. His dark hair was slicked back carelessly, and in his
heavy brown sweater he looked like a disgruntled bear.

"Heat's on." He held up his hands when Rob and Gus
began to clap. "But it's going to take a while for the building to warm up. So don't peel off your mittens just yet."

"Don't worry," Josie said with a shiver.

The door behind the reception desk opened and Roseanne
stuck her head out. "Olivia! It's the *Post* on the phone! I
think they're calling about one of those press releases Josie
sent."

Olivia raised an eyebrow at Josie. "See? I told you it
would pay off. Publicity never hurts, especially when it's
free."

She hurried back to her office, not even trying to hide the
grin that stretched across her face. Today was shaping up to
be a very good day. Maybe there was hope for this place yet.

A reckless voice in her head added, *And for you and
Rhys, too.*

At eleven o'clock that night, Gus took the elevator down
to the first floor. Josie was upstairs in bed—his bed, which
was still so amazing to him, he had to repeat it to himself
every once in a while—and he'd forgotten the bottle of wine

he'd left down in the walk-in. Josef had always let him store perishables in there, and Rusty didn't seem to mind, either. The minifridge in his suite was hardly big enough for essentials.

He pushed open the swinging door to the kitchen and then stopped cold. The lights were on, there was some kind of mess all over the stainless steel counter, and music was coming from somewhere.

Folding his arms over his chest and venturing further into the room, he sniffed the air. It smelled good in there, not like the ghost of dinner, but like . . . fruit. Or perfume. Or fruity perfume. What the hell?

He'd had suspicions about someone deliberately sabotaging the hotel, especially since that was clearly the case on Halloween, but he couldn't imagine even a really inept saboteur playing music while he or she worked. And leaving the lights on. That was just asking to be caught.

Taking another few steps into the room, he found an enormous pot simmering on the range and leaned over to inspect the contents more closely. It looked like . . . wax. Or really, really thick soup, which he sincerely hoped wasn't the case.

He turned around—just as Delancey Pruitt and Frank Garson came in from the hallway, with a shriek of surprise from Frank and a heavy sigh from Delancey.

"Gus," Delancey said pleasantly, considering the scowl creasing his forehead. "Can we help you?"

"Um . . ."

"Look, you caught us, all right?" Frank planted his hands on his hips and joined his lover in a scowl. "The kitchen upstairs just isn't big enough, and with Christmas coming I've got more orders than I can handle."

"Orders?" Gus said curiously.

"Frank's running a handmade soap and lotion company

from our apartment while I slave away in the public school system teaching tone-deaf children to play the triangle," Delancey said with more than a hint of weariness. "And it's doing well, if I do say so myself, but it's almost doing too well. In a manner of speaking. Thus the use of the kitchen after hours."

Frank gave a fierce nod of agreement, his floppy hair falling over his forehead. "The coconut rum soap is selling like hotcakes," he said in a conspiratorial whisper. "If, you know, hotcakes were made of coconut and rum."

"Uh-huh," Gus said blankly, but his mind was racing. "Are you doing Internet only sales, or catalog, too?"

"So far just Internet," Delancey said, pursing his lips as he watched Gus's face. "But we've managed to place product in a few boutiques around town, and they keep selling out."

"So a store of your own might be a good thing," Gus said carefully. Josie was probably wondering where the hell he was, but if this idea had legs, he was pretty sure she wouldn't mind in the end. "An exclusive brick-and-mortar place."

"Well, that would be fabulous," Frank said with a pleased smile as he smoothed his hair out of his eyes. "I can just imagine how I would decorate it, too. A nice soft green, with a lot of warm blues and—"

"The question would be whether or not the business warranted additional staff," Delancey said carefully, ignoring Frank's irritated frown. His cool blue eyes were fixed on Gus. "Overhead would be another expense."

"Unless overhead was, possibly, free of charge. At least at first," Gus added quickly, thinking hard. "In exchange for a cut of the profits, perhaps."

"Six of one," Delancey countered, but he was interested, Gus could tell.

"What are the two of you *talking* about?" Frank demanded. "Oh shit, this batch is already boiling." He shooed Gus out of the way to get to the pot.

"Let me think about it, talk to Olivia," Gus said to Delancey in a low tone. "Before we mention it to anyone else."

"Good idea." Delancey clapped him on the shoulder with a companionable smile. "Could work out that this benefits everyone, and wouldn't that be something of a miracle?"

Gus shrugged, and went to the walk-in to find his wine. Holding it up in good-bye, he said with a grin, "Hey, you never know when a miracle's going to walk in and kiss you."

Three days later Rhys shouldered his way through the crowd at LaGuardia, his backpack slung over one shoulder. All he had to do was collect his suitcase from baggage claim and he would be on his way to the hotel. Once upon a time he might have taken the subway, but he had the dosh now—he could splash out on a cab.

And have Olivia in his arms that much sooner. He hoped like hell she didn't have things to do this afternoon. At least not anything that didn't involve being naked with him.

He'd stopped fighting it. He was addicted to her, a junkie with only one sure fix. And he was jonesing for his right now, that was God's truth.

Baggage claim was, of course, a nightmare. He spent the first ten minutes growling under his breath as the empty belt rolled in lazy circles, and finally gave up and trudged to the newsstand for a bottle of water and a paper. Might as well scan the New York news while he was waiting, especially if it would keep him from going berserk on the baggage handlers.

He chose the *Post* and flipped through it idly, not really

reading, one eye on the luggage belt, until an item caught his eye. *Callender House: Old Is the New Black.*

Curious, he read on—and blinked in surprise at what Olivia had told the reporter who'd interviewed her.

"Callender House, that aging uptown behemoth, is undergoing some changes thanks to owner Olivia Callender. With a successful, and decidedly funky, Halloween ball launching a campaign to attract new business and update its image, Callender says she has plans to completely renovate and rename the hotel's restaurant, the Coach and Four, now that longtime chef Josef Vollner has retired. 'We want to honor the traditions that have been part of this place for so long,' she said, perhaps referring to the new Bohemian look of the lobby, 'but we're making some changes that reflect the times, too. A total redo of the restaurant is one of the biggest challenges, but not the only one.' With old-time charm oozing from its antique bricks, Callender House is positioned to satisfy the cravings of those who love a vintage aura and a loyalty to centuries past, and just might become the hip new destination spot this city has needed for awhile."

A total redo of the restaurant. He folded the paper and crammed it into one of the rubbish bins just as the luggage belt spewed forth the first load of suitcases. Disappointment and something close to betrayal clawed at his chest.

This would be it, then, he decided, scanning the belt for his battered suitcase. He should have known he couldn't trust anyone, not even Olivia.

Olivia, who had always seemed so genuine, true blue down to her bones. Olivia, who had gently reminded him when no condom was handy, and who had been determined to keep him out of the mess at the restaurant when Josef quit.

But this . . . Announcing she was going to renovate the

restaurant just days after he'd called her with the news that he was coming back to New York? Knowing he'd won the sodding competition and had all that convenient prize money just wasting for him to burn through it?

He spotted his case and wrestled his way through the crowd to yank it off the belt. Bloody hell. Some homecoming.

But . . . New York wasn't home, was it? Not really.

Except when it came to Olivia, he mused glumly as he walked outside to find a cab. Olivia had felt like home to him. And no matter how angry he was at the moment, the thought of checking in somewhere else, avoiding her, was as ridiculous as a dog riding a bicycle.

He had to see her. Had to touch her, kiss her, look into her eyes. Had to know, for sure, that she was just like the rest. Like the L.A. women who'd wanted their names in the paper as much as they'd wanted to shag him. Like Clodagh, fabricating a baby to keep him at her side. Like his mother, for God's sake, lying to him at every turn.

He raised his arm for a cab, his thoughts focused on Callender House. He would see Olivia first, then he would decide.

If she proved him right, he would walk out then and there. And he would cut off his arm before he trusted anyone again.

# Chapter 18

She hadn't asked him, Rhys reflected a week later, lounging with a magazine in Olivia's office while she answered e-mails. She still hadn't asked him to take over the renovation of the Coach and Four. In fact, she'd insisted that Rusty was coming into his own, and she didn't think he needed help handling the place.

When Rhys had walked into the lobby the day he flew back from L.A., he'd found her waiting at the reception desk, nearly trembling with excitement as he pushed through the revolving door. After almost two weeks, the sight of her, the feel of her, even the scent of her had been too exhilarating to ignore—he'd had her in the lift and on the way up to her apartment with barely a wave of greeting to anyone else.

He could, he'd decided, wait to find out anything about the restaurant until after they'd gotten good and naked.

And Olivia certainly hadn't disappointed him on that front, had she? He glanced up at her—she was biting her bottom lip as she typed, her hair in its usual cloud of disarray around her face despite her best efforts to tame it into place this morning. He'd woken her this morning with kisses—kisses that had turned into caresses, and more kisses, and then a fast and dirty shag that shook the head-board and made them both limp with pleasure.

Of course, that was the same way he'd woken her up every morning since he'd been back in town.

That first day back, though—hell, he'd given her no quarter. As if he could fuck the truth out of her, or something utterly mad like that. It made him a bit uncomfortable to think of it now—the first time, they'd barely been inside the apartment, and he'd yanked her pants down so quickly he'd ripped them.

And, unbelievably, she'd reacted as if it were the biggest turn-on in the world.

"Missed me, huh?" she'd whispered and tossed her panties over her shoulder.

Olivia. He grinned, watching her type, her brow furrowing as she wrestled with something she wanted to say. He really hadn't ever met a woman like her.

He'd been back for a week, and every day that passed he waited for her to bring up the subject of the Coach and Four. She'd told him everything else that first night, when they'd finally spent themselves making love and were curled in her bed, mugs of tea on the night table and the window cracked open to cool their heated skin. She'd come up with a charity Christmas bazaar and the possibility of an open mike night in the bar, since she'd heard Louise Gilchrist singing one night with an old friend of hers.

There was more, although he couldn't remember most of it at the moment. She'd mentioned the restaurant, of course, but never once had she said anything about him being the obvious choice as the new chef. Never once had she hinted about what his money could do by way of renovating the place.

And now, a week later, he was actually beginning to be—he winced to admit it—a bit hurt.

No promises, no commitments, he'd made sure she knew

that from the beginning. If not by saying so outright, then through sheer dint of saying nothing at all. Taught her well, he had—she was happy enough to have him in her bed, in her life, but she asked no questions and she made no demands.

Once, that would have suited him perfectly. Now . . .

He shut the magazine and sat forward, his elbows on his knees. Olivia looked up, curious but distracted. "You bored?" she said absently. "I just have to finish a few things here and then we can go out, if you want. Take a walk or get some lunch."

"Your call, love." He ran a hand through his hair as she turned back to the computer screen.

She was still the Olivia who'd knocked him over, literally and figuratively, but her agenda was definitely a bit fuller, wasn't it? Every time he turned around, it seemed, she had another scheme up her sleeve, another phone call to make, another to-do list scribbled on the back of an envelope.

Truth was, he was impressed. She was determined not to let her uncle intimidate her, and she was doing her damnedest to turn Callender House into a going concern.

It left him, however, feeling a bit like a lazy sod. He'd finally convinced her to let him cook the Thanksgiving meal next week, since it was just another day to him and would give the staff a much-needed rest.

"You'd do that?" she'd said, snuggling against him. "You *want* to do that? Because I'm sure I could figure out how to roast a few turkeys without burning anything down. I mean, it was my idea . . ." He'd finally silenced her with a firm kiss.

Bloody hell. She seemed to think he didn't want to do anything but shag her. A paranoid bloke would almost believe she didn't trust him with her sodding hotel.

Or her heart.

*       *       *

"Oh man, he's pissed," Davey said to Marty a few days later, snapping shut his cell phone. "I'm so fucking over this job. I mean, what the hell does he want us to do, burn the place down?"

They were sitting in a pizza place on Eighth Avenue. It was too warm inside compared to the frigid temperature outside, and the windows had fogged up with greasy steam. A blob of sauce had landed on Davey's shirt, too, but he hadn't noticed it.

Marty tore his gaze away from his friend and stared across the restaurant blindly. He was sick of the job, too. He'd pulled scams for Callender before, and roughed up a few people once or twice, but they'd deserved it.

He thought.

Olivia didn't deserve it. God, if he had a shot at a woman like her, he'd go to Mass every Sunday, just like his mother had always told him to. He'd fucking go to confession, even, although he hated to think of the number of Hail Marys he'd have to say just for swearing alone.

He'd never worked a job where he had to look someone in the eye every day and lie. Lie, and then make trouble for her, and lie some more. It was getting to him, and what was even more fucked up, it was getting to Davey, too.

Callender had all the money in the world, or at least that's what it looked like to Marty. What the hell did he need the hotel for? Okay, more money, and more money was never bad, but there were a million different ways to make it without screwing over his only relative.

Plus, he'd met a lot of the people who stayed at the hotel by now. The crazy little Russian lady was a hoot, as his mom would've said, and even the gay guys were pretty funny. They'd brought him a soda a couple of times when

Olivia had them all ripping up carpet on the third and fourth floors.

If someone was set on kicking his grandma out of the apartment building where she'd lived for thirty years . . . Well, in his family you didn't stand for that kind of shit. And if you were going to fight, you threw a punch and stood your ground, you didn't hide like a fucking coward and tie somebody's shoelaces together.

Or hire someone to do it for you.

He glanced down at the half eaten pizza on his paper plate and felt his stomach turn. Trouble was, his mom lived in one of Callender's buildings now. And Callender knew it.

"We better figure out something else to do," he told Davey. "Something to impress the asshole. Oh, and I gotta find a Duane Reade on the way across town. I need some antacids."


Limbo, Olivia had decided, was a pretty nice place to live. It was comfortable, at least. Not too hot, not too cold.

Well, maybe it was pretty hot, she thought the evening before Thanksgiving, turning over in bed and watching Rhys stride back from the bathroom, still gloriously naked. She never got tired of looking at his body, touching his body—he was all lean muscle, his abs and his shoulders sharply defined, his thighs gorgeously powerful, and his ass . . . She bit her lip, fighting a grin. And it was all hers.

Well, sort of. All hers for now. *Now* was a very important concept to keep in mind in limbo.

He'd come back, which was wonderful enough. Back to New York, to the hotel, to her. Even after winning, although that was still a secret only the two of them shared, he'd come back here, when he could have taken off for anywhere in the world. He'd missed her, and he certainly hadn't made any noises about moving on since he'd been back.

And that had to be enough, didn't it? She'd risen to the challenge of saving the hotel—she didn't want him to believe that she was waiting around for a white knight, for Callender House or for her. If what they had together wasn't going to be forever, well, she would live.

She could ask him to marry her, she'd thought one night, when he'd already dozed off, snoring gruffly beside her. She could ask him to . . . move in? Go steady? It was all so silly—she knew he wasn't seeing anyone else, and he all but lived in her apartment as it was. Even so, she knew she could take the reins, do the asking, be the one to fight for what she wanted.

She just wasn't sure she'd evolved quite that far yet. Especially when the idea of him saying no and leaving again made her ache in places she hadn't even known existed.

What she knew now was that she didn't need a daddy, or an uncle, or a grandfather. She didn't need a man to take care of things for her. But, oh God, how she wanted this one. Not to shelter her, but simply to love.

And she did love him, she thought as he sprawled on the bed beside her once more. They'd spent this afternoon in the kitchen, where he'd taught her how to make muffins and a coffee cake he intended to lay out for continental breakfast tomorrow. She'd decided to close the restaurant for the whole day, since they were serving dinner at two, and as if by magic every one of the usual dinner patrons, which meant Yelena and some of her local compatriots, had left word that they were eating at home tonight.

Sadly, there was no reason yet to expect an influx of other customers, so she'd given the staff off tonight, too. Rhys wanted to make pies for tomorrow—he'd left the makings out on the counter, in fact, so they could get the job done quickly. The amazing thing was that she knew it would be fun to watch him. Life with Rhys was never bor-

ing. She'd laughed harder making the muffins this afternoon than she had at the last funny movie she and Josie had
watched.

"You want to stay up here, love?" he murmured, trailing
a hand down her bare arm. "You look a bit knackered, and
I can handle a few pies easy-peasy. I am a trained chef, you
know."

He'd said that earlier today, and yesterday, too, and she
hated to admit that she wasn't quite getting the joke. So she
ignored it and said, "No, I want to come. Anyway, I'm hungry. We skipped dinner, you know."

"We did at that." He winked at her, and left a hot, hard
kiss on her belly. "Get your arse out of bed then, woman."

It took her a while to get dressed. She'd lost her bra
somewhere, and it turned out the cat had puked up a hair-
ball on her pants while she and Rhys were otherwise en-
gaged. Rhys sat on the bed watching, throwing out sly
comments about this shirt or that pair of jeans, judging
each on how well it showed off her body. "Oh yeah, those
are the right jeans, love. God, you've got a smashing behind, you know that?"

She was still rolling her eyes and batting his hands away
when they rode down to the lobby. They turned into the
hall leading to the kitchen, and found Marty and Davey
there, pale with surprise.

"What are you two doing?" she laughed, poking at
Marty's damp coveralls. "Work's over for the day, guys.
Take some time off and relax, you know?"

Rhys nodded and went into the kitchen without her, flipping on the light. "How about some pasta, love?" he called,
and walked into the pantry.

"Sure," she called back, and smiled at the guys. They'd fit
in pretty well on Angel's staff, even if they did tend to stick
together like Siamese twins. And they were always so ner-

vous around her, which she couldn't understand. Angel was their boss, for one thing, and she wasn't the yelling type, which they had to have figured out by now. "Are either of you coming to dinner tomorrow?" she asked. "You're more than welcome, as long as you don't show up with all twenty of your closest relatives. We're planning the meal for about fifty."

They answered in unison, a jumble of something about a grandmother and a girlfriend, so she shooed them home. She could hear Rhys running water in a pot. "Go on, guys. Clock out. It's a holiday."

Why did they look like she was the governor who'd just stayed their execution? She shrugged and wandered into the kitchen, where Rhys had already taken out a box of linguine and some fresh parmesan and tomato sauce he'd frozen a few days ago. "Ready to bake, Liv my love?"

She shook her head and pulled up a stool. "Can't I just watch? I think I flexed my culinary muscles quite enough for one day with those muffins."

He rolled his eyes. "Oh, excuse me, your highness. Rummage up some fresh basil for me, will you? Or is that going to be too, too exhausting?"

She smacked his rear end with a kitchen towel as she passed him to open the walk-in and stopped in surprise when the phone on the far wall rang. "Who on earth is that?"

"It's the house phone, love," Rhys said, squinting at the red light. "You want me to get it?"

"No, no." She tossed a package of fresh basil on the counter beside him and hurried to the phone. "This is Olivia."

"Oh, Olivia, thank God." It was Anna at the front desk, and she was whispering. "I tried your apartment but no one answered, and I didn't see you go out, and I thought Rhys mentioned something about making pie—"

"Anna," Olivia interrupted with a sigh. She was a sweet

kid, but Olivia was sure she was a wannabe actress. Any excuse for drama with Anna. "Is something wrong?"

"Um, is Rhys with you? There's a woman here requesting a room."

A woman? What did that have to do with Rhys? She glanced across the room, where he was busily chopping basil. "And the problem is?" she said evenly.

"She claims she's Rhys's mother."

Rhys's mother? Somehow, she'd never really given Rhys's family much thought. In her mind, he'd sort of sprung from a cabbage patch. A wickedly sexy British one, of course.

"What's her name?"

There was a pause, then papers shuffling, as well as a distinctly British and female voice in the background. "Um, Janet Spencer."

"Janet Spencer?" Olivia repeated.

And looked up in surprise to find Rhys swearing and clutching a bloody finger he'd apparently just sliced nearly in two.

Arms folded across his chest, Rhys stood to one side of the desk as Olivia helped Anna check in Janet Spencer.

She was . . . well, nothing like Rhys was putting it mildly, but she didn't want to be critical. In fact, she was afraid to say a word. Rhys was so furious, she practically had to smack him to get his finger wrapped before he marched into the lobby.

So many family relationships were screwed up, she shouldn't have been surprised at his reaction to his mother's name, but *screwed up* didn't quite seem to tell the story here.

"I tried to convince Gram to come," Janet was telling Rhys now, running a hand through hair that had been dyed a bright cherry red. "But you know how she is about her programs, and she's still never quite got the hang of flying, has she."

Rhys grunted in response.

Olivia shot a glance at him as the last of the paperwork spit out of the printer. The room was on the house, of course, which Rhys refused to accept. "Charge it to me," he'd hissed, and she'd nodded pleasantly while pretending to run his credit card. Damn it, she was going to have to have him pretend to sign for it, too.

"Are you not even going to give your old mum a hug?" Janet complained, crossing over to him and flicking a nonexistent speck from his shirt. Aside from the hair, she reminded Olivia of a hold-out hippie, in faded jeans and an Indian blouse, with sterling silver to rival Roseanne's jangling from her wrists and her ears. "Where are your manners, lovey?"

If Rhys scowled any harder, Olivia was afraid his face would actually crack under the pressure. Stiffly, as if he were being asked to embrace a rabid dog, he put one arm around his mother and squeezed her briefly before backing away. "It's late, Janet," he said. "For me, at least. I've got things to do in the kitchen. Someone'll see you upstairs, I wager."

He was gone before Olivia could say a word, and after a quick apology to Janet, she rushed after him. Anna would see the woman upstairs—they'd dispensed with the night porter long ago, since it was a wasted salary—and Olivia couldn't imagine any other unexpected arrivals tonight.

"What on earth was that about?" she said without thinking once she'd walked into the kitchen.

Rhys glared at her and went back to stirring the pot of pasta. "She wants something. That's why she's here."

"Maybe she simply wants to see you," Olivia said softly

and walked over to lay a hand on his arm. "Hey. You're beating those poor noodles to death, you know."

"She never *just* wants to see me," Rhys answered, but he put the spoon down and backed away from the range. "Believe me. I don't trust a word out of her mouth, especially not 'I love you.' "

He paced away from her, unconsciously flexing his injured finger. She wrapped her arms around herself and frowned, but waited until he'd turned to face her before speaking.

"Can you tell me why?"

He shook his head with a laugh that was too bitter to qualify as humor. "Why? Because she's lied to me all my life. She and Gram both." He came closer, his eyes as dark as smoke and blazing with fury. "Do you know until I was thirteen, I thought she was my sister? I'd called my gran 'Mum' all my life, and her Janet, all because she got herself knocked up at sixteen and didn't want to be a parent yet. Convinced my gran to raise me as her own, which worked just fine till I found my birth certificate when I was scrounging about in drawers for an odd pound or two."

Without realizing it, Olivia had clapped a hand to her mouth in shock. She bit the inside of her cheek when she felt tears well up, trying to stop them.

It was too late, though. Rhys had seen, and it had only made him angrier. "Your pasta's almost ready," he muttered and turned away.

# Chapter 19

Staring into the kitchen's walk-in the next morning, Rhys blinked. He hadn't slept well, and Olivia had tossed and turned like a leaf in a storm all night, too. He was knackered, out of sorts, and in need of another cup of coffee, immediately.

Maybe he was hallucinating. It happened, yeah? It wasn't unheard of. If he took a step back and cleared his head, he'd be all right, wouldn't he?

Except that when he did, shaking his head and shutting the walk-in door before trying again, the six fresh turkeys he'd bought yesterday morning were still missing.

They'd been right there, on the bottom shelf. He'd put them there himself when the market had delivered the order. Where the hell had six turkeys got off to?

He was scrambling, pulling apart the walk-in, making a hash of the vegetable bins and the other perishables, when Olivia walked in.

"Hey," she said softly, poking her head inside. "You were already gone when I woke up, and I—what are you doing?"

"Trying to find the sodding turkeys," he muttered, waving a handful of fresh parsley at her. "They've gone missing somehow."

Her mouth dropped open. "What do you mean, missing?"

"Exactly what I said," be barked. Guilt stabbed at him when he saw how she winced, and he straightened up to take her hand. "I'm sorry, love. I don't know what the hell happened. I didn't notice them missing last night when I put the pies away, but I was a bit distracted, yeah?"

She looked up, brow furrowed in thought. "The only time I was in here was to get the basil, but then the phone rang. If they were gone then, I certainly didn't notice."

"Who would steal turkeys?" He smacked the cold walk-in door furiously. "And what the hell are we supposed to feed fifty people expecting the sodding birds in all their glory?"

"The stores should be open, at least for a little while," Olivia said. "We'll just have to buy some more."

It sounded simple. It sounded logical, in fact. Crikey, he did need more sleep. It was New York. The shops wouldn't be shut, even today. Hell, he could get a shot of espresso while he was out.

He left Olivia preparing stuffing—with explicit, written instructions—and headed out into the gray, windy morning, determined to think of nothing but the sodding turkeys and the day ahead.

Anything but his mother. Even if she would insist on joining them for the meal.

And an hour later, Olivia was right where he'd left her, a fresh cup of coffee by her elbow, her hair piled on top of her head and cornbread crumbs dusting the front of her shirt. He was so frustrated and angry, he felt like whisking her upstairs for a long, lazy day in bed and calling off the whole meal.

"Success?" she said with a hopeful smile.

He held up three plastic carrier bags and shrugged. "To-furkey."

"Is . . . interesting," Yelena pronounced at dinner. "Different." She gave him a brilliant smile from beneath a silk turban fastened with a peacock brooch.

"It's utter shite," he leaned over to whisper, and she patted his hand.

"Stuffing is good." She shrugged. "And potatoes very good. Is just one meal, my love."

He couldn't help grinning at the way she pronounced the word—*luff*. He'd grown quite fond of the old bird.

And she was right, it was just one meal. Of course, it was meant to be a feast, a callback to a holiday tradition centuries old, and he was quite certain that tofu had no place at the Pilgrims' original meal. But oddly enough, no one seemed to mind.

Willie and Helen and Angel had rearranged the dining room to create five tables of ten, in a rough semicircle. By 1:30, everyone had gathered to sample the crudités and warm gougeres he'd set out, mingling around the piano and laughing as Olivia opened wine. Everyone had come, even eagle-beaked Mr. Mortimer, in a dour black suit and a red bow tie.

Frank and Delancey were there, Gus and Josie, of course, Louise Gilchrist and the sweet old Tartollas, a retired couple who had lived in the building since before Olivia was born. Angel had brought Theresa and the baby, who was still so pink and new, she looked a bit like a wax doll when she was sleeping, and Roseanne and Maribel and much of the staff. Everyone had dressed for the occasion, and Olivia had lit candles and graced the piano with great pots of fall mums and baby pumpkins.

It was quite nice, really, he reflected, sipping his wine as he sat back in his chair. Except for the utter horror of the tofurkey.

And his mother.

She'd latched onto Stanley Whitehead, Roseanne's assistant, and the poor man looked absolutely baffled. She'd worn one of her Indian caftans, and the big bell sleeves flapped at him every time she gestured.

Beside him, Olivia leaned forward to catch his eye. She'd put on a soft brown dress that clung to her curves, and a pair of amber earrings that caught the candlelight. "It's delicious, you know. Really."

"Don't lie," he said with a rueful laugh. "Not now."

A faint smile played around her mouth. "Well, I didn't say the tofurkey was delicious, precisely. But everything else is. And I can't wait for pie."

He slid his arm around her shoulders and pulled her closer. "I'm in the mood for another dessert entirely," he whispered, and grinned when she flushed scarlet.

"Oh, look at my naughty son," Janet said from across the table with a boozy laugh. "Save the snogging for later, lad. You're embarrassing poor Olivia."

He didn't think it was possible for Olivia to turn any pinker, but she did. His mum, meanwhile, was blissfully ignorant of the uncomfortable silence that had settled around the table. As usual.

What the hell was she doing here, anyway? She didn't know he'd won the competition, no one but Olivia did, so if she was sniffing around for money, she was grabbing at straws. Maternal love didn't enter into the equation—they'd gone months and months without seeing each other, which was always fine with him, but usually ended when she wanted something from him, like a bit of dosh or the use of his car or, once, an introduction to the owner of a restaurant where he was working, since she thought he was "quite dishy."

Josie piped up with an offer to pass round the potatoes for second helpings, and the rest of the table gratefully chimed in with thanks, which covered the awkward silence quite well. Olivia had taken his hand beneath the table and squeezed it hard. "It's okay," she murmured.

He shook his head. "It's not. I don't even know what she's doing here."

Drunk or not, his mum still had her hearing. She glanced up from the sweet potato puff she was examining and rolled her eyes with a weary sigh. "I'm here to visit with my only child. A naughty boy who never comes to see his mum anymore, I'll have you know," she informed the table at large.

Bloody hell. If the woman ruined this meal for Olivia, he'd have her head. "Why don't you come with me, Mum," he said, pushing his chair away from the table. "Let's go visit in the bar, yeah?"

"What's wrong with right here, love?" She pushed hair out of her eyes and sat back. "We're having a lovely meal, there's no need to scarper off just to chat."

Sod it all. He'd seen her like this before. She needed to be the center of attention and had long ago decided that since she hadn't made anything of her miserable life, she would bask in her son's success. She wanted to be the honored guest today—she'd probably clapped her hands in glee when she realized she'd arrived just in time for a big holiday meal.

And ten to one, she'd come only because she needed money, or one of her wanker boyfriends had roughed her up or caught her cheating.

"Mum, I've got something to show you," he offered, making his tone as pleasant as possible and rounding the table to pull her chair back. "Come on. We'll be back for pie."

"Do you see the shabby treatment I get?" Janet said this with a little laugh, playing it for effect, but there was a layer of bitterness beneath her words. "I had to ask the lad to give me a hug last night, yeah? And here I am splashing out for a plane ticket just to see him."

"One way, I warrant," Rhys said with a shake of his head. Fury had made a hard, hot knot in his gut. "Counting on me to send you off again, aren't you? First class, no doubt."

"Rhys . . ." Olivia had stood up, despair etched into her face.

"It's all right, love." He managed to keep his voice even, but when he lowered his head to speak to his mother, he didn't bother to disguise the venom in it. "You're making a bloody fool of yourself. If you had a lick of sense, you'd get up and leave the room this minute."

He straightened up, ignoring the hot flush on Janet's face and locked eyes with Olivia. "I'm taking a walk."

Josie was the one to hustle Olivia into the kitchen, but not until after Janet had staggered out after Rhys, her caftan fluttering like a white flag of surrender. "It's all right, honey," Josie said, pouring her another glass of wine and thrusting it into her hands. "It's not a holiday unless there's family dysfunction, right?"

Olivia couldn't help a snort of surprise at that. "You're right. I just hate to see Rhys this way, even if I do understand him a little better."

"Yeah, well, remind me never to introduce you to my mother," Josie said with a smile. "You okay? You want some help with the pies?"

"That would be good." Leaning over, she rested her cheek against Josie's. "Thanks."

They carried the pies out together—pumpkin, apple, and pecan, with a bonus spice cake Rhys had whipped up at the last minute—to a roomful of applause, and Olivia let a warm rush of gratitude spill over her. These were her people, her family, and maybe it was the wine, but she loved them with her whole heart at the moment. This was happiness.

Or it would have been, if Rhys hadn't been off somewhere brooding.

Still, the show, such as it was, had to go on. She watched the door for him as she opened more wine, and nodded in agreement when Roseanne offered to get coffee and tea going, and finally sat down with a sliver of each pie on her plate. Despite the horror of the tofurkey, she was actually pretty full, but the pies were too perfect to resist.

"Oh my God, so good," Frank moaned after a bite of the pecan. "The man should . . . well, he should be a chef!"

"He could definitely go into the pie business," Angel's Theresa remarked, forking up an enormous bite of pumpkin.

"Speaking of business," Olivia said to Delancey, "we need to talk about this shop idea some more. Gus and I discussed it the other day, and I think it's wonderful."

"What shop?" Yelena demanded. She'd brought an embossed silver flask of vodka downstairs with her, and added a generous splash to her hot tea.

Frank raised an eyebrow, but Olivia just laughed. "Frank and Delancey have started a soap business, and we're talking about them opening an exclusive shop here in the building."

"Soap? What kind of soap?"

Frank gave her the rundown while Olivia ate her pie, and

when he was done, Yelena announced, "Is brilliant! I open a shop, too, then!"

Choking on a bite of apple pie, Olivia held a napkin to her mouth and blinked at her. "What do you mean, you open a shop, too?"

"A tea room." Warming to her idea, Yelena sat up straighter, her turban bobbing as she nodded her head. "Yes, a real Russian tea room. Not like restaurant, no. Just good strong tea and maybe coffee, pastries. Perfect."

Josie caught Olivia's eye across the table and lifted her shoulders in question. It was actually kind of a good idea, Olivia thought with surprise. Tea lounges were more popular every day, and they could accommodate a crowd in one of the big rooms on the second floor. In fact, one of them was situated above the kitchen, with the service stairs nearby—renovating the room to add the kind of facilities a tea shop would need would probably be easy.

"Writers love coffee places," Louise Gilchrist put in with a nod of her head. "And if you decorate with a Russian scheme, it would suit the new look of the lobby."

She was right, Olivia thought in amazement, even though Yelena had chirped, "Tea! *Zavarka*, from a samovar!"

"I know a writer who would love a place like that," Gus said with a quiet smile, and Josie put her arm around him.

"I wrote a novel," Mr. Mortimer said, surprising them all. He'd barely spoken during the meal, which wasn't unusual, and Olivia took a surreptitious peek over his shoulder to see if he'd had some wine.

"You did?" Gus asked him with genuine interest.

"It's an erotic novel about ancient Egypt," Mr. Mortimer said, and it took Olivia a moment to realize he'd said it with an entirely straight face.

She glowered at Josie, who was hiding behind her napkin

in an attempt to keep from laughing. Gus merely looked stunned.

Before Olivia could think of any kind of response to his statement, Mr. Mortimer cleared his throat and added, "I've often thought this hotel is the kind of place that would be perfectly suited to a writer's retreat. Not everyone wants to head off to the mountains with a portable typewriter, you know."

"No, they don't," Olivia agreed, but her mind was racing ahead, picturing a whole floor renovated to accommodate a writers' colony of sorts, with a common room or a dining room, and Internet access, and . . .

"There's quite a history of literary tradition in the hotel, you know." Mr. Mortimer seemed to be enjoying the conversation—his pale cheeks were warm with color and his eyes were actually sparkling.

"There is?" Josie asked, truly interested this time. She put down her napkin and leaned forward.

"Oh yeah," Olivia said, with a fond laugh. "Writers of all kinds have stayed here over the years. Gus, and Mr. Mortimer here, are just our latest additions."

"Has anyone ever written down any of the stories about them, and the other people who have stayed here?" Gus asked, so suddenly that he spilled his water glass as he sat up straight.

Olivia shook her head. "I keep meaning to write things down, and I think my father made notes here or there in some of the records, but that's it."

Roseanne glanced up from the end of the nearby table, where she had rocked baby Isabella to sleep against her shoulder. "Tell them about the sword swallowers, honey. Everyone likes that story."

"No, no, the one about Frank Sinatra in the bar that

night with Mia Farrow, before they were married," Angel argued as he stroked his daughter's peach fuzz head over Roseanne's shoulder.

"What about Evelyn Nesbit staying here for a while in 1920?" Maribel offered. She stared into her empty wineglass wistfully. "Or was it 1921? She had such a sad life."

Gus's eyes widened and Olivia smiled at him. "Evelyn Nesbit stayed here?" he said.

She shrugged. "She was just one of many. Callender House actually has a fascinating history."

He nodded, and then got up without warning and walked out of the room, mumbling to himself.

"Is he coming back?" Josie said in confusion.

"You're asking me?" Olivia laughed. She pushed away from the table and groaned. She was past full, and on her way to the expected post-Thanksgiving drowsiness. "What got into him?"

At the next table, Mr. Mortimer tapped his temple with one long, bony finger. "Ideas."

"Well, another writer would know, I guess." Josie stood up and brushed off her skirt. "I think I'm going to check on him, though."

"And it's probably time to clean up," Olivia said with a sigh. The tables were littered with plates and wineglasses, serving bowls and platters, and the thought of leaving it all until tomorrow morning was very tempting.

Willie jumped up, with Helen and Maribel on either side of him. "No cleaning up for you, Olivia," he said, beaming at her across the table. "We wanted to thank you for having us, so we're cleaning up. Really. Go relax and enjoy yourself."

Oh, thank God. She grinned at them, but the truth was that cleaning up would have at least taken her mind off Rhys. Janet had never reappeared, and she didn't know whether that meant they were arguing somewhere or if Janet had given up and taken herself off to her room.

She wanted to give the woman the benefit of the doubt, but she hated the way she'd ruined dinner for Rhys. He hadn't gotten to hear any of the new ideas for the hotel. He hadn't even gotten any pie.

If she could have, she would have swooped in to rescue him this time. The problem was he needed to be saved from himself. From doubts and fears that had grown up right along with him, with good reason. There was nothing to do about that but make sure he knew he could trust her.

After leaning down to give Yelena a hug good night, she turned to leave the room—and found Rhys in the doorway, holding Uncle Stuart by the elbow like a child dragged off to detention.

"Look what I found lurking about outside," he said, his mouth set in a tight line. "One of our missing turkeys."

# Chapter 20

Olivia's heart pounded as she stared across the dining room at her uncle, dressed in his usual dull gray suit, which he'd accessorized with a glare of undisguised malice. "What are you doing here?"

"I wasn't *here*," he spat out, wrenching his arm out of Rhys's grip. He brushed off his lapels and took a step sideways, still glowering. "I was taking a walk. This street is still a public place, I'll have you know."

She raised her eyebrows in disbelief. "You live on Eighty-Seventh Street," she pointed out, "and your office is on Thirty-First Street. Either way, that's some walk on a chilly holiday afternoon."

"My exercise habits are none of your concern," Stuart said stiffly, and behind her Roseanne chuckled out loud.

"I don't give a flying fuck where or when you exercise," Rhys said in a low, dangerous voice, "but I do care what you do to this hotel, and to Olivia. Or at least what you pay others to do." He stalked closer to Stuart, and the effect was immediate—Stuart drew himself up to his full height, which was still a good five inches shorter than Rhys's six feet, and paled considerably.

"I don't know what you're talking about." His voice was

still as stiff as his posture, but his gaze bounced around the room, searching for a friendly face, if not an exit.

"I was taking a walk myself when I got a call on my mobile," Rhys explained, his tone silky but still unmistakably dangerous. "From a bloke by the name of Marty Kinsella, in fact."

Olivia gasped. Marty?

"Oh crap," she whispered aloud, looking at Rhys. "Last night, outside the kitchen . . ."

He nodded. "Seems they were recommended through a friend of your uncle's here. And he recommended them strictly to ensure he would have a few spies on the inside, as well as people he could ask to perform a bit of sabotage now and then."

"Olivia, I swear, I didn't know anything about this," Angel protested. He was pale and furious and had leapt to his feet as if he were about to march out and track the guys down.

She waved a hand at him. "Hey, I thought they were good guys, too. They were always here, always willing to help . . ."

"Well, that's the rub, you see," Rhys added. He was circling Stuart now, his hands behind his back, disgust written all over his face. "Your hired hands have had a change of heart. Today, it seems, the spirit of Thanksgiving got the better of them, and they decided to confess their sins. Apparently, six turkeys will be returned here tomorrow after a bit of holiday in Davey's mother's deep freeze."

"Idiots," Stuart muttered. He'd gotten his color back, but fury would do that to a person.

Olivia was pretty sure she was a nice mad red, as well. "You hired them to make trouble here? What exactly did you think they were going to do?"

"Oh, Christ, Olivia, I don't have to explain myself to

you," Stuart spat, but he flinched when Rhys glowered at him. "Don't you get it? You're a ridiculous child who's been given a toy much too expensive to play with. You don't know the first thing about making a profit, and you're just as nostalgic and absurdly sentimental as your father."

For a moment, Olivia was convinced Rhys was actually going to punch him. She could practically hear his blood boiling. Running across the room, she laid a hand on his arm and urged him backward a few steps.

"I'm sorry, and this is your business how?" she said evenly. She was sure it wasn't the wine this time—she wasn't in the least bit afraid of the man, and she wasn't positive that all of his efforts to intimidate her had been nothing more than some half-assed attempt to get himself out of trouble.

"You've screwed up, haven't you?" she said softly, staring him down. "You need the money from the sale of this place, you don't just want it. And since you have no legal basis for taking this hotel away from me, you thought you could simply scare me off like some little kid."

She could actually feel the pride in Rhys's grin, but for the moment she ignored it. "Did you really think a few overflowing toilets and some spilled paint was going to do it?" She shook her head, enjoying the powerful wave of outrage when he scowled back at her. "This place is my life, Stuart. My home, my family, my whole world. You might have scared me once, but you can't anymore. I have plans for this place, big plans. Shops, maybe a writer's retreat, renovating the restaurant, all kinds of things. And whether or not they succeed is my business. *Mine.* And I swear to you, I'll eat all of those missing turkeys myself before you ever see a dime from this hotel."

Behind her, the room burst into noisy applause, and she flushed with pleasure. And triumph, too. Because Stuart had actually slumped in defeat, all the hot air hissing out of his stiff frame like a deflated balloon.

"It'll never work, you know," Stuart insisted. A last-ditch effort to spread the hate, she guessed. "You need the backing of one of the big chains. You're going to sink cash into this place and never see it again."

"Well, at least she'll have some free labor for awhile," Rhys put in slyly. "Marty and Davey would like to keep their jobs, without pay, to make up for the trouble they caused. Since 'Olivia rocks,' as they say, and Mr. Callender is a . . . 'nasty old ass-wipe,' I believe were the words they used."

Olivia laughed at that, and the rest of the room joined her. Stuart was spluttering with rage, but when he protested that he was sure they wouldn't want his pay, Rhys shook his head. "No, they're quite willing to take your money, you idiot. Rather stupid of you to pay them so much in advance, don't you agree?"

Stuart pushed past him to leave, muttering to himself, but Rhys grabbed his arm. "One more thing, old man. Anything happens to those friends and relatives of Marty and Davey who live in your buildings, and you'll hear from me about it."

Stuart wrenched away again and stalked out, and Olivia threw her arms around Rhys.

"That was . . . incredible," she murmured, stretching up on tiptoe to kiss him.

His arms tightened around her. "I didn't do a thing, love. Just the messenger, over here. You've saved the day yourself, and pretty handily, I should say."

"I wonder why Marty called you instead of me," she said, leading him to a pair of empty chairs at the nearest table.

"I think he was too ashamed to tell you the truth," Rhys

said gently. "He nearly stumbled over himself a dozen times, trying to explain how sorry the two of them are."

"How did they get your cell phone number?" she wondered, sitting beside him, their hands still linked.

He gave her a tired smile. "They called the front desk, and Rob gave it to them when they asked. Some things work properly around here, you know."

"Rob!" she said, standing up. "I hope someone brought him a plate of food."

"Roseanne did, long ago, love." He sat back, his eyes dark and smoky again.

"You need some pie," she murmured, leaning toward him. She put her hands on his thighs as she watched his face. He looked so tired, and strangely sad.

"I'm all right, love." He kissed her forehead. "I think I'm going to go upstairs, yeah?"

She watched him walk out of the room, her heart sinking. What had just happened?

She loved him. God, she loved so much it hurt a little bit, in good places and bad ones. It was all she could give him, but she had no idea if it was what Rhys wanted.

When Olivia didn't come to bed by eleven, Rhys walked out of her apartment and shut the door behind him. She'd given him a key when he got back from L.A., and as he stepped onto the lift he fingered it gingerly.

Keys. Such a perfect symbol, yeah? They opened doors, and locked them. The person with the key was given power, wasn't he?

Strange that he didn't feel that way.

The hotel was hushed and mostly dark now, all the party-goers off to their beds—or the beds of their loved ones. Janet, he assumed, was passed out on hers, as she'd stopped ringing his mobile a few hours ago.

He'd have to bundle her back to London tomorrow, whether she liked it or not. The plane fare was nothing, if it meant she was safely across the pond. His life was here now, one way or another.

Tonight, he'd find out if he would live it with Olivia.

He found her in the deserted dining room, where just one row of sconces had been left lit. She was sitting at the piano with a glass of wine, her shoes abandoned on the floor beside her.

She was so beautiful. Well, he knew that the minute he picked himself up off the sidewalk, didn't he? But she was so much more than the dreamy princess in the tower he'd imagined her to be. Woman had an impressive vein of iron in her bones, and a heart as big as the planet. And she'd shared it with him so generously, he'd begun to forget that women like Clodagh existed in the same world.

He wanted nothing more than to take her in his arms, kiss her breathless, and whisper nonsensical words of love to her all night, just to hear her giggle. He wanted nothing more than her, for the rest of his life.

But she hadn't come up to bed, even now that the party was over and the dining room was empty, and he didn't have a clue why.

He walked into the room just as she plinked out a tune on the piano, smiling to herself in the dim light.

"Do you play?" he asked.

He'd startled her—her fingers landed heavily on the keys. "Rhys! I thought you went to bed."

"I was waiting for you," he said and sat down when she made room for him on the polished mahogany bench. "What are you doing down here in the dark?"

"Thinking." She looked up at him, and her eyes were full of questions, doubts, even fears.

She didn't deserve to feel any of that. He'd been the one

to doubt her, when she'd given him no cause. He'd been the one to hold back, when she'd opened her heart and her home to him. He was the one who needed to explain—and tell her how much he loved her.

Instead he said, "Why didn't you ask me, Liv? Why didn't you ask me?"

Bloody hell. He hadn't meant to say *that*.

She blinked in surprise. "Ask you what?"

"To take over the restaurant." He stood up and paced away from her, feeling like a total git, but wanting her answer just the same.

She set down her wineglass and got up, hurrying across the room in her stocking feet. Taking his hands, she pulled him to a stop and waited until he was looking at her to speak.

"Are you kidding?" she said.

That stung. "No! I'm not kidding," he said. "I was a bit taken aback, you know, reading about your plans in the newspaper instead of hearing about it from you, and then . . ." He stopped and shook his head. He felt like a stupid git, and now he sounded like one, too.

"I guess I thought you knew, or assumed . . ." she began, and shook her head. "There have been so many things I wanted to tell you, but I never knew what we were doing, where it would go . . . I kept reminding myself to be happy with *now*, you know? Not to think about the future. Not when I didn't have any idea what your plans were."

"You thought about the future?" he asked, trailing his fingers down her arm gently. "Our future?"

She bit her bottom lip. "Rhys . . ."

"I have, you know," he told her. "I haven't thought of much else in the past few weeks. Out in Los Angeles, I couldn't keep you out of my head. I kept thinking about what you were doing here in this blasted old place, what you were probably painting, what you were planning, when you might be sleeping . . ."

She turned her eyes up to him. The doubt was still there, a dark flicker, but hope was shining brighter. "You thought about all that?"

"I did." He put his arms around her, leaning down to whisper into her hair, "The day I came back, I didn't think I would survive until I got you upstairs where I could say hello to you properly."

He could feel her pleased blush, and her arms circled his waist, her fingers hooking in his belt loops.

"But, you see, that's why I was confused," he went on. "I came back, and you were talking about a whole new restaurant, and then you didn't ask me to help . . ." He let his words trail off into the quiet room. Yeah, he still sounded like a git. A helpless, hopeless git who'd fallen in love so hard, he was still dizzy.

"I . . . well, I wanted to do everything on my own, you know?" Olivia murmured, pulling away far enough to look at him. "You taught me that, somewhere along the way. That I had to wake up and look around and take charge of my life." She pulled away entirely then, her brow screwed up as she chose her words. "It was like a dream, you know? My whole life before I met you, just one long fantasy or memory, holed up here and not really paying attention to . . . well, anything. And when you made love to me . . ." She bit her bottom lip again, shy. "Well, it woke me up somehow. Everything was clearer, brighter, *real*. And as much as you seemed like some knight in shining armor, I knew I couldn't depend on a fairy tale ending."

"But I was here," he said, his voice thick with emotion. "I came back."

"Without one word about what it meant," she reminded

him gently. "Without one word about what you were going to do when it was announced that you won."

He deserved that, he knew. He shook his head, but she took his hand and pulled him back to her again.

"I'd thought about you running the restaurant practically since we met. How wonderful it would be, how perfect. But, well, when the time came I didn't know if you would say yes. And I couldn't bear to hear no." Her eyes shone with tears.

"But I was the obvious choice, yeah? I mean, I have the money to sink into the place, and I'm a sodding chef!" He shook his head, still incredulous. "I won the blasted competition. I just assumed . . ."

"The worst?" she said softly, her breath warm against his chest. "That people who love you want something from you? That no one *really* loves you, that all they want is what you can do for them?"

"Maybe," he admitted. He swung her into his arms, pulling her off her feet to bury his face in that glossy cloud of hair. "Doesn't matter now. I love you, Liv. I want to . . . well, I'd like you to consider me as a chef for the new restaurant. Please."

She was laughing, actually laughing—he could feel the gentle vibration of it against his throat.

"What's so funny?" he demanded. "I'm serious."

"I just . . ." She collapsed in giggles again. "I know you are."

Crikey, the woman had cheek. "Then why are you laughing?"

"You want me to consider you?" she said after a breath. "Are you kidding? I can't think of anything better. I just told you I've been dreaming about this for weeks."

"Well, it never hurts to be sure," he said with a sullen

pout, but she didn't let him get away with it, and smacked him on the shoulder.

"Believe me, I'm sure."

"You mean it?" he murmured, setting her down and kissing his way up her slender throat, along her jaw, the round curve of her cheek.

"Oh, I mean it," she whispered, and her head fell back as he steered her toward the closest table and laid her down on it. "Rhys . . ."

"Quiet, love, I'm rather busy," he said, sliding his hands up the soft fabric of her dress's skirt, revealing her long, slender legs in their silky stockings.

She made one of the vague little noises he adored, but she didn't protest when he reached up to tug her stockings down. He feathered breathy kisses down her thighs as he went, smiling when she trembled.

It was when he hooked his fingers into the waistband of her panties that she angled up on her elbows and looked at him from beneath her lashes.

"What are you doing?"

"Having my dessert," he whispered, and prepared to feast.

# Chapter 21

"Shh, it's coming back from commercial!"
"Someone pass the pretzels, please."
"Be quiet, it's on!"

It was two weeks later, and the hotel bar was crowded with staff and friends as the finale of *Fork in the Road* aired. Olivia glanced up from her stool at Rhys—he was behind the bar, overwhelmed by the attention. Gus had given him a baseball cap the other day, and he was wearing it now with the brim down low, over his eyes.

Tommy reached out with the remote control and turned up the volume on the big TV mounted to the wall. "Come on now, folks, quiet," he bellowed. "I've got the man of the hour back here, you know."

Rhys, it was interesting to discover, could blush, too.

She almost hated knowing the outcome of the competition already. For one thing, it had been hard not to crow about Rhys's success when the first of the two-part episode aired last week. They'd all watched that one here in the bar, too, to hoots of approval and generous applause when Rhys first appeared on screen.

"He was born to be a star," Frank had said wisely. "I can see him with his own show on that food channel now, you know. Huge hit, definitely. The women viewers would just eat him up."

Her eyes had widened at that idea, but Frank had patted her hand gently. "Never fear, sweetheart. The man is completely gone on you, and you know it."

That same day, she and Rhys had walked around the tenth floor, deciding on a new apartment.

"I love your place, Liv, but it's a bit cramped, yeah?" he'd said one morning shortly after Thanksgiving, when he'd tripped over his suitcase and spilled a full mug of coffee into the cat's bowl. Eloise hadn't slept for days.

He was right, of course. He'd checked out of his room the morning after Thanksgiving, and despite his relative lack of stuff, he was a huge male presence in her small space. And as much as she loved the cozy little place she'd made for herself, a studio was too small for the two of them. *The two of us.* It was still such a wonderful novelty to repeat the words to herself that she found herself doing it in the shower, at her desk, even on the street when she was out at the drug store or off to the library.

And it wasn't just a dream this time. Rhys had spent a day on the phone with a few friends and a shipping company and had arranged to sell some of his things, and ship the rest of it to the hotel. When the shipment arrived, they were going to move into the apartment she had grown up in.

"It won't be weird?" he'd asked her, when she'd opened the door to the big two-bedroom apartment she had loved as a child. She'd only moved out of it when she was in college, and trying to be "on her own" even if she was living in the same building as her father.

"It will be wonderful," she'd told him, and given him the tour of the spacious apartment, with its working fireplace in the large living room, its generous, if slightly outdated kitchen, and the two good-sized bedrooms with their view of Madison Avenue.

"We can renovate the kitchen, if you want," she'd told him, "although you will have the big kitchen downstairs to play in."

"Maybe I'll treat myself and get an Aga for in here." His eyes had lit up at the thought, even though she wasn't exactly sure what he was talking about it. "A bigger fridge, too. I don't want to be running downstairs every time I feel like making you pancakes."

"No pancakes," she'd groaned, slumping against the counter with a laugh. "Living with you is going to make me as big as a house."

"I know quite a few ways to work off calories," he'd promised with the wicked grin that melted her every time.

And then he'd proceeded to show her one of them, right there on the bare floor in front of the fireplace.

The memory washed over her in a warm rush, and she reached for her drink to hide the color on her cheeks. Josie didn't miss it, though—she leaned over and whispered, "Penny for your thoughts. No, wait. Make that a whole dollar."

"Wouldn't you like to know?" Olivia teased her.

"Actually, screw that," Josie said, flipping her ponytail over her shoulder with a pleased smirk. "I have my own thoughts, don't I?"

Olivia nearly spit her drink all over the bar. She certainly did. Josie and Gus had become inseparable.

He was working on a history of the hotel, it turned out. "A history of the hotel, but also of the city, as it changed, and really the world," he'd said a few days after Thanksgiving, scribbling in a spiral-bound notebook as he talked to her over coffee in her office. "I want to trace societal trends and world events through the guests that stayed here, through the hotel's changing amenities and traditions."

Okay. She wasn't really sure how he was going to do all of that, but she was more than happy to spend her lunch hour with him every few days, pulling out stories she hadn't told or even thought about in years. Roseanne and Josie had helped him cull through dusty boxes of old records, Josie swearing all the while that every once in a while a good bonfire wouldn't have hurt.

But she was happy to help Gus, and happy for him. "I think he was worried that he didn't have another book in him," she'd told Olivia one day when they'd escaped the hotel to treat themselves to manicures and lunch downtown. "And it was right there under his nose the whole time."

Not unlike Josie's feelings for Gus, Olivia thought privately. She'd been so cynical about men in general, about the possibility of love, that she'd never even considered looking at a truly nice guy until he was right in front of her.

"Bloody hell, this is embarrassing," Rhys muttered, slouching over the bar, a pint of Guinness untouched in front of him. "Look at me up there. I'm a complete git on telly."

He was anything but, Olivia thought, reaching over to touch his hand. On the screen, he was even more arresting, especially when the cameras were trained on him while he cooked, all concentration and focus, his eyes narrowed as he seared a piece of meat or chopped an onion with surgical precision. Her heart squeezed as she watched him on the TV, lining up with the other two finalists to face the judges. The intensity in his eyes was impressive—she would have hated to be one of the contestants trying to win against him.

Gus looked up from the notebook he was carrying

around night and day now, blinking in the dim light of the bar. "Is this it? Is this the end?"

"I'll let you know, sweetie," Josie told him, shaking her head. "It's going to be a long couple of months until this book is done."

Rhys grinned, and leaned over to whisper in Olivia's ear, "I don't think she minds a bit, do you?"

Olivia grinned right back and shook her head. "Not at all."

"Shh, they're going to announce who won," Roseanne barked from the other end of the bar, and all eyes turned to the screen.

"The dessert was the finishing touch," one of the judges was saying. "Showcasing all those American flavors with the pecans and the peaches, you really pulled out a show-stopper for the finale."

The camera panned to Rhys's reaction, and Olivia's heart raced. *Silly,* she thought. *I know he wins.* But he looked so strangely vulnerable as he waited. His jaw was set in determination, as if he was sure to win by sheer will power alone, but the tension of the competition showed in his tired, uncertain eyes.

"After much deliberation," Paula Chase said slowly, "we'd like to announce that *Fork in the Road* has a winner. And the winner is . . . Rhys Spencer."

The bar exploded in applause and rowdy cheers of congratulations, and Rhys sketched a bow, grinning like a fool all the while. Olivia pushed up over the bar to throw her arms around him. "Congratulations," she whispered.

"You already knew I won, silly girl," he whispered back.

"So I just like to touch you," she said with a laugh, and kissed him hard.

"Tell us, Rhys Spencer, are you going to Disneyworld?"

Tommy asked, chortling at his own joke as he held a fake microphone up to Rhys's mouth.

Rhys blinked in confusion. "Going where now?"

Olivia snorted, and waved Tommy away. "Leave the poor Brit alone," she said. "He's not going anywhere."

"How does it feel to win such a huge prize," Josie asked, beaming at Rhys from the circle of Gus's arm.

"Good," Rhys admitted. He took Olivia's hand and kissed it gently. "But I'd already won something better."

Damn the stupid blushing, she thought, smiling at Rhys. One day it would stop. Until then she was just going to have to get used it.

Rhys came out from behind the bar, shaking hands and accepting congratulations along the way. When he reached her, he swooped her in a bear hug that aroused another round of applause. He set her down just as Declan poked his head into the bar from his post at the front door.

"Um, Olivia?" he said, his eyes scanning the noisy crowd. "I hate to tell you this, but the nameplate outside? Just fell down again."

Olivia rolled her eyes as Rhys burst into laughter. Well, she couldn't win them all.

Take a look at Sylvia Day's
PASSION FOR THE GAME,
available now from Brava!

"Do not be fooled by her outward appearance. Yes, she is short of stature and tiny, but she is an asp waiting to strike."

Christopher St. John settled more firmly in his seat, disregarding the agent of the Crown who shared the box with him. His eyes were riveted to the crimson-clad woman who sat across the theater expanse. Having spent his entire life living amongst the dregs of society, he knew affinity when he saw it.

Wearing a dress that gave the impression of warmth and bearing the coloring of hot-blooded Spanish sirens, Lady Winter was nevertheless as icy as her title. And his *assignment* was to warm her up, ingratiate himself into her life, and then learn enough about her to see her hanged in his place.

A distasteful business, that. But a fair trade in his estimation. He was a pirate and thief by trade, she a bloodthirsty and greedy vixen.

"She has at least a dozen men working for her," Viscount Sedgewick said. "Some watch the wharves, others roam the countryside. Her interest in the agency is obvious and deadly. With your reputation for mayhem, you two are very much alike. We cannot see how she could resist any offer of assistance on your part."

Christopher sighed; the prospect of sharing his bed with the beautiful Wintry Widow was vastly unappealing. He knew her kind, too concerned over their appearance to enjoy an abandoned tumble. Her livelihood was contingent upon her ability to attract wealthy suitors. She would not wish to become sweaty or tax herself overmuch. It could ruin her hair.

Yawning, he asked, "May I depart now, my lord?"

Sedgewick shook his head. "You must begin immediately, or you will forfeit this opportunity."

It took great effort on Christopher's part to bite back his retort. The agency would learn soon enough that he danced to no one's tune but his own. "Leave the details to me. You wish me to pursue both personal and professional relations with Lady Winter, and I shall."

Christopher stood and casually adjusted his coat. "However, she is a woman who seeks the secure financial prospects of marriage, which makes it impossible for a bachelor such as myself to woo her first and then progress from the bed outward. We will instead have to start with business and seal our association with sex. It is how these things are done."

"You are a frightening individual," Sedgewick said dryly.

Christopher glanced over his shoulder as he pushed the black curtain aside. "It would be wise of you to remember that."

The sensation of being studied with predatory intent caused the hair at Maria's nape to rise. Turning her head, she studied every box across from her but saw nothing untoward. Still, her instincts were what kept her alive, and she trusted them implicitly.

Someone's interest was more than mere curiosity.

The low tone of men's voices in the gallery behind her drew her attention away from the fruitless visual search. Most would hear nothing over the rabble in the pit below and the carrying notes of the singer, but she was a hunter, her senses fine-tuned.

"The Wintry Widow's box."

"Ah . . ." a man murmured knowingly. "Worth the risk for a few hours in that fancy piece. She is incomparable, a goddess amongst women."

Maria snorted. A curse, that.

Suddenly eager to be productive in some manner, Maria rose to her feet. She pushed the curtain aside and stepped out to the gallery. The two footmen who stood on either side to keep the ambitiously amorous away snapped to attention. "My carriage," she said to one. He hurried away.

Then she was bumped none too gently from behind, and as she stumbled, was caught close to a hard body.

"I beg your pardon," murmured a deliciously raspy voice so close to her ear she felt the vibration of it.

The sound stilled her, caught her breath and held it. She stood unmoving, her senses flaring to awareness far more acute than usual. One after another, impressions bombarded her—a hard chest at her back, a firm arm wrapped beneath her breasts, a hand at her waist, and the rich scent of bergamot mixed with virile male. He did not release her; instead his grip upon her person tightened.

"Unhand me," she said, her voice low and filled with command.

"When I am ready to, I will."

His ungloved hand lifted to cup her throat, his touch heating the rubies that circled her neck until they burned. Calloused fingertips touched her pulse, stroking it, making it race. He moved with utter confidence, no hesitation, as if he possessed the right to fondle her whenever and wherever he chose, even in this public venue. Yet he was undeniably gentle. Despite the possession of his hold, she could writhe free if she chose, but a sudden weakness in her limbs prevented her from moving.

Her gaze moved to her remaining footman, ordering him silently to do something to assist her. The servant's wide eyes were trained above her head, his throat working convulsively as he swallowed hard. Then he looked away.

She sighed. Apparently, she would have to save herself.

Again.

Her next action was goaded as much by instinct as by forethought. She moved her hand, setting it over his wrist, allowing him to feel the sharp point of the blade she hid in a custom-made ring. The man froze. And then laughed. "I do so love a good surprise."

"I cannot say the same."

"Frightened?" he queried.

"Of blood on my gown? Yes," she retorted dryly. "It is one of my favorites."

"Ah, but then it would more aptly match the blood on your hands"—he paused, his tongue tracing the shell of her ear, making her shiver even as her skin flushed—"and mine."

"Who are you?"

"I am what you need."

Maria inhaled deeply, pressing her corset-flattened bosom against an unyielding forearm. Questions sifted through her mind faster than she could collect them. "I have everything I require."

As he released her, her captor allowed his fingers to drift across the bare flesh above her bodice. Her skin tingled, gooseflesh spreading in his wake. "If you find you are mistaken," he rasped, "come find me."

Here's Shelly Laurenston's
"My Kind of Town"
in the sexy new anthology
SUN, SAND, SEX
available now from Brava!

"There's blood everywhere."

Kyle Treharne leaned into the passenger side of the overturned car, the driver's side so badly damaged no one could get through the crumpled metal to extract themselves. Not even the female whose fear he could smell. Her fear and panic . . . and something else. Something he couldn't quite name.

"Do you see anybody?" his boss asked. Kyle readjusted the earplug to hear the man better. The sheriff's voice was so low, it was often hard to make out exactly what he'd said.

"Nope. I don't see anyone. No bodies, but . . ." He sniffed the air and looked down. "Blood trail."

"Follow it. Let me know what you find. I'll send out the EMS guys."

"You got it." Kyle disconnected and followed the trail of blood heading straight toward the beach. He moved fast, worried the woman might be bleeding to death, but also concerned that this human female would see something he'd never be able to explain.

Kyle pushed through the trees until he hit the beach. As he'd hoped, none of the town's people or resort visitors were hanging around; the beach was thankfully deserted in the middle of this hot August day. He followed the blood, cutting in a small arc across the sand, the trail leading back into the woods about twenty feet from where he'd entered.

He'd barely gone five feet when a bright flash of light and the missing woman's scent hit him hard, seconds before *she* hit him hard. He should have been faster. Normally, he would have been. That scent of hers, though, threw him off balance completely; and he couldn't snap out of it quick enough to avoid the woman slamming right into him.

Her body hit his so hard that had he been completely human, she might have killed him.

But Kyle wasn't human. He'd been born different, like nearly everyone else in his small town. They might not all be the same breed, but they were all the same *kind*.

Still, his less-than-human nature didn't mean he couldn't experience pain. At the moment, as he landed flat on his back with the woman on top of him, he felt lots and lots of pain.

Yet the pain faded away when the woman moved, her small body brushing against his. She moaned and Kyle reached around to gently grip her shoulders.

"Hey, darlin'. You all right?"

She didn't answer. Instead, she slapped her hand over his face, squashing his nose. Putting all her weight on that hand, she pushed herself up.

Between her fingers, he could see the confusion in her eyes as she looked around. Blood from a deep gash on her forehead matted her dark brown hair and covered part of her face. Bloodshot, slightly almond-shaped brown eyes searched the area. For what, Kyle had no idea. A cut slashed her top lip; and although it no longer bled, it had started to turn the area around it black and blue.

*Damn, little girl is cute.*

"Uh . . ." He tapped her arm. "Could you move your hand, sweetheart?" The question came out like he had the worst cold in the universe. "I can't really breathe."

She didn't even look at him, instead staring off into the forest. "Dammit. It's gone." Putting more pressure on his poor nose, the woman levered herself up and off him. "Damn. Damn. Damn." She stumbled toward the forest, and Kyle quickly got to his feet. "This isn't my fault. It's not."

*Poor thing, completely delirious from all that blood loss and muttering to herself like a mental patient.*

Then she stopped walking. Abruptly. Almost as if she'd walked into a wall. "Damn," she said again.

Knowing he had to get her to the hospital before she died, Kyle put his hand on her shoulder, gently turning her so he'd be visible. "It's all right, darlin'. Let's get you out of here, okay?" He slipped one arm behind her back and the other under her knees, scooping her up in his arms.

*Hmm. She feels nice there.*

Kyle smiled down at her and, for a moment, she looked at him with complete confusion.

Then the crazy woman started swinging and kicking, trying to get out of his arms. Although she had no skills—she did little more than flail wildly—he couldn't believe her strength after all the blood she'd lost. He quickly realized someone else had caught on to her scent, too, and was heading right for them.

Kyle gripped the fighting woman around the waist, dragging her back against him with one arm. Ignoring how much her tiny fists and feet were hurting, he turned his body so she faced the opposite direction; with his free hand, he swung up and back, slamming his fist into the muzzle of the orange- and black-striped Yankee bastard hell-bent on getting his tiger paws onto the woman in Kyle's arms. Tiger males only had to get one whiff of a female, and they were on them like white on rice. The fact that this woman was a full human *and* an outsider didn't seem to matter to some idiots.

A surprised yelp and the Yankee cat flipped back into the woods. Kyle rolled his eyes. He loved his town but, Lord knew, he didn't like the Yankees who often came to call. All of them were rude, pretentious, and damn annoying.

Kyle walked off with the woman, still trapped in his arm, until she started slapping him.

"Hands off! Hands off! Let me go!" After all that blood loss, she seemed completely lucid and quite insane.

Even worse . . . he'd recognize that accent anywhere. A Yankee. A *damn* Yankee.

Kyle dropped her on her cute butt, and she slammed into the sand hard.

After a moment of stunned silence, she suddenly glared up at him with those big brown eyes . . . and just like that, Kyle Treharne knew he was in the biggest trouble of his life.

No, no. *That* was not a normal-sized human being. Not by a long shot. Her Coven had warned her, "They grow 'em big in the South, sweetie," but she had no idea they grew *this* big.

Nor this gorgeous. She'd never seen hair that black before. Not brown. Black. But when the sunlight hit it in the right way, she could see other colors *under* the black. Light shades of red and yellow and brown. Then there were his eyes. Light, *light* gold eyes flickered over her face, taking in every detail. His nose, blunt at the tip; his lips full and quite lickable.

"You gonna calm down now, darlin'? Or should I drop you on that pretty ass again?"

Emma Lucchesi—worshipper of the Dark Mothers, power

elemental of the Coven of the Darkest Night, ninth-level Master of the Dream Realm, and Long Island accountant for the law offices of Bruce, MacArthur, & Markowitz—didn't know what to say to that. What to say to *him*. Mostly because she couldn't stop staring at the man standing over her.

Finally, here's a peek at HelenKay Dimon's
YOUR MOUTH DRIVES ME CRAZY
coming next month from Brava!

The world spun beneath Annie until her feet landed on the cold tile floor of the shower stall. Strong arms banded around her waist, holding her in place.

Every cell in her body snapped to life. The lethargy weighing her down disappeared with the screech of the shower curtain rings against the rod. A rush of water echoed in her ears as steam filled the room.

"Here we go," the stranger said to the room as if the nut chatted with unconscious people all the time.

He balanced her body against his. Rough denim scratched against her sensitive skin from the front. Lukewarm water splashed over her bare body from the back, making her skin tingle and burn.

A gasp caught in her throat as her shoulders stiffened under the spray. A scream rumbled right behind the gasp, but she managed to swallow that, too.

"This should help." He continued his one-sided conversation in a deep, hypnotizing voice.

He seemed mighty pleased with himself. And since he had stepped right under the water with her, a bit ballsy for her taste.

"This will feel better in a second," he said to the quiet room.

He wasn't wrong.

Firm hands caressed her skull, replacing the frigid ocean with bathwater. He rinsed and massaged and rinsed again. The sweep of his hands wiped away the last of her confusion. With that task done, his palms turned to her arms, brushing up and down, igniting every nerve ending in their path.

His chest rubbed against her bare breasts until heat replaced her chill. With thighs smashed against his legs, the full-body rubdown sparked life into body parts that had been on a deep-freeze hold for more than a year.

"Better?"

She didn't answer him. Wasn't even sure she could speak if she wanted to.

"Open your eyes and say something."

The husky command broke her out of her mental wanderings and sent a shot of anxiety skating down her spine. This was the part of the program where she ran and hid . . . and then ran some more.

Naked. Alone. Strange man. Yeah, a very bad combination.

"I know you're awake." He sounded pretty damn amused by the idea.

The jig was up. Okay, fine, she got his point.

Not knowing if her rescuer counted as a friend or foe, she played the scene with the utmost care. Only a complete madman would attack a vulnerable woman who didn't know her own name. If her stranger fell into that category, she'd scream and make a mad dash into the kitchen for the nearest sharp knife. The nearest sharp anything.

She groaned in pain that was only half false.

"Your eyes are still closed," he said.

*Yeah, pal, no kidding.*

"You aren't fooling me."

*Well she could certainly try.*

His hands continued to massage her sore flesh with just the right amount of pressure to bring her blood sizzling back to life. If he kept this up, her eyes wouldn't open. She'd be asleep.

She couldn't remember the last time she slept through the night. Actually, she could. It had been fifteen months, fifteen months of searching. The path led to Kauai. To the yacht. To flying over the side and into the water. To being in this shower.

"We can stand here all night for all I care," he said.

*Nothing that extreme. Maybe ten more minutes.*

He chuckled. "Doesn't bother me."

*Lucky for her she found an accommodating potential se-rial*

*killer.*

"Because I'm the one with clothes on," he pointed out.

Her eyelids flew open.